TARNISHED

ERICA CHILSON

· RUSTY KNOB · BOOK TWO ·

TARNISHED

Copyright ©2015 Erica Chilson

Wicked Reads
PO Box 29
Nelson, PA 16940

www.ericachilson.com/wicked-reads

Printed in the United States of America

First Printing, 2015

ISBN-13: **978-0692544679**
ISBN-10: **0692544674**

Dedication

To my faithful readers who bridge every genre just to read my words. I thank you for understanding that I believe even a written world should be diverse, with many from all walks of life, age range, physical appearance, educational level and societal class, and sexual orientation. Love is Love. Don't discriminate.

Titles by Erica Chilson

Mistress and Master of Restraint
-series order-

Restraint
Unleashed
Dexter
Dalton
Queen Omnibus*
Jaded*
Queened*
Checkmate*
King
Faithless
The Hunter
Integrated

-Coming Soon-
Hero/Empowered (tentative title)

BLENDED
-Series order-

Good Girl
Wildly Wedded Wife (Blended #1.5)
Widow
Wanton (Blended #2.5)

-COMING SOON-
Warped

RUSTY KNOB
Rusty Knob
Tarnished
Stainless (coming soon)

Royce Kennedy believes he has the town of Rusty Knob and its citizens in the palm of his hand. For altruistic reasons, of course. A real man takes care of his land and the people on it, whether they want to accept the help or not.

After fostering an orphan, adopting underprivileged kids, creating businesses to bring jobs back to the area, donating his time, energy, and money by founding the Community Growth: Life Skills Center, people are beginning to wonder if the man is running a campaign to earn the status of a saint.

Royce's family is getting frustrated by idly watching their patriarch spread himself too thin, because he won't allow them to shoulder his burdens or their own. Drastic measures are taken before the man can see reason. When the dust finally settles, Royce realizes he's been taking care of everyone but himself.

But there's a problem with sorting out your issues, with the clarity of mind, you can't hide from the good, bad, and downright filthy secrets buried in the depths of your past.

With dark, violent, depraved skeletons, Rusty Knob's patriarch isn't as pure of soul as he appears to be. Will he finally surrender and accept the help to buff the tarnish away?

Just because it's the moral thing to do, doesn't mean it's the right thing for you.

•JUNE•

I OPENED THE DOOR

"Royce,"' flows a breathy moan directly into my ear, followed by raspy pants of exertion. "Royce– baby." The needy tone of my wife's voice runs a quiver up my spine as I sink deeper and deeper into her. I lose myself, falling into the way every inch of her skin nestles perfectly beneath mine. It's an intimate comfort far greater than the need for gratification.

Tangled around my fingers, dark, silky threads turn to light, springy curls. Rolling into my lover in a wave, I rest my cheek against hers, knowing she craves to hear how she affects me. My muscles seize– body preparing to give her what she ultimately seeks.

Release and seed.

Demandingly so, fingertips clench, nails biting sharply into my ass, urging me on. "Don't stop... don't stop." Breathlessness blends into throaty moans of pure pleasure, voice finally twisting from my loving wife to the innocent seductress beneath me. Head jerking backward into the pillows, arching her neck, mouth opening wide, my name is released in a torrent as we explode. "R-O-Y-C-E!" The glorious sound warps, becoming frantic then blood-curdling.

Piercing pain shoots into my temples as my body is broken. Torn. Bloodied. Ruined. "Royce!" Willa's soft voice wavers until it's shrill and terrified. "Oh, my God! Donny, make it stop! Don't hurt him! I did it. It's my fault! R-O-Y-C-E!!!"

"I warned you, brother," Donny twists out with tears streaming down his cheeks– a baseball bat clenched in his fist. "I warned you, and you did it anyway. You'd be hurt, but Willa'd die."

My eyes open just as the butt of the bat travels toward my head. Jerking upright in bed, sheets stick to my sweat-coated flesh. I huff over and over again, trying to catch my breath. My heart beats in my throat, so rapidly I fear one day waking to a heart attack. My mind spins, emotions trying to catch up with my thoughts. Amazing and horrific portions of my life curl together into a nightmare.

For a few glorious moments I was with my Annie again– feeling her beneath me while I was thrusting inside her. I never thought I'd experience that again, except in my most cherished memories. The dream was so lifelike. Real. I could touch the softness of her skin. I could taste her delicate flowery scent on the back of my tongue. I could hear the way her breath would catch when my name rolled off her tongue. Lastly, most importantly, I could feel the force of her love and devotion. It was soothing and arousing. Then my greatest joy warped into a nightmare as Annie was torn from my life all over again.

I crave those snapshots of my life until I wake to learn I will have to suffer through the grief as if it's as fresh as the day she left me.

The love turned to lust. My Annie turned to Donny's Willa. My pleasure turned to pain. And then I awoke in a darker mood than the day before.

It was a trick. An evil, delicious taste of what I've lost that can never be found, and what I've tarnished and am trying to reclaim.

With a lunge, I roll to the side of the bed, understanding my adopted son more than he could possibly imagine. The convulsions start in my guts, until they become body-wracking. My back and stomach muscles clench and quiver painfully. I retch into my wastebasket, wishing I could change the past but knowing I never would even if I could.

I retch harder when I realize for the first time I wouldn't bring my Annie back to life. She would hate the man I've become. I would sicken her. I don't deserve her anymore, and she deserves more than a lowlife like me. Perhaps God took Annie in a fiery ball of agonizing hell to get her away from who I'd ultimately become. I hope Annie is at peace, and I'm glad my father didn't survive to watch both of his sons fall from grace.

The only change I would have made would have saved Willa, Donny, Sean, *and* me.

Woulda… Shoulda… Coulda…

Had I known they were for sale, I would have bought Warren, Willa, and Wynn all at the same time when they were little kids. Then I would have swallowed my pride. It would have changed the arc of our lives for the better– the only path that would have ensured Hayden and Hayley were created as well.

But I don't own a time machine, nor am I smart enough to make one. There is no changing the past. There is only *woulda shoulda coulda*, and I wouldn't change anything but the future.

I wipe my mouth off with the back of my hand, deciding to make a protein shake for myself this morning while I'm making Wynn's. In the past thirteen months, my son has slowly needed fewer and fewer shakes to combat the emotional vomiting, while I've needed them more and more.

We all suffer the consequences of our actions, but sometimes they take nine years to catch up with us.

I reach down for the wastebasket, and then make my way to my attached bathroom. "Dad?" Bren startles the hell out of me. I turn slowly toward my open bedroom door, knowing I had shut it when I'd gone to sleep.

"Brennan?" I can't look my son in the eye. I stare down guiltily at the puke splattering the inside of the chrome can clutched in my fingertips. "Did I oversleep?"

"No," is all he says. He doesn't move. I doubt he breathes.

I try again, eyes now looking through the trashcan but seeing nothing. "Did I shout in my sleep?"

Bren's, "No," has my eyes flicking up to finally meet his. My son looks exactly like me, finally filling out in the chest, but it's his mother staring back at me with unflinching sincerity and concern. His voice softens into a whisper. "I just felt it." His curled fists clench at his sides.

"I'm fine," I mutter lamely, feeling like the child. Bren doesn't blink. He looks deep inside of me, as if he already knows my dark secrets and he's okay with the vileness he sees because I'm his dad.

Bren steps forward, approaching me cautiously. "No, you're not. You're getting worse while everybody is getting better. Wynn might get sick once a week, but I hear you in here every morning upchucking your guts. Now you barely look at me."

"I…" My eyes seek out the corners of my bedroom, proving my son's suspicions right. "I'm fixin' to get ready for the day." I take a few steps. "I'll meet you down at breakfast."

I get as far as the bathroom door before Bren's, "Dad?" stops me.

I wait.

My son tracks across the carpeting with silent footfalls. "I was there, remember?"

Forehead pressed against the cool door, I close my eyes in defeat. "I remember. You saved Willa's and my life, and neither of us will ever be able to repay you that debt."

I huff a laugh at the irony. I was branded a hero when I was the coward. My son must hate me more and more every single time one of the townsfolk brings up how I saved the day. Bren is the hero who called 9-1-1 to save Willa and me while protecting Hayden and Hayley. I'm just thankful he never opened the twins' bedroom door like I'd ordered.

"I don't want a payment." Bren's hand settles between my shoulders. "I want you to look me in the eye. Willa's able to now, but you seem to have lost the ability. I know what happened; I was there."

Unable to answer him, I just press into Bren's touch. Tears slip free to carve across my cheekbones. "I can't look you in the eye because you'll see the truth, and I'm ashamed. You're one of the best people I've ever met, so much like your mother."

"I remember Mom," Bren says fondly. He releases a few chuckles. "I'm old enough to remember she was a yeller and far from perfect. Some things Willa and Penny do remind me of Mom, so don't go sanctifying her when she was only human." Laughing darkly, "I'm not that great, either. I'm about to join the family business in mistake making."

"Not true… aside from your lack of boundaries when it comes to privacy," I mutter wryly. "I know you think I've tried to replace you with Kade, and then Wynn, but that's not it. You were my first born, and I want to be the father for you that mine was for me, and I'm terrified you'll see that's a bullshit lie."

"I love you, Daddy." My son rests his forehead between my shoulders, and then his arms curl around my waist to hug me from behind. Then he cuts me off at the knees. "I opened the door."

I fall to the ground, body lurching forward to bounce off the closed bathroom door. Clutching the wastebasket to my chest, I retch like never before. I vomit until the vein in my forehead throbs, my eyes bulge from my skull, and my heart flutters on the verge of an attack. I pitch forward listlessly, but my son holds me upright before my face smashes to the floor.

"Shh… it's okay. I've got you. It's my turn to help you." Bren rocks me back and forth, both of us sobbing. "Shh… it was time I told you the truth. I start college in two months, and I've got to get you some help now because I've got a lot of shit I'm gonna have to deal with soon… I know you told me not to, but I had to leave Hayden and Hayley's room so I could let Corbin in to help. But don't worry, I made sure the twins were locked up nice and tight and couldn't see. Then I sat with you while we waited for the police and the ambulance."

With body-wracking convulsions, I retch like I'm dying. My son saw. My son saw what I have no true recollection of except from the police photographs. My son saw Willa beaten within an inch of her life with fists, a baseball bat, and a truncheon. Her violated body was sprawled on the floor next to mine, with the wooden truncheon *inside* me. Which means he knows I'm the reason why his uncle, who was a good man for the first forty years of his life, finally cracked and went insane.

With a deep breath, I put on my '*daddy*' uniform and step into our dining room. My mood changes instantly when I take in my family sitting around the table, with Bren and Wynn's yearbooks being passed around. My smile is no longer forced. It's ear-to-ear and strong enough to power a small city's electricity grid. I'm mirroring the huge smile on Brennan's senior picture, sitting front and center in the middle of the table. Next to that is the reject picture that didn't make it into the yearbook. Wynn is displaying his '*teenage Wynn*' attitude, taken in the dark months, as we've dubbed his asshole period.

"What's a manwhore?" Hayley parrots in a girly voice as she reads from Bren's yearbook, no doubt. "*They are going to write songs about you, my brotha. Songs sung at Pride Parades, and I'll be leading the march. Have a frantastic life, buddy. I hope Facebook is still in existence five, ten, fifteen years from now, because I ain't ever stepping foot back in Rusty Knob. I love ya like a brotha from anotha motha.* Franny writes weird," Hayley complains.

"My turn," is the only notice Hayden gives before he's tugging the book free. "*Fuck you– love Jackson. Positive! I'm going to cut your dick off– Jesse.*"

"That'll be enough of that," Willa says in a panic, snatching the yearbook and clutching it to her chest. A second later, she has the book open in her lap and her eyebrows are raised in shock.

"Dude, what did you do?" Wynn slaps Bren upside the head, punishing him with his own signature move. "I keep asking Jack, but he won't spill it."

"Dad?" Bren's eyes connect with mine across the table, when no one else knew I was skulking in the doorway. "Wanna make me a shake this morning?" Grimacing, he pushes the greasy bacon around on his plate, making my stomach revolt.

I step into the room, hand brushing the tops of the twins' heads. "Wynn, ya need one too?" Then I lean down to kiss Willa's cheek, and she surprises me by turning to the side to kiss the corner of my mouth instead. "Morning," I whisper in her ear, knowing she likes it. I jerk slightly when my voice cracks with lingering emotions.

"I'm good," Wynn answers, snagging Bren's bacon. His plate is loaded for bear and doused in the real maple syrup. He threw a fit in the middle of the grocery store last weekend when the kids tried to get Mrs. Butterworth's. I had to compromise by getting both. He's nearly drained the entire bottle in the past few days.

"It's a good thing you're playing college ball." I stare pointedly at Wynn's heart-attack-special, and then flick my eyes to make sure the little ones aren't eating unhealthy. "Hey, that oatmeal looks good." I nudge Willa in appreciation. "I think I'll fetch some for Bren and me."

Willa rests her palm in the center of my back and flashes me a big smile, like she somehow knew we needed something soothing and comforting for breakfast.

I hurry from the room, face flaming red from just that small touch. I listen to Willa as I fix my breakfast. "Okay, let's read some more. *Bren, you're proof you can't rehabilitate a hillbilly. No matter how much green is in your pocket– Duane.* Seriously, Bren, what the hell did you do to your friends?"

Serving spoon clattering to the countertop, fear strikes through me and has me shouting before I can filter myself. "You are graduating, right? Tell me you are, even if you have to lie to me."

"We're good, Dad!" Wynn shouts back. "Bren came in seventeenth in our class. Not great, but not last either."

"Do-gooder," Bren snarls. "The perpetual virgin managed to bypass Julie Hancock by a tenth of a point for the top spot. Ms. *I'm going to be a doctor*," Bren twists out in a snooty voice. "Let's see what's in your yearbook, Golden Boy."

"Me!" Hayden squeals, and then a clamoring flows in from the dining room that has me laughing silently.

I walk in with a bowl in each hand, chuckling at a little boy and a big boy fighting over a yearbook. Hayden lets go abruptly and the book jabs Wynn in the chin. Hopping in from behind, Hayley steals the yearbook while Wynn recovers.

Placing a bowl in front of Brennan, I slide into the seat next to him. He looks down and out, and I'm not sure if it's because of what happened between us this morning, or if he's been silently suffering for a while now. I squeeze his shoulder, hoping he realizes I'm here for him for anything, no matter how fucked up I may be.

Hayley darts underneath the table, and then pops out safely at the end. She crawls into her seat, adjusts her frilly dress, and then finger-brushes her fauxhawk. Prim and proper, she begins reading to us from Wynn's yearbook. "*Uncle Wynn, you're the bestest uncle*

I have, but Uncle Jeb is a close second. If you move away for college, I'll disown you. Huh? Copper is only five months old. He can't write yet."

"Sis," Hayden drawls, an eye roll hidden in his tone. He reaches to take the yearbook while she mulls that over. "Aunt Penny wrote it. *Hey, Rusty West! I'm gonna miss showering after practice with you. Best view in all of Rusty Knob. You've been blessed– Francis R. Parker, frantastic curiosities.* Huh?"

"You boys have some odd friends." Willa shakes her head, deciding it's her turn again, but I intercept the trade-off. "Royce!" she squeals, playfully slapping at my hand, giving me a glimpse of the wild girl I remember.

"My turn!" My eyes widen at the sheer amount of notes from Wynn's friends. His yearbook is covered in ink. I pick an entry at random. "Hmm… this one looks promising. *You little shit, I'll give you the college experience. I'll invite the roommate. You'll hire the limo. & we'll both get an education– forever a pervert, foster brother lover.*" I snap the book shut. "I believe that's enough for the day." I thrust the yearbook into a blushing Wynn's hands.

"Do tell." Bren turns to Wynn. "Do tell."

A deep, "Yes, do tell," has us all jumping in our seats. Kade makes his way into the dining room, snagging a piece of bacon on his way. "Torrid stories from Kentwood Area School District," he says cockily around a mouthful of pork. "My kind of breakfast."

"Uncle Kade? Did you write that?" Hayley calls him out, only making his grin bigger.

"Sure did," Kade says with a wink. "Best not read the bottom, left-hand corner of the back page."

"Oh, Lord." Wynn shoves his yearbook underneath his t-shirt, and then wraps his arms around himself. "What's up? What are you doing here?"

"What? Already sick of seeing me? Almost seven months together, am I boring you?" Taunting Wynn, Kade looks around at all of us, confused. "I thought Royce and I were meeting with Miriam Ross this morning. Am I wrong?" He steals Bren's untouched plate. "You lick anything on this?" As soon as Bren shakes his head no, Kade's loading it up with waffles, using the last of Wynn's '*precious*' maple syrup.

I'm surprised when Kaden doesn't get speared in the hand with a fork like Bren did yesterday morning. Must be Kade will pay Wynn back with the sexual favors displayed on the back page of the yearbook. I have no idea why Kade wrote a poem about the virtues of denim cut-off shorts.

Snorting at the absurdity my life has taken on, I decide to finally give an answer. "We're still on. We're meeting Miriam at nine downtown." My entire family is all in one place, happy and healthy, so I dig into my oatmeal with gusto. After a few mouthfuls, I decide the queasiness has abated and snag a few pieces of bacon before Kade and Wynn scarf it all down.

"Am I...?" Willa's confidence is still weak in all things except for cooking here at the house and for the fire department's auxiliary. "I mean..." She can't even ask if she's invited or not.

Typical Willa. The fifteen-year-old girl I met when my brother dragged Willa home is slowly erupting again. The confident, demanding young woman I knew– the same scary Gillette personality that popped out during Wynn's teenage asshole phase. Willa's lack of confidence makes me sad, but not as much as that broken girl she was for three horrific years. It's been a slow road of progress, but Willa's getting there.

"Hey," murmurs softly from my lips. I lean into Willa, and Wynn snaps into action. The older boys instinctively know to keep the little ones engaged so Willa and I can speak as privately as our dining room table will allow. I rest my lips on her ear, a trick I learned a lifetime ago that is Willa's off switch, or on switch, depending on the situation.

"Willa, sweetheart. I asked you last week. I haven't changed my mind. If I say it, I mean it. Remember?" She wants to believe me, and she'll never voice why she can't. "I understand," I say with great patience. "Donny was hot and cold, and I look and sound just like him. But my words are my own, as are my actions. I'll never let you go through this alone."

"I..." Willa's eyes flick around the room, taking in how Kade is chowing down while the boys and Hayley tease Hayden for having a crush on a little girl named Hannah. When Willa's vivid blue eyes finally settle on me, my breath catches like always. "Donny only hurt me once a month when he got frustrated, you know that. But... how could I trust him the rest of the month?"

"I'm not Donny," I whisper back, when I'd rather scream it into Willa's face. My guts twist up again, threatening to erupt oatmeal all over the table. "I was the one who stopped him from doing that." The *'which is what put us in the hospital, got a man murdered, and put Donny in prison'* goes without saying.

"Should I…" Willa's fingertips flutter along her hair, and then fall to straighten her blouse. "Should I dress nicer, more professional?" She's wearing a baby blue blouse and a pair of white pants that are chopped off below her knees. Whatever the hell they're called; I know they're not shorts, but not pants, either.

My smile is huge. I don't want Willa to think I'm laughing at her, but I can't help but be endlessly amused by her. She is one of the most beautiful women I've ever met. So young and innocent yet aged by her jadedness.

I've seen Willa staring at photographs of Annie, studying them, like she has to dress or act or behave a certain way. I don't want Annie's clone. All that would do is make me miss Annie more. I want Willa to be as chaotic as I know she is deep down.

A laugh slips out when I look at Kade, wearing a pair of dirty jeans and a XXL pink t-shirt with an ancient gray and white flannel over top– the flannel he keeps trading back and forth with Wynn during the weird mating dance they play. To top the '*I don't give a fuck*' sundae, Kade's shirt has a big rooster with **Cock-a-doodle-doo** printed across it.

Professional? Ha!

"Dress however you wish." I reach up to stroke Willa's earlobe. My grin gets brighter when her eyelids droop. "You know how much I love you in white." My tone is loaded with innuendo from over our lifetime together. "I want you to be comfortable. So no worrying about how you look instead of having a voice this morning." I lean forward and breathe into her ear. "You'll be surrounded by your family, so don't fret over the people you don't know. Okay?"

"Okay." Willa's smile is magnificent, open and innocent– the young woman she should have been, which is why we need to get this show on the road.

"Time for school." I push away from the table. "Time for the adults to go to work."

Kade groans loud over that, after having a six-month hiatus where he sat on his ass tying flies and playing video games. Depressed, I couldn't get him to work. The asshole knew he had me by the balls. I either paid for his mortgage, or he'd move back in here– with Wynn. Unlike Wynn, Kade has no issue opening my wallet and taking out whatever he needs, which is why they got into no less than four fist fights this past month. I didn't allow Wynn to be alone with Kade after each fight, fearing explosive make-up sex.

But I'm eighteen!

Wynn doesn't see the darkness lurking beneath Kade's surface. I recognize it because it matches my own. I didn't care how much whining and teenage asshole Wynn I had to put up with, he was not going to be taken advantage of by Kade. I love them both, and I won't allow them to destroy each other like Willa and I did– and we took Donny and Sean with us.

I'm un-depressing Kaden Marx this morning, especially since I know it will only get worse once Wynn runs off to college. Not allocated in his scholarship, I just paid for Wynn's room and board last week. I'm positive Kade was envisioning kicking me in the nuts when he found out. Oddly enough, Wynn seems really excited to get away. But that's probably because Jack's his roommate.

Willa and I enter co-parent-mode with practiced ease. Backpacks, lunches, homework and shoes accounted for. Wiggly, cuddly goodbyes that simultaneously hurt because I don't want to let them go, but offer a feeling of relief because I can breathe for five minutes without having to take care of someone every second.

At almost eight, Hayden and Hayley are big kids now. They march out the door to join the horde of children flowing down the sidewalk, and I trust them enough to let them go.

… But Bren doesn't. "Later, Dad." I get a wave, but Willa gets a peck on the cheek. "Later, Willa!" Then he's off to keep pace with the twins, trailing them a hundred feet behind so they feel independent.

Willa and I roll our eyes at each other and groan. We start picking up the table while Wynn and Kade say their goodbyes for all of seven long, excruciating hours. It's a drawn out affair, anywhere from a minute to fifteen.

I'm not in the mood to play voyeur today while they do their foreplay bullshit with the flannel shirt exchange. I'd like to keep my oatmeal down. Something about seeing my foster son and my adopted son doing cutesy talk makes me want to retch in my mouth. Which entertains the hell out of Willa.

My fingers twist in the collar of Kaden's flannel. With a rough yank, I jerk it off his back. "Here," I thrust the nasty thing at Wynn, scared to death they have sex while wearing it– or whatever the hell you call whatever they do at Kade's house when they think I'm too stupid to notice. "Put the dang thing on and get your ass to school. It's your last week, and you should be with your friends, not debating who is going to miss who more."

Carrying a stack of plates, Willa's riotous laughter trails after her from the kitchen. "Sometimes I wish they were both little guys, because even I want to kick their asses. I prefer Bren's random hookups. At least they don't do the walk of shame by the breakfast table."

"I'm still a virgin." Wynn goes on the defensive. "Mostly."

"Ain't no shame in that," Kade volleys back. "Same here."

Pointing at Wynn, Willa shouts in her momma voice, "Git out!" slipping back into her former diction. "Git out and git yer ass ta school. Yer gonna give yer dad an aneurysm."

Immune, Wynn laughs while slipping Kade the tongue for shock-value. Almost taking Kade to the floor, the chair tips sideways. They maul one another to get a rise out of Willa and me. "Git!" Willa gives a swift kick to Wynn's big ass, knocking him loose of Kade's mouth. "Git before I grab the hose and turn it on ya."

Tugging on that foul flannel shirt, "Going..." Wynn sings, happier than usual. "Going," he keeps it up all the way to the front door. "Gone!" he shouts from the sidewalk.

"You!" Willa points a butter knife at Kade. "Git yer ass up ta Wynn's room and put on one of his nicer outfits, but dab on some deodorant first. You stink." She gives an exaggerated shudder. "Nasty. We're meeting a bunch of important people today, and you're supposed to be our new director. You can't show up flaunting how much you crave cock and are scared of soap."

I let Willa go off because there are only three people on this earth she does this to: Warren, Wynn, and Kaden. With a respectful authority given to the twins, and a teensy bit to Bren. But she lets those three fools have it with both barrels, and I hate to admit but it makes me harder than hell.

I miss this take-charge side of Willa. I don't dare let my mind drift back to a time when I was someone she told what to do, because those are some of my fondest and most shameful memories.

Also immune, Kade just stays at the table, reaching for his fork to continue cleaning his plate. "I'm older than you are, Willamina, remember?"

Charging forward, "By seven whole months. Whoop-dee-doo. Then act like it, ya bum. Git up! And don't do nothing nasty in Wynn's room. I knows how you are."

Turning around to face the wall, I laugh into the back of my hand, but my body is quaking violently. "I just... can't." I bust out laughing as Kade stomps from the room, Wolverines pounding up the staircase.

Out of reflex, I reach out and grab Willa as she walks past. I hook my arm around her waist to draw her against my chest. I bury my face against the side of her neck, laughing so hard my belly hurts.

"I've known that little peckerwood since I was four," Willa goes off in a serious tone. "He used to brandish his willy, flicking and waving it at me when he pissed in the yard. You just know he's up there jerking off on Wynn's pillow, or something equally nasty."

"Willa," I gasp out, barely able to breathe. "Lord, help me." I squeeze her tighter. "Kade's a guy. We're nasty creatures by default."

"So you think Kade's tugging on his willy up there right now?" Willa looks up at the ceiling, her face twisted in revulsion.

All I can do is laugh harder– wheezing. I have to press Willa closer to me to push on my aching stomach muscles. "Knowing him, he'll probably wipe it on the doorknob when he's finished." That does it, Willa breaks down with me. Clutching me just as tight, we laugh so hard tears are spilling from our eyes.

"I think I'm gonna pee my pants." Willa runs off, still laughing. "Dang kids ruined my bladder."

Exiting the house and then locking up, I call out. "Do you have everything we need, Kade?"

Kade's overdressed to rub Willa the wrong way, wearing a pair of dress pants, a lavender button-up, suspenders, and an oversized yellow bowtie he must have snagged from the Halloween costume trunk.

Kade has a real issue with authority. He doesn't like to be told what to do, and turns into a self-righteous prick. But if he wants to look like a moron, then I'll laugh at him instead of getting angry.

Hazel eyes squinting up at me from the driveway, "You mean the busywork you used to distract me?" Kade calls my bluff. "Yeah, I got it. It's in the Durango– c'mon, we'll take my car."

"Nah," I mutter, trying to hide my grimace. I'm not getting anywhere near the shaggin' wagon. "I'm teaching Willa to drive, so she has to chauffeur us everywhere."

"You don't know how to drive?" Voice drawn out and incredulous, I want to beat Kade for upsetting Willa. But he's digging the files and laptop out of his backseat before I can lay into him. He pops out like a good boy who did as he was told, so I let it go.

Evil smirk twisting her lips, Willa palms the fob while walking backward. I miss a step, nearly tripping from the naughty glint in her eye. Kade's footfall lands wrong, and he catches himself before he tumbles to the ground. Willa and Wynn share a few expressions and their attitudes mirror one another. No doubt Kade just figured that out and doesn't know what to do with the knowledge.

"Well, see..." Willa flashes Kade a predatory look. "Seeing as how I was only fifteen when I was hitched, and the only thing my husband wanted out of me was proof his dick didn't fire off blanks, I never got my license. Never had a car. Never had a job." She narrows her eyes like she's envisioning punching Kade in the nads. "But you know the rest of the story, Mr. Woe-is-Me."

Chuckling to himself, Kade gets into the passenger seat. "I'm 6'4", my ass ain't fitting in the backseat," he answers my glare. "You can get your jollies off once we get to the new building."

"And to think…" I crawl into Willa's car, squeezing into the backseat. "I chose you as my son, and this is how you repay me?"

"Guilt trip, much?" Kade peeks at me over his shoulder. "We need a game plan going in."

"I'm freaking the fuck out." Willa's voice breaks as she pulls out of the driveway, and I fear Kade sitting in the front seat isn't a good idea. We've yet to graduate to the kids tagging along on our rides. But she surprises me as usual. "Lawyers. Bankers. People from the government. I don't want to make a fool out of you, Royce. Maybe I shouldn't have come."

"But then who would have driven us?" Kade bops Willa on the nose. "I was dressed like a gay bum for a reason. How you look or where you came from doesn't have a thing to do with the brains in your head. Those assholes had the same education I did, and I can guarantee they don't have a lick of sense."

"It's true," I pipe in from the backseat. "I'm self-taught by trial and error, things I learned by repetition. When I have to cut through all that red tape mumbo jumbo with the government, they make it seem like something that took me five minutes to complete will take nine employees with multiple degrees a month of constant work. Which is why we're doing this project in the first place."

"I hear ya on that." Kade grunts. "Fuck you very much, Kentwood Area School District, for making my degrees obsolete."

"That's on you, mister." Willa points at Kade, and I freak the fuck out that her hands are no longer at ten and two. "You should have kept it in your pants, but you knew that already. I bet you did it on purpose so you could bitch about losing the job you were too yellow to quit."

Kade flips around to glare at me. "Can I push her out of the car? Ballsy Willa is like a combination of Warren and Wynn with tits, and I can't handle seeing my best buddy and my boyfriend like that."

Laughing, I direct Willa where to park. "Front of the building, behind Warren's old beater."

"Oh, hell no!" Willa snarls. "No. I ain't parallel parking for nothing."

"Well, if you hit anything it will be Warren's car, so you're fine. You can't scratch something that is covered in rust with its tailpipe and fender hanging to the ground." I stare at Warren's deathtrap, deciding that it's going to the junkyard sooner rather than later. We can't have Penny and Copper riding around in it.

"I bet I can park better than you," Kade goads Willa. "If I can do it on the first try, you have to stop bossing me around."

Gillette pride activated. Willa parallel parks. On the fourth try.

I crawl out of the backseat, practically folding myself in half. I decide it's high-time Willa learned how to drive stick shift just so we can take my truck from now on.

Willa did a piss-poor job, but it's her first time, so I'm giving an A for effort and leaving the car crooked to the curb. Let's just hope no one clips the front bumper sticking out into the lane of traffic.

Kade and Willa are bickering back and forth about how to parallel park while I take in our newest venture. Rusty Knob is a failing town, just like every other town in the United States. Government influence and conservationists murdered the coal and logging industry in our area. Then all major industry fled overseas. Our people have nowhere to work, but they still need to eat. They either left the small towns and moved to larger areas to find office and service work, or they starved while begging for government aid.

If you drive down any main street, you'll see buildings that have stood the test of time lie empty. Empty. Empty. Bank repossession. Going out of business. Liquidation sale. Empty. Empty. Dilapidated and boarded up. Struggling to survive while the owner uses their second and third mortgages to try to keep their fourth-generation legacies alive.

With my money, I could have filled Rusty Knob's buildings with businesses that would have sucked my wallet dry while giving a handful of townsfolk jobs. But in order to keep them afloat, the rest of the townsfolk wouldn't be able to afford to shop there. It was an impossible situation.

Driving down our streets and looking at our failing town is demoralizing, removing whatever sense of community spirit we have left. The business owners are committing suicide or falling into alcoholism to cope, splitting families and ruining lives. So instead of bleeding me dry to pay a few employees, I found a way to employ many while giving back to the community. A way to heal the infection that runs so deep in Rusty Knob.

I bought an entire block on the left-hand side of Main Street between our two stoplights. I relocated all the remaining businesses to the right-hand side so the street now looks bustling and prosperous.

My idea is a business plan to tie communities together from tax-deductible contributions using the empty buildings in our small towns. Our people need to know how to take care of themselves.

They need an education that doesn't involve debt they can't pay back because they can't get a job after leaving college. Ninety percent of the population can't squeeze into ten percent of the highest paying jobs.

There are jobs out there that will always be necessary: laborers, service jobs, and office work. There is no shame in honest work, and the wages you earn are enough to live on if they aren't wasted on unnecessary expenses.

They need to learn how to survive.

"Looking awfully serious there, Royce." Warren pats me on the shoulder to gain my attention. "You've been teaching us ignorant bastards for years. It's about time you do it on a grander scale."

"Even if they won't let us go non-profit, I'm still going to see this through." I turn around to face Warren and the source of the constant babbling. My expression softens as I gaze down at the pink-cheeked baby boy gnawing on his own thumb. Spit bubbles pop and form as he makes noises like he's talking to us in his own language.

My arms itch to hold Copper, but his daddy isn't one to pass him around. "This little feller hasn't let me get a lick of sleep this past week." Warren rubs a palm over his son's shock of red hair. "I think he misses his momma. Don't fret, Momma will be with us night and day come Saturday after graduation."

"I bet you're proud." My heart does a backflip for my sons and their friends, but it squeezes a bit when I realize how much I'm going to miss them come August.

"Honestly..." Warren gazes down at his son while he speaks softly. "I didn't think this day would come. If it hadn't, I would have blamed myself and Penny would have resented me for life." Getting emotional, he takes a deep breath. "Proud doesn't cover it."

"You gonna miss being a stay-at-home dad?" I bite back a laugh at how Warren refuses to part with Copper. Penny has to fight him off to spend time with the little guy after school.

"Oh, hell no!" Warren repeats Willa's earlier words, and they sound identical. "My boy is coming with me no matter where you send me. Penny can just follow her ass behind us."

Willa and Kade's bickering cuts off the second they realize they have an audience. Copper is like a homing beacon. Their eyes get droopy when they catch sight of him, then they're walking toward us with goofy grins on their faces.

"How's my nephew?" Willa tries to lift Copper from Warren's arms but is unsuccessful. "War..." she whines. "He needs to socialize."

"Socialize?" Warren arches his eyebrow. "Have you met our families? The Franklins are shoved up my ass day and night. Copper and I have to evacuate to Kade's house to get some peace and quiet."

"How's my godson?" Kade reaches right in and pries the feller from his daddy's arms, and Warren has no choice but to let him go. Cradled to Kade's broad chest, Copper nestles down like he belongs there. "Uncle Kade is your favorite. C'mon, admit it. Jeb is too small and Wynn looks too much like your daddy. You love me best."

"How come you let Kade and Wynn hold him but not me?" Willa's whining again. "I have to fight Penny for two minutes when you're in the shower, and all those dang little sisters of hers steal him from me."

"I don't *let* them do anything," Warren complains. "They take him." He retrieves his son, only to pass the baby to his sister. "I'm just happy they give him back."

Willa looks up at me through the lace of her lashes while rubbing her cheek on the top of Copper's red curls. "I'm not giving him back." She flashes me a mischievous grin, and then walks to the entrance of the **Community Growth: Life Skills Center**.

Brain dead, I follow after Willa. "I want a turn."

"I think this project should be connected to the school system so it can receive additional funding," Miriam Ross interrupts the banker, Clyde Lomax, and the lawyer, Arnold Hinsdale, who are arguing over the benefits of non-profit.

"No!" Kade's voice overpowers mine. "No way, Miriam!" My son turns to me with fury etched across his features and issues me a warning. "If you give them any power, I'm out. Let's get real, those bastards only fired me because I'm gay." He glares me down. "Your sons are *gay*."

Sighing, I gaze around the long table and occupied folding chairs acting as our meeting room while we get this project up and running. We're housed in the central most building, which used to be an insurance office a few years back.

"I invited you all here today because I need community backing, not financial backing." My words soothe Kade some, but not enough to get his back from being ramrod straight. Even sitting, he's towering over everyone. "The Life Skills Center will not be beholden to anyone. We will not play politics, knowing any money we receive will have an agenda attached. We won't be connected to any religious affiliation because I don't want God's Word interpreted to fit a specific standard."

"Listen." Warren adjusts Copper in his baby sling, and then leans forward to address everyone, much to my surprise. "This is for folks like me and Willa. Sure, we went to school, but what we learned at home overrode whatever you teachers taught us. Our loyalties were with our momma and daddy, not with some snooty know-it-all looking down their nose at us. So if you have any say in this, it'll be high school all over again but with adults."

"You can't…" Willa looks down at her hands, but she doesn't stop speaking. "You can't make us feel stupid, or we'll stop coming 'round. If we need help, you need to show us how to help ourselves, not do it for us because you think we're too ignorant."

Sensing Kade's rising anger and Willa and Warren's erupting emotions, I take charge and hope everyone will hear what I'm saying. "The Life Skills Center is *not* an educational system for adults. It's survival. It's making the most of the life you were given. Kade, pass out the list of services you came up with."

"As a director, it will be my responsibility to find volunteers to teach specific classes. Most of this is common sense, pure and simple. Just because you've never learned something, doesn't mean you're incapable of learning."

Kade passes a stack of paper to Miriam, and so forth. With fifteen members of Rusty Knob's community surrounding this table, it's a mishmash. Several business owners are scowling, realizing they may lose money once this is up and running. The banker is shaking his head left and right, muttering '*no*' underneath his breath.

"I was briefly a teacher in Kentwood Area School District, and I despised the politics in the system. Most teachers put in requests for supplies and ended up buying their own, and that is the bullshit I want to prevent. What good is Home Economics and Shop class in the eighth grade? I didn't need to know how to sew a stuffed animal when I was thirteen. But at eighteen, I needed to know how to balance my checkbook and how to shop at the grocery store."

"I know you're thinking that's our parents' job, and I will teach my children this myself. But what if your parents didn't know and were too prideful to admit it, so it went untaught?" Willa still won't look up from her hands, but she's found her voice at last. "Every generation is teaching their children less and less about this stuff, and we're getting more and more ignorant. Being book smart is not the same as knowing how to take care of yourself. Our kids need to know calculus, but they need to know how to change a tire more. Every day I feel stupid over all the things I wasn't taught."

"It was a rude awakening coming out of college and buying my own home, having to pay some dude two-hundred bucks to change the broken flush chain in my toilet tank. Wynn laughed at me when he found out, saying it would have taken five minutes and a two dollar part. But I didn't know, so I lived on Top Ramen for the rest of the month to offset the cost."

I scan down the list Kade printed off. "It's the small things that destroy families, and money is usually the root of it. If you lose your job, you feel like you let your family down. Everything out of your wife's mouth sounds like a complaint. Your kids need this and that and you feel like a failure because you can't afford it. So you look to the bottle for some relief, not realizing you're wasting your money on something you didn't need while destroying everything you've ever built. I want our community to know there is hope, even when they are down and out."

"No one should have to live like that," Warren says with conviction. "I hated how hopeless I felt when our house was falling down around our ears and we couldn't afford to hire it done and we didn't know how to fix it ourselves. So you sit while your life crumbles down around you, looking for anything that is an escape. Except the escape traps you in an even worse fate."

"Our program will teach valuable lessons, like money management." My fingertip scans down the list, but I decide to speak from experience instead. "The less money we had, the more Annie *wanted*. She'd go buy something to fill the void. It would be something cheap and worthless, only a few bucks here or there. Easily broken and forgotten. But it added up to where we could have had something of value. Most people are too blind to notice. It's only a cup of coffee, or a cigarette, or a couple beers because I only have a twenty dollar bill and it's not enough to pay the electric bill. So they spend it to feel better. But written down, they would see they just spent an entire mortgage payment on bullshit throughout the month. You can be poor and still have *more*. It's all about value and worth."

"Penny was spending too much on cookies and pre-packaged snacks, and she didn't realize she could make the same things at home for a quarter of the price." Willa finally looks up, and stares right at Miriam. "So I taught her how to bake some things and make air-popped popcorn, and how to clip coupons and buy groceries that are on sale. She'd cry to me how she wanted cable but couldn't afford it. Now, instead of throwing money away at the store, she has TV to watch at night and food that isn't filled with preservatives."

"I know all of this sounds like it's the 1950s, but maybe we need to remember a few things our grandparents used to know. No one has to sit around waiting for someone to help them when they have the tools to help themselves. Instead of wasting money on simple tasks because it sounds easier, do it yourself so you have the money when you really need it."

"I thought it best to group classes of a similar nature in the same space." Kade scans his list. "Set up hands-on stations instead of barking instructions that will fall on deaf ears. Like simple home repairs happening at stations around the room. Or different recipes in a cooking class. Or showing how to balance your checkbook at one table, while at the next discussing how to clip coupons or create a monthly budget."

"I thought..." Willa stumbles over her words, so I reach over to grip her hand before she wrings them raw. "I thought it would be good to do things in real-time. For those with even a quarter acre of usable land, we could help till their garden. Later we could harvest, and then show them how to put the produce up for winter. We don't need to buy it if we can grow it, and it would occupy us from doing destructive things."

Kade winks at Willa, and then takes the floor. "With the advent of the internet, things have been simplified, but we've lost touch with living. I could order groceries online and have them delivered to my front door. Convenient and awe-inspiring, sure. But since I can't afford my mortgage because I'm unemployed, what good is that to me? I need to know how to stretch my dollar, not pay quadruple because it's a novelty. Technology is sucking us dry, and we don't even realize it. We're buying what we don't need at the expense of what we do need."

Reaching past Kade, I snag the folder I organized for this meeting. "We will be privately funded by tax-deductible charitable contributions. We will also be hosting Narcotics and Alcoholics Anonymous, Al Anon, and various support groups. I've contacted counselors across four counties for their help. Kade is organizing an LGBTQ support group open to sixteen-year-olds and older, and Willa would like to start one for victims of domestic violence."

"I highly doubt you'll get much community support when it comes to Kaden Marx and his queer crusade," Conner Stevens blurts out without filtering his thoughts. While sounding bigoted, it was more of a statement of truth. We're sitting in Conner's former building. After the decline, he had to move his insurance practice to his home. His choice, given by Banker Lomax, keep the failing building and dwindling clientele and lose his house to the bank– he chose the roof over his head and to work from home.

Every person in Rusty Knob has a similar story, and it's made them bitter.

"If any of our donors disagree with our policy of not having an affiliation to anything, they can keep their money. No agendas will be run during our program. All funding will go toward paying for upkeep on the buildings, wages for our directors, and supplies for our volunteers. We will provide an inventoried monthly statement down to the last cent."

"And who will be your directors?" Arnold Hinsdale asks with narrowed eyes and a scowl pulling at his lips.

"You're looking at 'em." I don't back down as I point to Kade, Warren, Willa, and myself. "We're here in Rusty Knob for life, and we would rather live in a thriving town than watch it cannibalize itself."

Clyde Lomax snorts. "Three hillbillies and their king?"

"Who better to understand the people who will use this program than the very ones who would have utilized it in years' past when they needed it most?" Miriam comes to our defense. "They get what we will never understand– what it means to be hungry." She turns kind eyes on me. "Royce, I agree with your stance. I won't push the issue on government funding, but I want to be able to refer both volunteers and people in need."

"And that is precisely why you're here," I say with a smile, glad someone is finally getting with the program. "We're going to start small, helping Kentwood County. After the kinks are worked out, we'd like to branch out. Share our business plan with other counties so they can clone what we're trying to achieve. Every town has empty buildings rotting because the banks won't release them for purchase."

"I'm in," Miriam and Conner say at the same time.

Banker Lomax just gets up from the table and walks out the door, because what we're proposing is to live within our means and not accrue the debt he's peddling.

"I assume I'm here because you'll need a lawyer?" Arnold Hinsdale perks up. The eager, evil light in his eyes twists my guts.

"No," I utter bluntly. "I've had a team of attorneys since Annie and my father's accident. They will be handling the legal side of things. I need you to refer us to your clients because they need our help more than they need yours."

"And how do you figure that?" Arnold spits, face flushing red with anger.

Kade goes on the attack. "If your client is doing jail time, obviously he's in need of positive change. Most of what you do are divorces, DUIs, and homeowners fighting with the bank to keep their homes. I'd think that is self-explanatory."

Ignoring the snide battle Kade and Arnold engage in, I turn to Carol and Karen Jacobs, a pair of sisters who run our local H&R Block branch. "I'd appreciate it if you'd pass out our business card when your clients do their income taxes. You'd know whether they needed us by their lack of yearly income."

"Oh, Royce," Carol cries as she reaches across the table to snare my hand. "This is needed. Badly. I can't make it through tax season without breaking down from the harrowing stories my clients tell me. So needed."

"Some of their stories…" Karen shakes her head sadly. "The shit they deal with would have never happened if they knew better. The elderly folks get taken advantage of, and the young'uns make more mistakes than good choices." She releases a bitter laugh. "Last week, I could have used a class in Television Installation. It took three minutes for the tech guru to hook my TV to the DVR and DVD player. When he handed me a bill for a hundred and fifty bucks, I wanted to puke."

"Exactly!" Kade shouts excitedly. "Jack or Duane would have done that for free, and shown you how to do it yourself next time. Hell, it took Wynn two minutes to fix the riser to my back steps, and Lord knows how much that would have cost me."

"Well," I stand from the table, effectively ending the meeting because Copper is starting to get fussy. "I guess Community Growth: Life Skills Center is a go. We'll proceed forward, and I'll be in touch with what I need from each of you on your end. I need everything ready for our grand opening on August eighth."

"Why that date?" Carol asks, causing Warren, Willa, Kade, and me to flinch.

In a stiff voice, I force the words out between quivering lips. "I felt it only fitting to open on the anniversary of Don and Annie Kennedy's deaths, since it's the settlement for their accident backing this endeavor."

"I'm so sorry." Karen's voice is so sympathetic that I find myself spilling the rest of it.

"It's also the fifth anniversary of Willa's attack." I gaze at Willa to center myself, leaving out how I was the one violated and left for dead. I see the questions spinning in the townsfolk's heads, so I head them off at the pass. "Donny and I always spent the anniversary together, as we have every year since. No son should be alone on the day his father died… I just happened to walk into a nightmare five years ago."

"What happened to–" Willa censors herself, and only Warren and Kade catch on. "*Me* is why we need this program. Domestic violence. Alcoholism. Poverty. Ignorance. I was in an impossible situation, and I barely survived it." Her final words croak out. Emotions getting the best of her, Willa covers her mouth with the back of her hand and makes a run for it.

I move to follow, but a chubby baby is pressed into my arms. "Sometimes you make it more *real*. You feel me?" and then Warren is chasing after his sister.

"Hi," I whisper to Copper, looking straight into his bright, blue eyes. I turn my back to everyone so they can't see the expression on my face. "I hope you recognize my voice, because this is the first time I've held you and I promise I'm not a stranger."

Finding me nonthreatening, Copper shoves his pink thumb into his mouth and starts gumming it and making spit bubbles, curious eyes never leaving mine.

"Thank you for coming," Kade takes over like I hoped he would. "I hope y'all will keep in touch. I'd like to have a meeting a week from Monday. So if any of you have any suggestions, email me and I'll mull them over. If you're not interested in our program, don't let the door hit you on the ass on your way out."

I press my cheek against the top of the boy's baby-fine coppery hair and ignore everyone as they leave. "You're such a good baby. So patient. So unlike your parents. I hope they don't drive you insane, little feller." Copper makes a cooing sound and snuggles deeper against me. "Aww… you like me."

"That baby is a flirt," Kade walks up behind me. "Give him a bit of attention and he owns you. He already has my dog wrapped around his tiny finger." Kade settles his palm in the center of my back, and I stiffen. "I don't know why you continue to lie to me, Dad. I lost an entire semester of my sophomore year at Penn State because I had to take care of Bren while you were in the hospital and then while you healed at home."

"I wasn't in the hospital. I was just there for Willa." I barely breathe as the lie lands, not daring to move. Kade's fingertips curl into my back, like he's furious and trying to make a fist. "There are some things a son should never know about his father. Let's leave it at that."

"There are times when a father shouldn't underestimate his son." Kade's voice is so quiet I have to strain to hear him. "The courtroom may have been closed to the public. The case files may have been sealed to protect the identity of the victims. But to think my own father thinks me stupid hurts the worst."

"It wasn't about you, Kade." My words are cold, and I regret them instantly.

"I know," Kade grits back. "But to be frozen out, to have read the transcripts and know what had happened to you. You of all people refused to get help, refused to let me in, when you expect me to accept your help and give you total access to my private thoughts... I was twenty during the trial, and I took care of Bren while you were with your lawyers, and you froze me out."

"Kaden?" I turn around, Copper clutched to my chest.

Hands spread out to stop me, "Don't!" Kade looks me straight in the eyes, more defiant than ever. "You always wanted to know why I acted like I resented you... well, there ya go. That's why." He walks backward toward the exit. "Maybe if you'd let me in, I'd do the same."

"I–" my eyes flick to the baby's, like he can tell me what I should say to make Kaden feel better.

"Ya know what?" Clearly fed up with my shit, Kade flings his hands in the air. "You're thirty-nine. Warren and I are twenty-four with Willa joining us soon, and the boys are eighteen. But do you know what we all have in common?"

"We're all adults," I blurt out.

"Yeah, *that*." Kade rolls his eyes. "We've all made mistakes and you helped us deal with them. Maybe we feel worthless because you won't let us return the favor."

I'm walking forward before I realize it, but my son is turning away from me. "Kaden."

"You're a human being, Royce. It's time you accepted that fact." Kade leaves me standing alone, and all I can do is follow. I catch the last of what he's saying. "You need to take a few of your own classes."

Hackles rising, I hate how Kade manipulates the ever-loving fuck out of me. "Seriously? What do you expect?" I snarl as I stalk after him. "We split a six-pack while I spill the grisly details about being raped while my hysterically crying brother beat his wife so she'd pass out and not have to witness it? That sound like a fun time to you?"

Kade turns on his heel, glare lasering through me. "How about you explain why such a good guy cracked in the first place? Hmm? Sean? What the fuck happened to Sean? One week we were eating Sunday dinner, and the next you and Willa are half dead, Sean is dead, and Donny won't be out of prison for another nine years... but you still visit him once a month."

I turn belligerent because I do *not* want to have this conversation right now. Ever. "You guilt-trip worse than a grandmother– always trying to cut my balls off. I'll die before I answer any of that," I mutter defiantly as I step onto the sidewalk.

"I'm not stupid!" Kade shouts, sound splitting my ears. I curl my arm over Copper's head, never wanting him to hear raised voices. "And neither is he!" Kade points at Warren.

Having a faceoff similar to ours, Warren is leaning over Willa, whose arms are crossed over her chest and her lips are drawn into a tight line of defiance. No doubt they are having a similar interrogation.

"I don't know about that," I grumble. "Warren can act pretty stupid. Nice try, but he ain't getting shit out of Willa. Out of the two of us, she's less likely to tell the truth."

Kade reaches over, taking Copper from my arms. The baby fusses for a second, but settles down immediately against Kade's broad chest. His, "When Willa's sober," has my knees buckling. My arm is braced in Kade's unforgiving fist to keep me upright. "And Willa wasn't sober for nearly four years. I know everything, Royce. Every-fucking-thing."

Eyes bulging out of my skull, body weak like I'm going to pass out, I mutter listlessly, "Then why are you doing this to us? Leave well enough alone."

"Well enough? Because it's time," Kaden whispers with tears glinting in his eyes.

"I've had a rough day, son." I take a deep breath, and then start for Willa. "Can I have the rest of the day without being emotionally tortured?"

"Dad?" Kade grips my bicep lightly to stay me, while clutching Copper to his chest with his other arm. "It's time. You and Willa have been dancing around this for eleven months." He releases a bitter laugh. "Make that eight? No, almost nine years. I'm going to put one-hundred-percent of my focus into the Life Skills Center because I believe in it. Wynn's going away to school, and I want him to experience it without having half his heart and soul back here worried about you… and Bren. Bren's got his own shit going down, and he can't handle yours."

"What do you want me to do?" Warren steps away as I stand at Willa's side. She looks less worse for wear than I do. She's used to her brother's tactics, whereas I'm not used to Kade reaching the end of his rope.

"Gimme my boy," Warren orders, reaching to take Copper from Kade. "If you ever yell while holding him again, I'll kick your teeth in. Got it?"

"Got it." Kade glances away in shame. "Dad– Willa? Ya gotta move on. Get some help. You can't keep this lie going."

"I don't see how not giving the violent details is lying," I burst out, flabbergasted. "We have the right to privacy."

Kade points at Willa and me, fury etched across his features. "*They* have a right to not live a lie. Tell the truth and be done with it."

Willa and I are both stunned stupid. She reaches for my hand, never before initiating that small gesture of comfort. I wrap my hand around hers and squeeze tightly to center myself.

"We're walking home," Kade orders Warren. "You're not getting in that car with my godson ever again. I'm calling the junkyard to tow it away."

"What the fuck am I supposed to drive, asshole?" Warren keeps snarling underneath his breath, but he's removing Copper's car seat while he's doing it. "Penny is gonna shit a brick if I can't drive Jeb and the girls back up to Franklin Holler every evening."

"I'll drive you tonight." Kade takes the car seat so Warren can carry Copper. "Penny's getting a graduation gift. Look for a hefty deposit into your account come tomorrow morning."

"What the fuck?" It's my turn to snarl. "Stop accessing the fund, or I'll remove your name from it! Are you bastards blackmailing me now?" Willa tugs on my hand to keep me from committing homicide in front of my new center promoting survival.

"Royce," Kade talks down to me like I'm an idiot. "When you're upset, it makes you feel good to give things to people in need. I saw you eyeing this car, and I heard you bitching about it. You're really, *really* upset right now, so you need to give a big gift."

"Thanks!" Warren says enthusiastically as he carries his son down the street toward my house. "I'm glad Willa hasn't convinced you to go into therapy yet, or I might have missed out on a new car."

My glare is piercing, but it only makes Kade laugh. "Hey, don't shoot the messenger. I'm just doing your work for you, cutting out the middle man. I promise not to go overboard at the center."

"I'm telling Wynn," I threaten, and I only succeed in making Kade's grin larger. He walks away from me after detonating a bomb and then leaving me to do the cleanup. "He hates it when you spend my money." I turn to Willa. "Did that actually just happen?"

"Welcome to my world," she mutters sarcastically. "They tag-team you by making you feel like shit. Then when you're at your weakest, they go in for the kill. It's classic Warren and Kade. They planned this, no doubt."

Dumbfounded, I just stare after my son, finally seeing him clearly. Kade always said I wouldn't want to hear his private thoughts. Now I'm terrified.

"You know, I hate Kade's guts," Willa admits.

"Really?" I squint, just making out Kade blowing kisses to Copper.

"I mean, I love him like a brother." Willa sighs, seeing the sweetness I'm seeing. "But sometimes I want to punch him in his fucking face."

"I bet Wynn feels the same way most days, aside from the brother part... Therapy?" I prompt. "What was Warren talking about?"

"Lunch?" Willa evades.

"Therapy?" I try again.

Willa proves she can't be swayed while sober. "Lunch. Driving lesson. Be home before the kids get out of school. I'm cooking dinner while you're in your office. We're having pulled pork and baked potatoes. Strawberry shortcake. Dishes and homework. Sit around the bonfire. Then sleep. Nowhere in there is talk of therapy."

"Yes, ma'am."

"I'm really proud of you, you know?" I murmur to Willa as we all sit around the bonfire. Hayden's curled up in my lap, softly sleeping. When he begins to stir, I skim my fingertips down my boy's cheek, trying to coax him back to sleep.

"I should have learned to drive almost eight years ago," Willa replies flippantly. She gazes down at Hayley's head resting on her lap. "Our daughter will never have to go through this. This sick feeling of learning things kids do when you're a grown woman with half-grown kids. Do you have any idea how embarrassing it was when Wynn was driving and I couldn't? He's five years younger than me."

"That doesn't mean you shouldn't be proud, just the same." This time I skim my fingertip down Willa's arm, then Hayley's pink cheek. "No one has ever thought any less of you."

"I don't want a handicap because of what happened." Willa's words are soft and quiet, but for the first time I can hear the underlying anger. "*I've* thought less of me. I can't be proud of myself for learning something I should've known already. I can't keep blaming Donny and Momma and Daddy, either."

"You better not be blaming yourself," I order in a commanding tone. I stroke the back of her hand to lessen the punch of my words.

"I don't want to have this conversation right now. Dr. Cassidy is helping me work through this."

My eyes flick over to rest on Kaden, and now I understand how he feels with me. If Willa doesn't want to talk, she shuts down. Nothing will force her to open up. I never realized I do this to my kids, and I have no buddies to open up to. Donny was my best friend, with Corbin and Sean as his buddies. Once they were gone, I was too terrified to connect with anyone else.

Kade's being an asshole because of me– I just know it. I want him to treat me as he did his father, but I'm not treating him as his father did. The connection flows both ways.

Willa catches me watching Kade while he scribbles furiously into a notebook using the firelight to see. "Hey, Wynn?" She calls out. "Did Kade tell you Warren's getting a new car tomorrow?"

"Huh?" Wynn's chisel slips and he curses underneath his breath. "Since when? They ain't got no money." Wynn hands Kade the director's nameplate he's crafting. "This what you had in mind?"

"Yeah…" Kade's fingertip glides over the letters as he gazes down reverently. His eyes flick up to Willa's, pleading with her not to start any shit. In Willa's own way, she's defending me. "It's perfect, Wynn. I love it."

Wynn takes the nameplate back, and his chisel goes back to work. "Car?"

"I… um…" Kade stumbles over his words, so I protect the tranquility of our bonfire time.

"I didn't like Copper riding around in that deathtrap, so they're getting a new family car as a wedding-baby-graduation present," I say on the fly.

"Oh, that's so sweet, Royce." Wynn looks at me like I rise and set the sun. Kade snorts, but he flashes me a relieved smile.

"Nice," Willa drawls. Hayley wiggles in her sleep, hand slapping her momma in the chest. "Now I see why Penny calls you Rocky," Willa says with a girlish giggle.

We all go back to what we were doing: Willa and I gazing down at the children in our laps, Kade working on something for the center, Wynn crafting the nameplates, and my first born is gazing into the fire like it holds the secrets of the universe.

Bren feels my gaze, and it breaks him out of his trance. He looks terrified, lost, and alone. I move to go to him, but he shakes his head no. "I need to take a walk– gotta get out of here so I can think straight."

"Hide-a-key is by Suicidal Tendencies' foot," Kade mutters, never looking up from his notebook. "Either hook Pervert on his run or take him for a walk. His food is in the pantry. Don't let the fat hog fool ya– he only gets a cup and a half of dry food. Sleep on the couch 'cuz my sheets need washed and you don't wanna know what's on 'em. Perty has to sleep with you, or else he shits on the floor out of spite. Beware, he snores and kicks in his sleep."

"Brennan?" My voice wavers. "You don't have to go. We won't bother you in the house."

Bren's, "I need a change of scenery," is cut off by Kade's, "Let him go, Dad."

"I'm fine, Dad." Bren leans down to flutter Hayden's hair. "Nobody is dying. No one is sick. I'm still graduating. But I'm trying to figure out what I'm supposed to do with the rest of my life.

So don't worry about me." He gives a tug to Hayley's fauxhawk. "I'll be back before breakfast."

We all stare after Bren as he crosses the yard. Watching my son walk away tears my heart out. Kade yelling startles all of us. "If you have anyone over to– talk –Perty has to stay in the room with you."

Bren's laugh is dark and pain-filled. "Or else he shits on the floor? Got it. Good night."

Wynn, Willa, and I turn on Kade as soon as Bren is out of sight. "You know?"

"I'm being a big brother," is all Kade says. He picks up his pen again, and begins scratching out words in his notebook. I'm stunned speechless and Willa is making odd, flabbergasted noises.

"You either tell me, or I'm gonna rip your dick off." Wynn grabs the pen out of Kade's hand, and then points at him with it. "Bren has been a lunatic for the past two weeks. Our friends won't speak to each other. We only have a few days left and should be together. I need to fix it."

"You can't fix it." Kade calmly reclaims his pen. "No one can." He leans forward to write in his notebook. "Bren has to figure out what he wants to do, and the people he loves are going to have their feelings hurt. But the choice is his."

"I can help!" Wynn cries. "Dammit, Kaden!"

"You *can't*," he stresses with finality, causing my guts to twist in on themselves. "Bren can't talk to you or Royce because you'll try to fix it for him, or tell him what you think he should do. With something like this, only Bren can decide. I'm not influencing him, that's why he came to me. And I'm not going to break his confidence, because then no one would trust me to keep my word again."

"If my son needs me–" I grit out between clenched teeth, feeling utterly helpless.

"Then he'll come to you." Kade is firm with me and I oddly take comfort in it. "Bren was telling the truth; no one is in mortal danger. He's just... *conflicted.*"

"I'm tired." Wynn hops up from the ground and begins gathering his supplies. "I'm going to bed."

"I'll go with." Kade makes it two feet before three people glare at him for different reasons.

"Unless you're going to tell me what's up, you can keep your ass out of my bedroom," Wynn snarls.

"No," I bark out, startling Hayden awake. "Remember the house rules?"

"I'm tired." Kade rolls his eyes at me. "It's been a shitty day. I want to shower and go to sleep. I'm not up for *that*. Besides, look at him." He points at Wynn's furious expression. "He's not gonna let me sleep until he bitches at me."

"Yeah, but in the morning…"

"What?" Willa looks around, confused. "Morning what?"

"A pissed off hormonal teenager in bed with–" I shudder at the thought.

Kade flashes me the naughtiest smirk I've ever seen, and then releases an evil cackle. "*Two* hormonal guys."

"Gross," Willa and I grumble at the same time. "No, follow the rules," I warn.

"Royce," Wynn sounds exasperated. "Like either one of us have followed your rules at all. I've slept with Kade four times in the past week. Only this is the first time we're letting you know it's happening beforehand."

Impersonating her brother, "*But I'm eighteen and a half!*" Willa stops me from murdering my sons by mocking Wynn's favorite saying. "If you still add that half year, you're too young to share a bed."

"Bitch," Wynn says with affection. Sour mood broken, Wynn's laughter floats after him as he crosses to the back porch.

"I promise to be as quiet as a church mouse," Kade taunts us. "It's not like you heard us this morning, or last night, or yesterday afternoon. Seriously, I'd suggest hiring a cleaning service to fumigate Wynn's room of the sex stench when he moves to the dorm."

"Good night, Kade," I say none too kindly, but then I crack a grin.

"Good riddance, Kade," Willa mumbles beneath her breath. "Do you think we'll get rid of him once Wynn moves?"

"Nah, he's here to stay." My smile is genuine as I revel in having Kade all to myself, getting to know him on a different level without him being distracted by Wynn.

"Drat," Willa teases me. "You have some work you need to do on that boy before my brother graduates from college. I don't want Wynn spending his life with that man-child."

"I think the center will take care of that." I hope and pray. "They're good for each other. They balance each other out."

"Yeah, but there is something seriously naughty about the pair, like they could get into some trouble if they're not careful."

"Trouble?" My head tilts back as I release a deep laugh to the sky. I can practically feel my eyes glinting with amusement. "Wynn is your baby brother, Willa. I'm the only person on this planet who knows just how naughty you can get. Mixing Kade and Wynn equals depraved."

I lean back against the log, hugging a sleeping Hayden to my chest. Bubbles of laughter keep spilling from my lips, but they get cut off when a pair of soft lips press against mine. I still, breath hitching in my lungs, unsure what to do as I allow Willa the freedom of choice.

The tentative kiss lasts all of two seconds, but it rocks me to my core. Willa leans away, lips still parted from our kiss yet smiling blindingly. Both of us are blushing in the firelight like innocent teenagers.

"Now *that* I'm proud of." Standing, Willa hoists Hayley up against her chest, and the little one wraps her arms around her momma's neck and hooks her legs around momma's hips. "Naughty? Pretty sure I was depraved with you…"

NOCTURNAL VISITOR

Warm and comfy, I have to be dreaming. Giving me a bit of a chill, sneaky fingertips tug at my sheet, lowering it until my thighs are bare. "I thought men slept naked," Willa's disappointed, pouting words swirl around inside my head.

I bolt upright in bed, heart beating out of control from the shock. "Christ!" I clutch my chest, fearing a heart attack. "Dang it! I'm getting too old for this shit. I'm not dreaming, am I?" I reach blindly to switch on my lamp. In the process, my hand knocks a glass of water off the nightstand to land on the floor with a piercing smash. Soft light spearing the darkness, Willa cringes, hand covering her face.

"What are you doing in here?" I demand of the young woman sitting on the edge of my bed. "How did you get here?"

Scrubbing at her filthy face, Willa's finger snags in her uncombed hair. "I wal–ked," she slurs, yanking her finger free from her rat's nest.

"You what?" I squawk, not fearing Bren will hear me since he's staying over at Franny's house. "Willa, are you high? What did you take? How did you get here? Why are you here? Are Wynn and the kids alright?"

"I'm so sorry." Willa bends at the waist, sobbing into her hands. I take a good look at her– a good look. She's destroyed herself. Ruined. Flashes of the young girl I met years ago play out in my mind, and it makes me sick.

I did this to Willa. Me.

My hands flutter around, unsure of what to do with Willa after so long of trying to reclaim her. I have no idea how to help her since she's sunk so deep. Her feet are bare, black as soot but not marred in anyway. So she didn't walk from Gillette Holler. Her skin looks thin and yellowed. Her body is shrinking away, not the vitality a twenty-two-year-old woman should have. Her silky blonde curls are ratted and snarled, not seeing a drop of water and soap or a brush in more than a month. Tears make tracks in the caked-on dirt on her cheeks. She stinks. A vile scent of sickness and drugs, and misery and regret.

My fists clench in my sheets, not knowing what to do but knowing I need to do something. This is the end– Willa can't go on living like this. I can't go on living in this stasis, waiting and wondering, fearing for the twins' lives at the same time as watching Warren, Willa, and Wynn suffer so.

Willa's eyes connect with mine, and for the first time in a long time, they hold clarity. She's ready. "War's at Kade's place, figuring out what we need to do. He told me to stay in the car, but I couldn't."

"So you came to me," I mutter underneath my breath, stunned. "What's going on?"

"Wynn–" my cellphone interrupts Willa.

I blindly reach to silence it. "What about Wynn?" I look to see who's calling and my heart sinks. With the flick of my finger, the phone is answered and pressed to my ear. "Wynn? It's two in the morning. Did something happen?"

I hold an entire conversation on autopilot, nothing sinking in, as Willa stares at me with eyes filled with a wealth of guilt and shame. Call ended, my cellphone lands on my mattress, forgotten.

Rage spikes my blood. Pure, unadulterated rage fuels my courage. I don't walk on eggshells. I lose every ounce of patience I possess. I blink, only to find my fists clenched around Willa's bony arms, when I haven't initiated touching her in years, hating how she would shrink back and cry out. I always waited for Willa to touch me first. But not tonight. I squeeze this side of breaking bone and she doesn't fight me.

I snarl into Willa's face, spittle flying. "What did Wynn do?" Grimacing, she shakes her head no, matted hair flopping into her face. I squeeze tighter, until her face contorts in agony. "What. Did. Wynn. Do?"

"Dad?" Bren's bellow hits my ears just as my door is swinging open. "Fran and I were taking a walk and Kade and Warren were running down the street calling out for–" My son finally registers the tableau happening on my bed. "Oh…"

My hands release Willa, not giving a fuck that she lands on the floor in a pile of filthy skin and bones. I step over her wailing body and grab a pair of jeans out of my dresser drawer. My mind spins with solutions. Fury making me only see red. I slip my jeans over my boxers and abandon looking for a shirt.

"Call your brother and tell him I have Willa. Make sure he gets Warren's ass in this house in the next three minutes or I'm cutting him off financially for life." I stare my stunned son down. "You

repeat that word for word. Go!" I don't bother making sure Brennan follows through. The kid always does as he's told.

No longer gentle and kind, I reach down to grip Willa's arm. Hauling her to her feet, I drag her to my bathroom. Propelling her forward, I toss Willa into the bathtub, not giving a shit when she releases a pain-filled grunt.

"I'm sorry," she mutters on repeat, every few words slurring together. I can tell this is as sober as she's been in years and it won't be long until the effects of detox set in.

Voice laced with fury and sarcasm, "I'm glad to see you love Wynn more than you love your own kids." I jerk the faucet handle to the hottest setting. Instantly a spray of scalding water descends on Willa. She hovers in the bottom of my bathtub with her hands over her head like I'm going to kick her.

Even seeing Willa in a position my brother used to put her into way too often, when I was the one she ran to for help, doesn't lessen my anger. I know I'm breaking our bond of trust and comfort, but we're way past easing Willa into anything.

As I'm dumping the contents of a bottle of shampoo on her head, she sputters up at me. "It wasn't Wynn... When Momma slapped Hayley, I–I– I snapped. I couldn't take it no more. I got into a fight with Momma, and Daddy had to tear us apart."

My eyes zero in on Willa's bloodied lip, and I swear once again how I'm going to kill Corbin Gillette one day. But then I remember why he still breathes. I want that man to suffer until his dying breath. I'll take every fucking Gillette from him if I have to. I'll make them happy and flaunt them in his face, showing him how he is a pathetic, worthless excuse for a human being who couldn't take care of his own flesh and blood. But I could.

Corbin had no right to take from me what he did. To take from Donny and me. To take from Willa. Justice. I might not be putting a bullet in Corbin's head, but I've been plying him with beer just so I can watch his body cannibalize itself. I derive sick enjoyment out of watching him deteriorate.

"It took Wynn trying to blow his own brains out for War to finally snap." Willa's still blubbering as my mind takes a vengeful vacation up to Gillette Holler, where I see Corbin looking confused over the loss of every one of his children. To me. They are all mine now. He has no one except for his toxic Cora.

Evil exists, and it's only human nature for me to want to witness my revenge.

But I'm not evil, only human. "I'm going to take your clothes off you," I warn Willa to steel herself. Her big blue eyes pop wide open, filled with terror. "I have never hurt you. I will never hurt you. All I've ever done is save you at the risk of ruining everyone else, even if I couldn't save you from yourself."

Courageously, Willa begins unbuttoning her stained blouse with shaking fingertips. I stand over her, half leaning into the bathtub as the shower rains down on us. I watch, noticing how time, age, children, and drugs have taken their toll on Willa's body. She's no longer the curious child I laid with. She's a grown woman who is going to take my help, even if I have to force her.

"You're incapable of making the decisions I've allowed you to make, Willamina." I take her blouse from her, and toss it onto the tile floor. "I promised I'd never force you to do anything. But maybe if I loved you more than fearing you'd hate me if I broke my promise, I would have. Because there are some things you have to do, whether you want to or not."

"Dad?" Bren calls from my bedroom, knowing better than to enter my bathroom. "Warren and Kade are with me."

I look down at Willa. "Are you okay with your brother helping you wash and dress, or do you want me to do it?"

"Where will you be?" Her voice quivers as if she's cold, but she's sitting in sweltering water.

"Kade and I have some arrangements to make, and I have to put Bren into action." I reach down to help Willa struggle out of her soaked jeans, stretched out underwear pulling away with them. There's a bruise blooming on her hip, and I want to kill myself knowing it was from when I tossed her into the bathtub.

I hate myself even more when Willa takes off her bra. I notice she's fuller, more womanly. I remember how her breasts fit directly in my palms and how they swelled when she was pregnant— the satisfaction I felt as the twins suckled at her nipples. Sick in the head and heart, I turn from Willa.

"I'll give you some privacy and send Warren in." I grab a towel to dry my back and chest off. "Don't worry, Willa. I promise I will put your welfare above any promises I made in the past."

"That's what I'm terrified of but am counting on," she whispers as I leave the room.

Warren brushes past me in a rush to get at his sister, nearly knocking me off my feet. "What did you do?" Warren bellows. "Why did you run from me? Why did you come here?"

Willa's, "We need help," breaks me.

Suffocating, choking on a sob, I bolt past my sons, fist landing in the center of my bedroom door. The force propelling my hand all the way through it.

"Hey… hey… hey…" Willa's worried voice draws me awake. "Shh… it's okay. It's gonna be okay, Royce. I promise."

It takes me a moment to blink off the delirium. I wake in the same way my nightmare began. "I'm not dreaming, am I?" Willa's leaning over me, curls loose and clean, skin fragrant and healthy. An innocent white nightgown made seductive with its transparency. "What are you doing in here?"

One corner of Willa's lips curves up into a sardonic smirk. "Is this where I'm to ask you if you sleep in the nude?" She pats her hand in the center of my chest, directly over my heart, the only thing separating our skin is the thin sheet. "I could feel you were hurting. I can tell the memories are riding you more now that I'm letting them go. It's time we talk about therapy."

"Willa?" I roll my eyes, but I reach up to rest my hand over hers– the comforting warmth seeping into my bones. "I thought you said we weren't going to talk about therapy?"

"That was yesterday." The other side of her lips curves up to widen her smirk. "The last thing on my list was sleep. It's morning. A new day. I'm stronger now, and it's my turn to help *you.*"

"Please, take a seat," Dr. Cassidy gestures to the leather sofa as she slowly lowers herself into a matching chair. Willa sits next to me, pulling a pillow from behind her back to clasp to her chest like a teddy bear. "First, Mr. Kennedy– may I call you Royce?" I nod my head in a quick jerk yes. "Are you okay with Mrs. Kennedy joining us?"

Eyes narrowed, I turn to Willa. "Why didn't you let the doctor call you Willa?"

Dr. Cassidy covers her mouth with the back of her hand, a trilling laugh slipping out. "No, Royce, I call Mrs. Kennedy Willa. I'm just getting the formalities out of the way."

"Oh," I mutter, eyes still on Willa. She's comfortable here, and I can tell she trusts the doctor. I kept envisioning a mother or grandmother looking woman, who I'd never want to know my dark secrets. But Dr. Cassidy is in her late forties, very professional with her bifocals and clinical air. She's what comes to mind when you think *doctor*.

"Willa said she couldn't progress any further in her therapy unless I came. Something about how she can't fill you in on my memories."

"That is very true." Dr. Cassidy shifts in her chair, picking up a tablet and pen. "Frankly, I'm surprised you're joining us today. For the past year, you've sat in my parking lot four times a week. I was beginning to wonder if you wanted me to go out and drag you in here for a session." Dr. Cassidy has a sarcastic, evil edge about her that puts me at ease. "Maybe an engraved invitation?"

Willa leans forward. "That's my fault. I–I–I didn't think Royce was ready yet, so I didn't ask him to join us."

"Ah… I see." Dr. Cassidy's eyes flick back and forth between Willa and me, with a tiny smirk on her face. "You both protect the other. Royce, that's why I asked whether or not you wished for our initial session to be in private. But I fear I won't get the whole story unless I can watch both of your reactions to your truths."

"I–I–I…" It's my turn to stutter. "No matter how much it hurts, we need to get this out. If Donny were with us, I'd say the same thing in front of him. We can't hide behind the lies anymore."

Dr. Cassidy looks stumped, like the way I think is baffling. "Willa said you don't blame Donny, how you don't blame Sean. She said no matter what she says, you won't let her take responsibility for her actions, nor do you blame yourself."

"I blame her father," I blurt out before I can edit myself. Since it's out, I go with it. "Corbin Gillette is at fault."

"Did you tell Royce what you learned?" Dr. Cassidy turns her questions on Willa. "He might not hold this grudge if he could be more sympathetic toward your father's kneejerk reaction."

"No," Willa breathes.

"Probably for the best. These types of things go best in a controlled environment. Just as how I said I'd like to be present for when you finally tell your children the truth."

Willa shakes her head emphatically, and I'm confused since I never thought we'd tell them. I turn to the side, jerking the pillow from behind my back. I wrap my arms around it and squeeze. I wonder if all of Dr. Cassidy's patients hug her pillows. There is a bunch of teddy bears hanging out by her desk that draw my attention. I hope she brings them when she forces me to tell the kids the truth. I'll need one then.

"How about we start out easy, hmm?" Dr. Cassidy's smile matches the bright and easy tone in her voice. "Royce, tell me about how you and Willa met."

"Ha! Easy?" Willa and I share a bitter laugh.

ᰒ9 years agoᰒ

"Roy!" Sean shouts from the driveway. "Roy! Get rid of the kid. We gotta book it to Don's. He's got a surprise for us."

Hiding out behind the barn, I'm hanging up a basketball hoop for Brennan to practice with. "Just ignore him," I mutter to Bren, trying hard not to laugh. My kid's face is scrunched up, hating it when my friends stop by and whisk me away. My son loves to be shoved up my ass, just the way I want it.

"You'll go to Uncle Donny's." Bren pouts, flashing his brown puppy dog eyes. "We were gonna play Horse."

"Roy? Where ya at, bub? Stop playing hide and seek!"

I put a finger up against my lips. "Be vewy, vewy qwiet." I mimic Elmer Fudd. "Sean's hunting wily wabbits."

"Jeez, Dad." Bren rolls his eyes, and then he starts giggling. I reach over, turning into the tickle monster. "Yer givin' us away!"

Sean follows our laughter, finding Bren and me rolling around on the ground, wrestling and tickling the shit out of each other. I wish I could bottle the sound of my kid's happiness.

Hands tucked on his hips, Sean stares down at us smiling brightly. "I always wanted a little squirt, but…" My buddy leaves that trailing off. Sean Probst is a couple years older than me, same age as my brother and their buddy, Corbin Gillette. They take pity on me a few times a month and give me a good time up at my brother's place, making me ditch my boy with his friends.

Sean's an odd duck– in his thirties and never married. He doesn't seem to have much use for a woman, so I doubt he'll ever have a kid. I like him anyway. Real nice feller. Corbin Gillette, on the other hand, is a mean sonofabitch who gets belligerent and ornery when he drinks. But I don't get much choice in the matter, seeing as how I never made any friends besides Annie. Now that she's gone, my brother's taking pity on me.

"What's the surprise?" I roll over to my knees, and then stand. I reach down to pluck Bren off the ground, steadying him on his feet. "You never know with Donny." I huff a laugh, remembering that time he bought a horse only for me to tell him it was a mule. "He got a goat this time?"

"Better," Sean says cryptically. "Fetch the squirt and drop him somewhere." Loping across my yard, Sean shouts over his shoulder. "I'll meet ya at Don's."

I pop an eyebrow at the kid. "Franny or Jack?"

"Jack is camping with Duane and Jesse." Bren has a way with making normal words hold emotion. Right now, he's *very* disappointed in me. "I told them no because you said we were gonna play Horse on the new hoop."

Bren's guilt trips always make me miss my Annie. She was the queen of guilt trips, and she taught her son well.

"Well, what if Uncle Don got a new dog?" I rest my hand on Bren's bony shoulder. "Hmm? What if he got a new dog and I have to make sure it's not vicious?"

"If he's nice, can I pet him?" Bren's face glows and his voice pitches higher. "Please? Can I? Can I?"

"Sure, kid." I look away, trying hard not to laugh. *What if there isn't a dog?*

"Dad? I'm nine. I ain't slow," Bren deadpans. "C'mon, ya need to drop me off at Franny's. You owe me big time, 'cuz his sisters use us as dolls."

"Dolls?" I pull my keys from my pocket, following after my boy.

"*Dolls*," Bren stresses. "Sometimes the makeup doesn't wash off, and Franny loves it." He looks at me in exasperation, silently saying, "*Look what you put me through.*"

"You like Franny, though, right? He's your buddy." We hop in my truck, and drive two streets over to Francis Parker's house. I'm shifting into park and Bren still hasn't answered me. "Brennan? You like Franny, right?"

"Yes, Dad. He's my best friend." Bren turns to look out the window. "Franny's different, like Sean." His quiet, hesitant words don't compute, because I don't know what he's getting at. But kids are more perceptive than adults sometimes. "He likes to play dress-up and be his sisters' living doll. I put up with it because someone has to protect him."

Bren opens the truck door and hops out. "I'll see ya later, Dad."

I watch my son stride up the front walk, and just before he gets to the door, I roll my window down and call out, "You know I love you, right? Just sometimes I need to play with my friends, too."

"I get it." Bren knocks on the door, still staring at me. "I love you, too." The door opens with a high-pitched girly squeal, and it's coming from Franny. Brennan waves me off, slipping inside to play dress-up.

I crank the radio up as high as it will go. I roll down both windows, loving the way the wind rushes inside the truck. The ride is smooth until I get outside of town and turn off the main drag. The tree-lined, dirt road is narrow, and it's a thrilling ride going up and down the hills when driving too fast.

Hillbilly roller coaster.

The sense of freedom is intoxicating. Knowing I'll begin missing Bren in about twenty minutes, I savor it.

My brother lives on our old land. Daddy sold it off years ago when I needed cash to buy a place in town. Annie's daddy had a laundry list of demands, and living in town was one of them. When Daddy and Annie died, one of the first things we did was buy back our birthright.

A flatlander had bought it, and he tore down the house and outbuildings. He and his buddies would show up during hunting season with their travel trailers. With the land a blank canvas, Donny wanted a modular home and a barn. Feeling guilty because it was my fault that asshole destroyed our home, I gave my brother whatever he wanted out of my share of Daddy's money. Since Donny's like me, it wasn't too extravagant.

I pull up next to Sean's car, surprised to see him waiting outside for me. "Donny built a fire pit!" I get excited as I jump out of my truck, taking note that's the only new addition to the land. "Is that the surprise? I can't wait 'til Bren's older and appreciates ours."

"You think the surprise is a fire pit?" Sean smirks at me like he finds me amusing. "How cute. Guess again."

I slowly turn in a circle, seeing nothing else out of the ordinary. Besides Donny's flatbed with the welder on the back, only Corbin's rust-bucket is in the driveway. "Why'd you wait out here for me?"

Rubbing his hands together in anticipation, I notice his bruised knuckles. "Oh, I know what the surprise is, and I wanted to see your reaction up close." Sean swaggers up the gravel, and I get what Bren meant about him being different. As I said, Sean's an odd duck. "You ain't gonna like it… but maybe you'll be jealous." Fury leaks into his voice. "I know I was."

Sean walks onto the small porch. He stands to the side, arm out like a gameshow host. "Voila," he sings as he twists the doorknob. "Feel free to kick his ass some more."

My eyes drink in every available surface. Nothing looks different– same furniture I dragged in here last year. My brother's sitting in his favorite recliner, sporting one helluva shiner on his left eye and a split lip. Neither one of us are very tall, but unlike me, Donny's not stocky. He's just a little guy, and I want to pummel Sean for punching him.

Sean moves to stand behind Donny, like he plans on protecting him from me after telling me to go ahead and beat him. If it came down to a fight between Sean and me, he'd lay my ass out.

"Oh, hi!" I step forward to greet the young girl sitting on the sofa with Corbin. "You must be Corbin's little Willa." I don't really look at her while I shake her tiny hand. My eyes are on my brother, waiting for the punchline.

"She ain't *my* little Willa no more," Corbin grunts. He has one arm wrapped around the girl's shoulders while the other is bringing a beer can up to his lips.

Movement catches my gaze, Willa's slowly sliding down to the edge of the sofa, getting as far away from her father as she possibly can. She seems sedate, but ready to bolt if given the chance. She keeps eyeing the door, looking for escape.

Eyes flicking to my brother, "What did you do?" I demand. Donny tries to get out of the chair, but Sean shoves him back down. "What's going on?"

"We good?" Corbin asks. He stands from the sofa, drains his beer, and then tosses it into the kitchen like the bastard he is. It rattles to the floor, nowhere near the trashcan. "We better be. It's too late now. You've already tarnished the wares." He makes his getaway…

"You forgetting something?" I gesture to the girl trying to shrink into the couch.

"Daddy?" Willa blurts out, but then her eyes are flicking all over the place, taking inventory of her surroundings. She looks at me, then Donny. She shrinks away when her eyes light on Sean. She flits across the room to the kitchen, getting as far away from the exit as she can possibly get. "Tell Momma I hate her, and tell War and Wynn I'll be fine and I love 'em."

"Yeah," Corbin grunts. "I thought so. I'd rather stay 'ere, if I was you," he grumbles underneath his breath as he leaves. The door closing heavily has us all jumping out of our skin.

"Explain," I order like I'm in charge. Donny's the one who gives the orders, usually passed down from Sean.

My brother's tongue-tied, and Sean is wearing a sadistic smile on his face. I decide to change my course of action. "Hey, girl. How about you and I have a bit of a visit?" Willa nods her head rapidly, deciding I'm not a threat. "There's a bench on the back deck. It's none too comfortable, but the view sure is breathtaking."

The girl takes a deep breath, obviously relieved I chose the exit that didn't involve walking past my brother and Sean. "What'd you do?" I demand again, but don't get an answer.

"Hey, Roy?" Sean calls out after me as I cross the kitchen. "Go on out there and chat awhile with your new sister-in-law." I miss a step, stumbling. I catch myself on the counter, praying this is all some sick game they're playing.

Surely Sean's joking. Donny's been married twice already, and neither marriage lasted more than a year. Kelly and Nicole left in a fog of rumors and speculation. Both women moving away shortly after the divorce.

I find Willa sitting on the bench, back ramrod straight with pride. She's gazing out over the landscape to the hills beyond. I use the opportunity to look her over. She's a tiny little thing, but rugged, like she could be scrappy. Soft blonde curls frame her heart-shaped face. She's wearing jeans and a t-shirt that look to be undisturbed.

I settle next to Willa, leaving a bit of space between us. She turns her face to gaze at me and my breath catches in my throat. I freeze, understanding Sean's jealous comment. But I'm not jealous of my brother; I'm mesmerized by Willa's clear blue, intelligent eyes.

"It's true, ya know?" She's a blunt little thing, like a ballpeen hammer. "Yer brotha and I are wed. Not that I wanted to, mind you. But I guess it's too late for that now."

"Too late?" My eyes bulge out the more she speaks. "Not that you wanted to?"

"Nah, I didn't want nothin' ta do with this business. But Daddy said we gotta eat, and I was his meal ticket." Willa pierces me with her gaze. "Do ya got any idea what it's like to be someone's meal ticket? Do ya?" She looks me up and down, taking my inventory. "Too bad Daddy didn't find you first. I bet you woulda had more sense than to take me like a dog."

"What?" I gasp, nearly choking on my tongue. I don't know whether I should laugh or scream. I do know I'm going to murder my brother first, though.

"Daddy drug me from my home with my brothers calling after me. I fought. I was kicking and screaming, and I got a few good licks in 'cuz daddy couldn't *tarnish the merchandise*, he said. A pen was shoved in my hand, forcing me to sign the license, and then I was carted here to the back bedroom– my new room –and taken like a dog for all of two seconds."

"Jesus Christ, you keep saying that, but I don't think you know what you're saying."

"War, my oldest brother, he raises coonhounds. I know exactly what I'm saying. It sure as shit ain't what I saw my brother doing to all the neighbor girls. They seemed to enjoy it more than he did."

"Lord, help me," I pray, eyes looking heavenward. "I don't want the details. I take it you weren't a virgin."

Quick and sharp, Willa smacks me across the face. Stunned, I hold my cheek while she stares at me in indignation. "I ain't cheap," she snarls. "I was worth twenty thousand."

"Twenty thousand?" Okay. Remembering Annie when I finally breached her, she bled a bit. "Are you doing okay? Ya know?" I vaguely gesture to her *area*. "Down there?"

"I'm sore." She pouts a great deal, putting Bren's attempts to shame. "But I'll deal. Your brother was quick. Maybe a minute or two from start to finish after I stopped fighting him."

Wait. "Did Donny force you?" My eyes flick all over Willa, noting there is nary a scratch on her perfect skin. "Did *he*?"

"Donny was arguing with me about it. He slapped me like a bitch, but then I decided to get it over with. If I woulda tucked my tail and ran away, Daddy woulda beat me to death. So what's spreading my legs for my new husband compared to that? If I'd known there was nothing to fuss about, I would've just bent over the second we walked into the room."

"Are you sure Donny finished?" I scrub my face with my palms. "I can't imagine trying to do *that* with someone who didn't want me back. I mean, the whole process involves *wanting* to do it."

"My husband's willy was hard!" Willa shouts, offended. "I'm not ugly! I'm not stupid neither. I knows me some things. I knows what needs to be done, and it happened." She glares at me with icy eyes. "I washed it outta me. Didn't want it in me."

"Motherfucking bizarre," I drawl. "Didn't see this coming… Listen, I gotta talk to my brother."

"Yeah, yous better. But don't let me alone with that Sean character. I'ma be in my bedroom if you need me." The girl walks off like she already owns the place.

"Hey, Willa?" I call after her. "How old are you? Eighteen? Twenty? A hundred and five?" It takes decades to perfect that attitude.

"Fifteen," she says with pride– the screen door slamming is her explanation point.

ᏸ❧Present❧Ꮾ

"I missed you," I say with a smile, forgetting where we are. My palm cups the back of Willa's head, drawing her mouth to mine. I kiss her smiling face, her tears mingling with mine.

"Wow…" Dr. Cassidy breaks into the moment. I move away from Willa. I scrub my face with my palms, clearing away the tears and embarrassment. "You don't allow yourselves to remember that time, do you? Is it because it's too painful?"

"I wouldn't say it was painful exactly." I look to Willa, and I know we're feeling the same unexplainable emotion. "It felt good to revisit it just then, though. But at the same time, it's confusing and frustrating and shameful and painful. It's just… too much."

"We've explored losing your virginity before, Willa, and you said it wasn't a big deal. Was that the truth, or was it too painful to revisit?"

Willa laughs, and it's sweet and free. "It wasn't much of anything. I mean, I grew up in the hollers. If it wasn't for Warren and Daddy, I would have lost it a billion times before then. We don't really put a price tag on it like you nice ladies do. It wasn't about God. It wasn't about respect. It was about not getting knocked up by our cousins, our guy friends, or our neighbors. Sex equaled another mouth to feed, and it wasn't worth spreading your legs for someone who couldn't feed ya."

Dr. Cassidy is rendered speechless, but all I feel is relief. *This*. This odd, unique, blunt creature is the Willa we've all missed, and I pray to God she leaves this therapy session with me.

"Donny was my husband, and it was my duty to pull up my nightgown, roll on my side, and let him thrust inside me for about two minutes every night. I didn't know I was missing something until I was taught otherwise." Willa laughs hard, snorting. "God, the night Donny realized I'd learned a new trick, it freaked him the fuck out. He seriously didn't want me to get anything out of it because it threw him off his game. He never touched me again after that."

"I have to hear this." Dr. Cassidy leaned forward. "There has to be a story there."

"Another time, Tabitha," Willa says with a naughty smirk that manages to be as shy and bashful as it is cocky. "I don't think you can handle it today."

"You're probably right." Dr. Cassidy fans her flushed face.

My eyes squint in Willa's direction. "You've never brought this up before in an entire year of counseling?"

"If it was directly tied to you, Willa was always very vague about the details. But I was given the bullet points." Dr. Cassidy picks her notepad and pen back up. "Royce, could you please share the conversation you had with your brother regarding his new marriage?"

"Do I want to? No." I take a deep breath, finding anything dealing with Donny difficult to voice. "Donny was– *is* –my best friend. So you have to understand how hard this is for me. How much guilt and shame I carry over what I did to him, and how I feel he was justified in the pain he felt. It wasn't his fault. Just another form of domestic violence I still don't understand. But he did what he did, and if we hadn't done what we did, none of this would have happened. But what we did, Willa and I, we did it out of love for Donny."

"That wasn't the only reason," Willa interrupts me with the truth.

"Shush now. It's my turn to talk."

❧9 years ago↙

Marching into the living room with purposeful strides, I shout, "Get out!" at Sean. He just shrugs and walks out of the house, but I never hear his truck start up. Then a sick feeling sinks to the pit of my stomach. "Willa? Hey, Slap-Happy?"

Willa appears from the hallway, looking put out. "Would you like some coffee?"

"Do you even know how to make coffee?" Donny has the balls to ask.

"No." Willa narrows her eyes at her new husband. "I ain't stupid. I can figure it out. I can read."

"Does your momma talk to your daddy like that?" Donny volleys back.

"What do you think? Daddy's your buddy." Willa wanders into the kitchen, never really answering Donny. Cupboards slam and water runs.

"I guess we're getting coffee." I sit down on the couch across from my brother. "Do you think Cora talks to Corbin like that?"

A snort flows in from the kitchen.

"Something tells me that hellcat is being good," Donny grumbles, looking guilty and filled with regret. "Something tells me my palm is gonna sting a great deal."

"Just don't let Sean near her." I point at the bruises Donny's buddy left behind.

"This?" Donny points at his shiner and split lip, and another snort hits my ears. "Is a wedding gift from my wife."

My neck jackknifes, hitching to the side so I can look into the kitchen. I find an innocent Willa humming to herself, coffee can cradled in her palms as she reads the instructions on the back.

"Don't start beating on her," I warn Donny. "I can tell Corbin has. A lot."

"Girls like that," Sean says from the front porch, voice flowing in from the open window. "They will test their boundaries. The girl knows better than to pull this shit with her daddy. You were too soft with her already, and she'll own your nuts. Get a kid in her gut and give her something to do."

"I'm the only one here who's had a wife and kid." I stomp over to the window and slam it shut. I lock every window leading out to the porch. "I don't like how Sean influences you. It was you and Corbin for the longest time, then Sean came out of nowhere. If anyone has your nuts in a vise, it's that odd duck."

"I thought you hated Corbin?" Donny looks over his shoulder, watching his new wife like she's invading his home.

"I do. That's saying something, ain't it? I like Sean when he's not around you." I lean forward to squeeze my brother's knee. "What did you do, Donny? Why?"

"I–I–I…" Donny's lost his voice again.

Willa sashays in, still humming to herself. She has a bowl of Cheetos tucked in the crook of her arm, the handles of two coffee mugs in one hand, and a bottle of beer in the other. This girl would make one helluva waitress. She plops a coffee mug in front of me, and then one in front of Donny. The Cheetos land on the center of the coffee table. She drops down onto the sofa next to me, getting into my personal space, and then twists the cap off the beer. She takes a large swig, sighs in pleasure, and leans back on the couch.

Donny and I stare at Willa like she's grown a second head. "What?" She takes another swig. "I've had a rough day."

I grab the beer out of her hand. Tilting my head back, I drain the bottle in a couple of swallows. "Me too. Thanks." I slam the bottle on the coffee table.

Willa glares at me, getting up from the couch.

"Grab another one, and I'll drink that one too," I warn. "Married or not, you're a child."

Petulant, Willa steals my coffee, takes a sip, grimaces, and then grabs the Cheetos bowl to wash the taste away.

"Why?" I beg my brother to answer. "Why did you do this to yourself?"

"Hey!" Willa yells at me, but I ignore her.

I lean to the side so I'm all Donny can see. "Why?"

"I needed a wife and Corbin needed money," Donny whispers, not wanting us to hear the truth.

"Let me get this straight…" I sit back up. "You paid." I look at Willa, remembering how she said she wasn't cheap. "You took twenty grand out of Daddy's trust to buy yourself a hillbilly child-bride, when you could have went to the bar and picked up any girl, even married ones, because you've got more than enough money to take care of a harem of wives. Explain this to me."

"Sean was telling me–"

"Fuck Sean," I snarl. "Leave him out of it."

"Corbin has a wife and kids to feed, and we got more than we could ever need. So instead of lending him money we'd never get back, we made a trade. I needed a wife because I'd like some kids, and he needed some money because his disability isn't enough."

"Corbin is thirty-four-fucking-years-old and never worked a day in his life. What exactly is the nature of his disability?" I see Willa out of the corner of my eye. "Sorry. No offense."

"None taken. My daddy is a worthless sonofabitch." She crunches on a handful of Cheetos. "His only disability is being a violent, lazy drunk." Willa looks at her new husband and says sarcastically, "No offense, but you have shit taste in friends. Brothers? That remains to be seen."

"Wow…" I sigh while rubbing my sweaty palms on my jeans. "What's this kid bullshit you keep spouting? Your wives left you because you didn't want kids."

"I want kids." Donny gazes at me with earnest eyes. "Look how much I love Bren. My wives left because they couldn't give me kids." My brother looks toward the porch, and then shudders. "Kids are important to build a family. I want Daddy to live on in my children too."

"Yeah, but why…" I look back to Willa, who's watching us like a tennis match. "Her?"

"Sean said–" Donny raises his hand to stop my *Fuck Sean*. "I always went after older women, remember? Nicole was forty-five, maybe her eggs dried up. Corbin said his daughter was willing." Willa snorts loudly. "So I decided the younger the more fertile."

"Dammit, Donny!" I pound my fist against my thigh. "Sixteen is the age of consent. Corbin and Cora were the ones consenting. Why?"

"I won't bug the girl none." Donny looks guilty as fuck. He gestures to his maimed face. "These bruises were from Willa trying to get after her daddy. I didn't want Corbin to snap and beat the piss out of her. I didn't take advantage of her. After a minute or two, she said to get the consummating over with. So I did. It didn't hurt her none."

"She's *fifteen*!" I shout in outrage. "How did your dick get hard?"

Both Willa and Donny glare at the sides of my face. "I'll have you know–" Willa's bitching gets cut off by my brother's, "Don't even. I'm not a moron."

"Brennan said the same thing to me earlier, and you two sounded exactly the same, but fuck if I get what you're talking about."

"You're a guy who hasn't gotten laid in three years. Your dick would have gotten hard," Donny challenges me, and it makes me uncomfortable. "Not even you are *that* good."

"But Willa's so charming," I mutter sarcastically. "How could I possibly resist this caustic creature?"

Calculating eyes baring me naked, "Don't go there," Willa warns in a sultry voice that utterly terrifies me. "You best hope I never take a shine to you."

"Willa, please," Donny whispers as softly as possible. He looks to the front windows. "You better hope Sean never hears you say that." He reaches over to grip my hand, squeezing hard. "Don't do it. Don't go there. Sean might hurt you, but he'd surely kill Willa."

"What the fuck?" I come to my feet in an instant.

"Sean is very loyal," is Donny's only explanation. "Don't worry. He'll leave when you do. He's just being snoopy."

"He better," I grit out between clenched teeth. "I gotta get outta here before my head explodes. Does anybody need anything?"

"Surprise me," Willa says with a bright smile. "My daddy forgot to pack my stuff."

"Of course he did," I mutter beneath my breath. "What about school?"

"I'm a married woman now."

"Christ." I stare at my brother, and we share a look. Both of us a heartbeat away from being ill. "This shit is what happens when you let assholes like Corbin and Sean influence you, Donny. This is *not* a joke. We're stuck with Willa for life– all the Gillettes."

My brother looks like he's going to cry, so I back off.

"I won't be mean to Donny as long as he's not mean to me." Willa sounds her age, and I can see the toll this is taking on her.

"I'll leave you be. It's your honeymoon, after all."

My brother winces, but Willa snorts in reply. I swear she mouths, "*I'm not a dog.*"

❧Present❧

"What did you do after you left?" Dr. Cassidy asks, placing her pen on top of her notepad. "Did Sean follow after you?"

"Sean was already gone before I left the house. We were so focused on the conversation at hand, we didn't hear him leave." I squeeze the pillow in my arms, looking for comfort. "I picked my son up, and his little friend too. Both of them were wearing makeup, and I didn't make them wash it off, which made Franny happier than a pig in shit. We played five rounds of Horse, because we had to play until Bren could win. Then I showed the boys the power of the bonfire. We told ghost stories and ate roasted hotdogs and toasted marshmallows all night. The next day Franny helped me pick out some stuff for Willa, and we delivered it. Bren took one look at Willa and thought she was his cousin, not his aunt."

"Did that go well?" Dr. Cassidy tries to gauge Willa's reaction.

"I felt guilty for all of the pretty things Royce showered on me, but was most thankful for the school books he brought. Later, Royce helped me study them. But on the second day of my marriage, I spent my time playing with Bren and Franny. It made me miss my brothers."

"Oh, Willa…" Dr. Cassidy clasps her chest, like her heart hurts.

"Something good came out of it, though. Bren went to school looking for Wynn. Started trailing after him, wanting to know him because of me. It took Bren a few years to get Wynn to notice, but they're as close as brothers can get now."

"How does Bren see you, Willa?" Dr. Cassidy coaxes her to open up.

"I think… and this will sound odd because of how close in age we are. But I think Bren is starting to see me as a mother-figure. He didn't at first when I came home from rehab. He was frightened of hurting my feelings. But now, it's going smoothly. He listens when I speak, like he cares about what I have to say." Willa starts to get choked up, and I long to protect her from the pain. "I like how Bren sees me. It makes me feel good. Makes me feel proud. That's not something my brothers can give me. That's only a form of respect your child can give."

"You should feel proud," Dr. Cassidy says firmly. "I know you barely hear me when I say that, but it's still the truth."

"I don't– I don't recognize this girl Royce is talking about. It's like he's telling a story about someone else. She's not me and I'm not her anymore. But I don't like who I am, either. I wish there was a way to bring back the parts of her I love, without bringing the ignorance with her."

"Willa," I pull her into my side, wrapping my arm around her shoulders. "We'll keep rubbing the tarnish away every day, and she'll shine through brighter and brighter. I promise."

"Okay, here we go, boys." I run my tie between my fingertips. "Every father should teach his sons how to knot a necktie properly."

"I can think of a better use for that tie," Kade grumbles underneath his breath, causing Wynn's face to bloom a bright shade of red.

"Well, I'm sure. But seeing as how I've given you this lesson almost a dozen times, I fear you'd be the one being trussed up." I yank a reluctant laugh out of Bren. Finally. The boy has been catatonic all week. Kade flashes me the stink-eye for embarrassing him. "So, ya put it around your neck like this…"

I swing the tie around my neck so the tails fall to my chest, then I shimmy it until the skinny side is longer. "Pay close attention. Now wrap the tail around from beneath, and tuck it up and over… just like this…" When I finish up the knot, I look up with a wide grin.

Bren's tie is crooked, but otherwise done correctly. I give it a tug to yank it right, and pat it into place. I lean forward, resting my forehead against his. "So proud of you, son. So proud." I wrap my palm around the back of Bren's neck and hold him to me for a moment, imprinting this slice of time into my memory bank. My son gets a bit misty-eyed, so I hand him a hanky.

"Thanks, Dad," croaks from Bren's throat, then he turns to have some privacy while he sniffles.

"And look at you…" Wynn flashes me a Gillette smile filled with big white teeth.

"Do I get a '*so proud of you, son*' for getting my tie right?" Teasing me, Wynn puffs out his chest and grins. "You're too short to do that forehead cuddle with me, though."

"Ever the Golden Boy." Kade grunts begrudgingly. "Does everything perfectly on the first try."

"Hardee-har-har." Wynn rolls his eyes.

"You're jealous of your own boyfriend?" Bren flips around, tears drying on his cheeks but wearing a smile on his face. "You suck at everything, that's why."

I bite my tongue to stop laughing. Kade's tie is wadded into a ball around his neck. "You're more of a hands-on type of guy who takes a few times to learn." I try to fix it and give up, yanking it off his neck. I grab another tie from my closet and do it myself. "There. You sure have grown up to be a handsome sonofabitch. I never met your daddy and momma, but they did good."

"Lumberjack Casanova's not very bright," Bren teases. "College educated idiot who's still a virgin and has never swung an axe."

"Brennan," I warn, knowing how easily Kade will take that to heart. "Some of us learn differently."

"I've got a house, a semi-potty-trained pug, a job I love, a hot genius for a boyfriend, and a bratty-ass little brother. Who cares how bright I am?" Kade grumbles to himself about little assholes. "I'm doing good for myself." He looks down at his discarded necktie. "Just not very good at this. I better go fetch my yellow bowtie."

"Christ, no!" Brennan recoils. "You're not going to embarrass us on our day."

"How'd I do, Daddy?" Hayden tugs at my shirt sleeve. "I'm not gonna embarrass Uncle Wynn and Bren, am I?"

We all try to keep a straight face as I crouch down next to Hayden. "Perfect, son. It's perfect." I straighten his little boy clip-on tie, and then roll up his shirt cuffs to match how Kaden's are above his thick forearms. "I think when your hair grows back in, it'll no longer be Gillette blond." My fingertips flutter across Hayden's fresh, summer brush cut– a Kennedy tradition on the last day of school.

"I want hair like yours and Brennan's but I wanna be big like Uncle Wynn," Hayden puts in a request that ain't ever happening.

"Sorry, Kiddo. You're only getting half of that wish, so which are you gonna pick?"

"I wanna look like you," he whispers softly like it's a secret. "Even if I have to be short."

"Wish granted." I peck a kiss to his forehead, and then rise. "Being tall is overrated anyway. It's easier to kiss girls when you don't have to crank your neck."

"That ain't never been an issue for us." Wynn hitches his thumb between him and Kade. "But it's probably a good idea for Hayden."

"Imagine either one of those fools kissing a short guy or girl." Bren doesn't look very far down to meet Hayden's gaze, commiserating. "They'd look like a cast member from TLC's My Giant Life."

"Bitch," Wynn whispers with affection.

"Franny's wearing off on you, bro." Bren's eyes fill with tears again. "No more calling people a bitch. It'll hurt too much."

"Sorry," Wynn mutters, looking away. But not fast enough before I see his nose wrinkle in a sniffle.

"Good God!" Kade rolls his eyes. "My high school graduation day was the happiest day of my life. You little shits are fucking nuts. I'm the certified fag in the room and I'm not bawling my eyes out because my boyfriend is moving in a few weeks. Man up, pussies."

Kade stomps from my bedroom, boots echoing off the stair treads.

"In other words…" Bren's gaze is locked on the doorway Kade just exited. "He's gonna go hide out in the downstairs bathroom until his puffy eyes go down."

"More than half of our LGBTQ group is graduating today," Wynn explains Kade's odd mood. "He had to remove us from the group last night– Miriam Ross demanded it. He'll be getting a fresh crop come fall, though."

Making a dying sound, Bren darts from the room. Hayden is licking at his heels, but gets cut off by a closing door.

"Have you figured out what's up with him yet?" I've had Wynn on Bren duty all week. I've lowered my standards by asking him to use sexual favors on Kade to get the details.

"No," Wynn pouts. "Kade tricked me three times in a row, saying he'd tell me afterward." He manages to blush and look flabbergasted at the same time. "All I can figure, Franny moving away this afternoon is hitting Bren harder than I expected."

"They have been friends since the sandbox." I can hear Bren being upset in his bedroom while Hayden keeps knocking and asking if he's okay. It's tearing my heart out. "Today should be a happy day."

"I'm happy!" Wynn says with a big, genuine grin. "I'd be happier if Bren and Kade weren't being buzzkills." He shrugs. "There is so much to be thankful for. I almost didn't get to experience today. So I'ma take whatever I can get. It's why I was okay with rooming at school."

"Believe it or not, that was Kade's idea." I didn't want to let Wynn go, but Kade convinced me otherwise. It was the first selfless act on Kade's part I've witnessed. It was so noble it made me forget all the selfish ones.

"Ready?" Now it's my turn to get emotional. "I can't believe this day has arrived." I clasp Wynn on the shoulder. "You're officially a grown man. Dammit!"

"I'm as ready as I'll ever be." Wynn is radiating excitement, practically vibrating out of his skin. "Let's get this show on the road." He walks out into the hallway, movements playful, almost dancing. Cupping his hands around his mouth, "Royce said I'm a grown man now!" he bellows down the staircase. "Ya know what that means, ya old, ornery bastard?"

Kade's insane laughter bubbles up from downstairs. "Wrong graduation, ya little shit."

"Nice try, son." I slap a disappointed Wynn on the back, and then jog down the steps. "Drag your brother out of his depression chamber... I mean his bedroom."

Kade's leaning against the front door, laughing silently with an evil smirk twisting his lips. "I ought to make Wynn wait. I'm the epitome of patient. I only let Warren win the grand because I couldn't take it anymore, but I could've if I tried."

"Don't play games," I warn Kade, and his face transforms from amused to serious. "It'll happen when it happens. It doesn't have to be a special date or time, or the perfect setup or setting. You could just be sitting around doing nothing with Wynn, and you'll just know. It'll be perfect because you love each other."

"You're such a sap." Kade ribs me, but he's blushing. "There was no way your time with..." He makes a whistling sound while pointing up above. "Was perfect."

Laughing uncomfortably, I rub the back of my neck. "It was, though. Even with why we were doing it. *She* chased the hell out of me, had these innocent seduction skills. So when it happened, it was pure fucking chaos, and I needed that in my life. Still do."

"Still need what?" Wynn asks as he hops down the stairs two at a time, with an entourage trailing behind him.

"Balance," I answer with all honesty. "Surreal. My first born is a grown man today, and I was blessed to have Kade and Wynn as well." My eyes widen in amazement. "I'll need Dr. Cassidy to talk me down the day Hayden and Hayley graduate. Dammit!"

"I'll keep your shit together. Promise." Willa takes my breath away. Every day she's a new version of herself– a better version – and I've loved each and every one of them. I'll never be bored, that's for damn sure.

Dressed in an innocent, white sundress, miles of tanned, healthy skin and long, flowing hair, I have to blink to make sure Willa's real. She steps to the side, showing off her mini-me, and a sharp bark of laughter is yanked from my chest.

"Baby girl, what'd you do?" I put my hand over my mouth, containing my laughter.

"It's a Kennedy tradition," Hayley says in her girly voice, shifting side-to-side on her feet while twisting her fingers in the hem of her frilly dress.

All the Kennedy kids are sporting a summer buzz cut. I did Bren, Bren did Hayden, and they both took turns at my noggin with the clippers. But Hayley? Hayley no longer has a fauxhawk; she has the real goddamned thing. "Well, gotta say, you do a mohawk justice."

"It's time!" Wynn shouts, tugging at everyone he can reach. "I want my fake diploma. I wanna give my speech. I want to be done with high school. C'mon!" He shakes Bren silly, finally knocking a bit of the melancholy off of him. "I'm the first Gillette to graduate high school and get into college, and I earned my own way!"

Enthusiasm contagious, "Let's put Wynn outta his misery." Kade's words are sarcastic, but he looks more excited for Wynn than Wynn is for himself. "Bren?"

"Yeah?" My normally happy boy is the most miserable sonofabitch I've ever seen. If his head hangs any lower, it'll be dragging on the floor.

"Put your troubles in your back pocket." Kade wraps an arm around Bren's shoulders, herding him out the front door. I feel a tinge of jealousy that my son won't come to me, but not as much as the relief I feel that they have each other. Donny and I were like that for each other forever and a day ago, and every man needs a brother. "You can take your troubles back out tonight and suffer with 'em. You've worked for twelve years for this. There are no do-overs. Enjoy yourself today."

Wynn flashes Willa and me a look that screams '*see how awesome Kaden is?*' "God, my baby brother reminds me of a puppy. I give him two semesters before his ass is back in Rusty Knob."

"Thanksgiving break," I counter. "Winner gets to pick which bedroom we'll use." I hedge my bets with a passive-aggressive way of asking Willa to share my bed from now on.

The Gillette in Willa can't pass up a challenge. She stabs me in the chest with her fingertip. "You've got yourself a bet, mister." Then runs the tip of her finger up my neck, and turns back into slap-happy Willa to seal the deal.

"I haven't been back in this dump since they fired my ass," Kade grumbles underneath his breath as he wiggles his large behind to fit into the auditorium seat.

Our group is crowded into the third row– it's a packed house. All three schools in the district are *bang, bang, bang* One graduation right after the other today. We're second up, having the afternoon. I feel bad for the folks who have to go to all three.

"Your fault," Willa says every time Kade brings up how he was fired for not keeping it in his pants for a few more months. "You got what you wanted, so quit your complaining."

Warren stretches his arm across several seats to high-five his sister. "Glad you've got the balls to say it for me. I didn't want to ruin our friendship."

"Are you shitting me?" Kade glares at Warren. "You say it all the time… gimme the kid." He takes Copper even though Warren doesn't want to let him go. "At least this little feller still loves me."

"Ba-by," Hayley whispers, face going soft. She offers her finger as a temporary rattle. "I want more cousins. Can't wait 'til Copper's bigger so I can boss him around."

"What about you?" I turn to Hayden, nudging to get his attention. He wanted the aisle seat so he could see around the bald guy in front of us. "How do you feel about babies?" He just shrugs, not impressed. "Yeah, I didn't care for 'em until I had my own."

Miriam enters the stage, walks up to the podium, and taps on the mic. Kade stiffens. "Am I having a PTSD flashback?" Willa issues a taunting laugh, and Warren echoes her. Poor Kade.

"Welcome friends and family of Rusty Knob's class of 2015!" Miriam shouts into the mic amongst a chorus of cheers.

"This is even more generic than when I graduated," Kade whispers loud enough to be heard from four rows away, meaning Miriam heard. "Wynn and Bren are gonna shit a brick when they graduate college. I went from forty-seven in my high school graduating class to over six thousand when I graduated from Penn State. It was a whole 'nother world."

Willa sinks lower in her seat, and I can read her like an open book. I twine her fingers with mine, and then press the back of her hand to my lips. I keep her hand in my lap, trying to comfort her.

"I…"

I whisper in Willa's ear to soothe her. "Our children will have a life we never got to lead. Neither one of us graduated from high school, but look where we're sitting today. You're still a young woman. You can do whatever you want, and I will support you."

"It's like with learning to drive when I should have already had my license for years. There is nothing to be proud of when I should have already done it."

"Look at Warren," I gesture with my chin. "If that ain't pride shining through, then I don't know what it is." Warren's face lights up the entire auditorium when Penny walks onto the stage with Wynn right behind her. Two kids later, Bren is ambling forward.

"Look at your momma and Uncle Winnie the Pooh," Kade imitates Penny, making Copper's little, chubby hand wave to the stage. "There's Jack! Look at that bratty Bren scowling at us. He's a dimby-wit. Oh, here comes Francis. He's so silly. He's gonna get his ass lynched."

The auditorium goes dead silent for a heartbeat, and then erupts into pure chaos. Francis Parker walks onto stage to take a seat, wearing a rainbow graduation gown instead of the red they were given. Seated, Franny tips his head down, allowing the top of his cap to show a message.

F. U. R. K.

With a satisfied smirk stretching his lips, Francis challenges the town.

"Just like Josh Truman." Kade reminds us of the kid who outed half of their group, including the superintendent's son, was bullied but fought back by calling them all out, and then left for Rhode Island. "Only Franny was smart enough to book a flight out of here before the dust settles."

With the patience of a saint, Miriam waits for the crowd to die down as the last of the students take their seats. "Well, that was out of the ordinary." She raises an eyebrow at Kaden, recognizing his signature written all over Franny. "Our very own Wynn Gillette has prepared a speech for us today. Rusty Knob's valedictorian, 2015 Basketball State Champion, and recipient of a basketball scholarship to West Virginia University." Miriam gestures to the podium, and then takes a seat on stage.

"My God, Wynn's glowing like a supernova." Mesmerized, Kade's pupils are blown. "I will not be held accountable for my actions after graduation."

Striding across the stage like he owns the place, Wynn turns on a dime to face the auditorium with a huge grin stretching across his face. He clears his throat twice, lifts his index cards, and memorizes a few lines. His lips twist into an expression I've never seen grace my son's face before. A warped mix of excitement and fury, tarnishing what should have been a proud moment.

"I prepared a speech for today," Wynn begins in a defiant tone. "It was going to be poignant, proving how eloquent of a speaker I am after growing up in the hollers. I was going to hit on how isolation breeds ignorance, not a lack of intelligence. I was going to put a voice to my struggles, being the youngest of poor white, abusive, drunk trash. How I was adopted at seventeen. How through all of that, I maintained a high GPA and led our basketball team to victory."

Wynn raises the cards in his hands, and tears them down the center while wearing a rebellious smirk— the microphone picks up the audible ripping sound, causing it to echo around the auditorium. Speech fluttering to the ground, he releases all of the pent-up rage he's held on to for far too long.

Hands gripping the edge of the podium, Wynn leans into the microphone with eyes blazing fury. "I agree with Francis Parker. Fuck you, Rusty Knob!" Slowly enunciating, words quiet, they hit their intended targets like ammunition fired from a gun. "Fuck! You!"

Deafening silence rings throughout the auditorium, and I have no idea where Wynn is leading with this, and no one else does either. I crank my head around wildly, trying to gauge the reaction from the crowd.

"Rusty Knob?" Wynn cups a hand to his ear. "Can you hear me now? You've been mighty deaf lately. For the past seven months, I've either been called a faggot or patted on the back for being courageous. Both reactions were insulting— both insinuating something is *wrong* with me. Whether we're at fault or not, it doesn't change the fact that this school fired my boyfriend because we're gay. So fuck you!"

Kade leans forward, releasing a noise I hope to never hear again. I yank the idiot back by the collar before he crawls on stage.

"But I owe you a thank you," Wynn circles back, finally having our undivided attention. "Thank you for the education, for allowing me to make the most of it. I hope your eyes and ears are now open to the sources of education all around you. I'm no longer ignorant, so thank you."

Wynn reclaims his seat while whispers roll through the auditorium, all versions of *'what the fuck was that?'* Miriam has everything under control. Whatever speeches and events planned for the ceremony are cut in the wake of the chaos weaving its way through the auditorium.

Miriam walks to the farthest part of the stage near the steps. One of her helper monkeys on the school board hands her rolled up fake diplomas from a woven basket. Child after child crosses the stage, exiting down the stairs to join their family members as a high school graduate– an adult.

Jessica Arnold is the first to cross the stage, appearing to be physically ill. Three kids later, Jackson Duncan strides forward with an air of *'I don't give a fuck'*. He grabs his diploma without shaking anyone's hand, and jumps off the end of the stage. Penny Gillette walks on rubbery legs, so petrified we can see her shaking. After saying a meek *thanks*, she makes a beeline to Warren and Copper. Wynn floats across the stage, kisses Miriam Ross on the cheek and refuses to shake her crony's hand– Hayden dominates Wynn's time at the end of our aisle, having to inspect the fake diploma. My son walks like he's headed to his own execution, and I wait for him to join us. But he congregates with Jack and Jesse. And then there is Francis Parker, cartwheeling across the stage.

Kade groans like he's dying. "That kid... I swear to God he's begging for a hazing." He shakes his head left and right. "After you've had dog shit flung at you from a moving car, you keep your gay tendencies to a minimum."

"Do you really want to do cartwheels?" Warren grimaces when Kade slaps him upside the head for being an idiot.

"Wait... What?" I turn in my seat abruptly. "Are you saying someone did that to you?"

Leveling me with his unflinching gaze, Kade breaks my heart. "Dad, the past seven months have not been easy for Wynn and me. I wasn't locked in my house for no reason. Sure, I was depressed– depressed because of what happened whenever I walked outside. Nothing like a redneck tossing shit at me. A *'gift'* he said, because I love ass so much, I ought to love what comes out of one too."

Kade looks to me with haunted eyes. I have no way to erase what he's been through, so I keep my mouth shut.

"Why do you think I want Wynn to get his ass out of here? I'm protecting him the only way I know how. Maybe by the time he graduates from college, the Life Skills Center will have made a difference. And if it doesn't, Wynn will be older, smarter, and stronger by then."

"Son, I-I-I…" I stammer, having no idea how to fix this for him. My eyes seek out Wynn, who is chatting animatedly with Hayden, oblivious of what Kaden is discussing.

"All the kids in my group came out to support Wynn and me, and they've been bullied every fucking day. Look at 'em!" Kade points to Jack, Franny, Jessica, and Bren. "They're miserable as fuck, but happy to be getting the hell out of here."

It takes all of my control to force my voice to sound neutral instead of betrayed. "Why didn't you tell me?"

"Because you would have leveled this town to the ground." Kade's expression says it all. He knows what happens when my shit spirals out of control. People either go to jail or wind up dead. "That's why. It was nothing we couldn't handle, and we were watching your back for once."

"What–" Hayden being flung over Wynn's shoulder stops my words.

Proving he has impeccable hearing, "We handled it, and I'm perfectly happy!" Wynn leans down, over several of our seats, with the widest grin I've ever seen. "C'mon, watch us toss our caps to the sky." Moving away, he takes off with Hayden riding piggyback.

"Wait for me, Uncle Wynn!" Hayley crawls over us and scampers through the crowd.

"If the golden boy calls, we shall follow." Kaden rises first, looking impatient. "Stop blocking traffic, old man. I don't wanna miss it."

We empty to the front of the school, into the circular lawn created by the exit and entrance driveways. The crowd surrounds the forty-some brand new adults wearing caps and gowns. Wynn's halo of blond hair is a head above the rest. I can just make out Penny at his side, with Copper being held in her arms. My boy is in the center of a huddle, being supported by his friends.

Hayden and Hayley steal Willa's and my cellphones and capture the moment on video. With a big whoop, the caps are flung into the air, signaling the end of an era and the beginning of another.

We all crowd in, offering congratulations and hugs. Groups break off and empty to the parking lot. Willa and I stand back, taking it all in. Penny and the baby are being swallowed by Hayden and Hayley and Warren, chattering so fast she can't answer.

"Can we stay with you tonight, Aunt Penny? Tomlin and Hannah live next door and they're having a campout. Can we? Can we?"

"Ask your momma and daddy." Penny laughs, flashing us a look that she's okay with it.

"I don't know. It's your first sleepover," I drawl, making them wait a bit.

"Daddy!" Hayden shouts. "Please, we're big kids now."

"Too big," Willa whispers, getting choked up. I tug her to my side, wrapping an arm around her waist. "You mind Aunt Penny," she warns. "And don't go getting into any trouble."

"Oh, they'll mind," Warren drawls, eyes twinkling. "C'mon, brats. Copper has got to get home to catch a nap before he starts wailing."

"I'm proud of you, Penny," I shout as she leads my kids away. "So proud."

"I'ma get you a little '*I'm proud of you*' sign to put in your back pocket, and every time you wanna say that to someone, you gotta pull it out." Penny teases me, but she glows from the compliment. "I'll bring the twins back on Sunday night. Give you two some privacy."

"Do we need privacy?" I whisper in Willa's ear, earning a giggle. "We still have three young men to deal with."

"I'm pretty sure two of 'em will be honeymooning across the street from Penny and War." She points at Wynn tugging Kade around by his tie. He keeps turning around and kissing Kaden on the lips to piss the townsfolk off.

Never one who was agile, Kade almost upends by tripping over his large feet. "Little shit, you're gonna regret that." Kade catches my eye. "See ya at work on Monday, and not a second sooner."

"You two have fun," I call back.

Reminding me of a spooked horse, Wynn's blue eyes bulge from his skull. "Holy shit!" He rotates to catch my gaze while speaking to Kade. "Royce didn't tell me no."

"You're a man now, remember?" Kaden taunts Wynn. "Git in my truck before I make a bigger fool of myself."

"No calling 9-1-1 on us!" Wynn teases me as he lopes across the lawn toward the parking lot.

"There won't be a need, ya little shit," Kade says gruffly. "Wrong graduation."

A laugh huffs out of me at the devastated expression that crosses Wynn's face as he slips into the passenger seat of the Durango. Kade waves at us, visibly amused, and then he's ducking inside his vehicle.

"No idea if Kade is joking or not." I look down at Willa with a bemused expression. "It pains me to say, Kade is patient enough to make Wynn wait, and I feel bad for the kid not getting what he wants. But then I feel grossed out after I remember what the kid wants in the first place. The father in me ought to be happy about waiting. But the man in me understands how Wynn feels."

Willa laughs, shaking her head back and forth. "Lord knows with that asshole. My guess is college graduation because Kade is selfish and will want Wynn to wait as long as he had to wait. But if Wynn would just learn to let go and tap into the Gillette in him, Kade wouldn't stand a chance."

"Christ." A shiver works its way along my spine as my eyes cut to the one person who has made me lose my mind.

Willa smiles sweetly at me– innocently. "Two down, one to go…"

Face twisted up in agony, Bren is in an embrace with Franny, fingers clutching at the rainbow gown. I can hear Francis laughing through his tears, but Bren just keeps squeezing him tighter and tighter.

"I ain't ever stepping foot in this town again, but that doesn't mean you can't visit me in California. My sisters have lived there for years with my grandparents. They will welcome you into the fold. I'm sure they miss their living dollbaby."

"You know I can't right now," Bren's voice is rough and gritty. "I wish your family wasn't pulling out of Rusty Knob."

"Well, we can still visit. I'm willing to go to Pennsylvania or Ohio, but unless I'm driving through or flying above West Virginia, I'm not stopping."

"It won't be the same," Bren mumbles into Franny's shoulder, squeezing him so tightly it has to be leaving a bruise. "We've been partners in crime since we were three. You've been with me through everything. Skype, texting, and Facebook aren't enough. Seeing you every few years and noticing how we've changed is gonna kill me."

"We're on to bigger and brighter…"

"Shut up." Bren's words don't hold any weight. "You're not even upset."

Franny's laughter is contagious, and soon my son is laughing through the tears. Pulling back, we all gasp in shock when Bren plants a big, sloppy kiss on Franny's parted lips.

"Holy fuck!" Franny shouts, eyes bulging from his skull. "Had I known leaving would gain me a kiss from you, I would've moved sooner. And tried for tongue."

Jack walks over with Jessica in tow. He's smiling ear-to-ear when I was scared he'd be jealous. "Bren's stingy when it comes to boys, so you better have imprinted that kiss into memory." They curl into a group hug, saying their final goodbye, knowing they might never see Francis again.

Franny is the first to pull back, slipping away unnoticed by his friends. His rainbow gown becomes a streak of light as he runs across the schoolyard to his parents' idling car, already packed and ready for the airport.

"That's so sad." Willa sniffles, pressing closer into my side. "Bigger and brighter, I believe. But it's still so sad. I'll never forget the first time I met that kid almost a decade ago. I wish he could have stayed in Rusty Knob. Franny brought life to this place."

Jessica is next to pull away. She rests her hand on my son's back, pausing as if she wants to say something. But she thinks the better of it, and shakes her head no. Then Jesse's walking off, leaving Bren and Jack embraced, faces buried in the crook of each other's neck, fingers clenching shoulder muscles.

"We'll leave them be." I take Willa's hand. "Bren will wander home when he wanders home."

Voice thick with barely suppressed tears, "That suspiciously looks like a goodbye, too," Willa whispers to me as we head to her car.

Heart breaking for my son, I breathe, "I reckon it is."

As I bend down to get into Willa's car, I catch sight of someone lingering on the edges of the school property. Looking healthy for the first time in nearly a decade, Corbin raises a hesitant hand.

I hate myself. I hate myself for feeling bipolar. I'm simultaneously furious and relieved that Corbin Gillette looks to be cleaning up his act. Furious, because I wanted him to die a slow and painful death. Relived, because I love his children enough to want them to have a real daddy and because I want this burden of guilt to be lifted from my soul.

The largest part of me is still reeling from not having any real justice, while a small kernel longs to thank Corbin for carrying around such a large debt– a debt that turned an asshole into a monster in the name of loyalty.

Unable to stop myself, my chin raises and lowers in acknowledgment, my involuntary way of waving back to Corbin. As I shut the car door, Corbin Gillette slips back into the trees.

The only way of reclaiming my manhood was to believe stealing all of Corbin's children from him was an act of revenge. I know it wasn't Corbin who violated me and left me broken and almost dead. But his act of loyalty took my brother away from me, and I hate him for that. But when I look more closely to my motives, I believe taking care of Corbin's family was my odd way of saying thank you for defending my honor.

"Ya want another marshmallow?" Willa blows the flame out, leaving behind a charred blob of sticky sugar. "Mmm…" she groans, eating it right off the stick. It's my turn to groan when she sucks her fingertips. "They're best burnt."

"I can't believe you don't like s'mores." I grab the stick out of her hand and jab another marshmallow on it. "Who doesn't like s'mores?" I wait for it to catch fire, and then hand the flaming blob to Willa.

"The chocolate never melts. It's like *hard*." Willa pulls a face. "We should keep the chocolate bars next to the fire."

"Smart woman," I mutter appreciatively, trying to ignore the signals my body is throwing out. "For the past few years, I've been obsessed with having the kids shoved up my ass… I thought I'd be more upset."

Grinning, Willa covers her mouth with her palm, hiding her laughter and the melted marshmallow she's chewing. She takes a big swallow to clear her mouth. "I thought it'd be weird, just me and you." She points between us while wearing a funny, little smirk. She distracts us both by grabbing a few Hershey Bars out of the cooler, resting them on a rock next to the roaring fire. "I didn't like remembering, ya know? I spent a lot of time trying to forget."

"I just blocked it out." It's my turn to feel odd. I have no problem talking to Willa, but it's never just the two of us with all the kids running around. This is the first time the house has been empty in over a year. "It hurts to remember, because not only did I lose Donny that day, I lost you, too."

Eyes turning glossy, Willa slowly reaches out to cup my cheek. "I wanna remember, Royce. I wanna remember who I was so I can see how far I've come." Her hand drops to her lap, and she stares at it instead of me. "I want you to remember you too. You're not an old man, no matter how you act now. You should be more than just a daddy and protector of Rusty Knob. You need friends who aren't your children." Willa finally meets my eyes, and I can tell she's been waiting to speak to me about this. "You forgot who you used to be. A bit gruff and surly, but playful too. I miss him, Royce. I miss you."

I cover my surprise with a joke. "You saying I acted like Kaden?"

"Yeah, you did. I miss him. *You*," she mutters softly, a world of emotions in her voice. "I loved bickering with you. It's why I ride Kade's ass so much. I think it's what drew you to him in the first place." Sitting on her heels with her hands in her lap, Willa opens her mouth, and then shuts it. She pulls this routine a few times before she gets the courage to continue. "Did I ever tell you how I was never frightened of you?"

"Such a strange thing to say." I release an uncomfortable chuckle. "It makes me sad that girls have to be afraid of men in the first place." I poke Willa in the knee with the marshmallow stick. "Go on."

"Obviously, even when Donny was slapping me around, I was never scared of him. The word *prey* glowed in my head when I met him. So between Donny and Daddy, I picked Donny. Sean was at the house when we showed up, so I chose the bedroom with Donny over being in the living room with Sean."

"Oh, Willamina." I clench my chest, heart breaking and repairing itself a billion times over. "None of that should have *ever* happened to you."

"And *you*," she reminds me. "But it did, and we've got to deal with it, so Dr. Cassidy says." Willa's tone is filled with the strength of resolve. "I've had to work this out in my head to sort through it. Sean reminded me of a beautiful dog. Loyal, cunning, charming. But you could just sense that he didn't belong to you, that beneath the surface he was waiting to bite your face off. He was the loving pup you raised, and you didn't realize until it was too late that he was a predator."

"I always thought Sean was off. With Corbin, it was in-your-face obvious that he would bite you, but he'd shake your hand afterward and apologize. But Sean, I didn't realize until I couldn't stop it."

"Daddy can be rotten but he's harmless. I know that sounds fucked up to say. But after meeting someone like Sean..." Willa takes a deep breath. Neither one of us wants to talk about this, but we have to. We're never alone, and it's not the same when Dr. Cassidy forces us.

"So I'm sitting on the couch with my daddy, and I could tell he was regretting it. Not regretting Donny. I've come to terms with the why of that. Daddy picked someone who could take care of me and treat me right but also give a bit back so they didn't have to struggle so hard. Daddy should have worked, but he was doing what he was taught. So I can't blame him too harshly."

"But we'd only known Sean for a little over a year…"

"Yeah, I think that's what Daddy was picking up on. I could sense it immediately, but it probably slowly creeped up on Daddy. So that's what you walked into… and you walked in, and I–" Willa covers her face with her palms, laughing at herself. "Good God, I took one look atcha and… yeah. I was sitting with a dumb dog, a beaten dog, and a rabid dog, and all I could think of when I first saw ya was siccing them on each other so I could go play with the fox."

"Willa?" With a fingertip beneath her chin, I tilt her head into the firelight so I can get a good look at her. "As a Gillette, I know you see yourself as ignorant trash. I see the same mindset in Warren and Wynn, and even Penny being from the hollers. You have no idea how intelligent you truly are."

"I ain't," she argues with me.

"You *are*," I stress, gripping Willa's chin tightly between my fingertips. "There's common sense, and there's book smarts. But then there's survival of the fittest. Kade, he's a fighter and he's educated, but he ain't got a lick of sense sometimes. You and Warren, you are the craftiest people I know. Even your daddy. It's focusing those smarts that makes you unstoppable."

Willa perks up a bit. "Like Wynn?"

"Like Wynn," I agree. "But that doesn't have a dang lick to do with diplomas or degrees. You took one look at Sean and recognized the darkness none of us could see."

Ashamed, Willa turns away from me, but I can still hear the guilt riding her voice. "But I was too loyal to Donny to tell you, and look where that got us."

"That's the crux of it all, ain't it? By being loyal– keeping secrets and promises – we're betraying those we love most."

Face whipping around to gaze at me, "I want to remember, Royce," Willa cries. "I can't break those promises, even now. But if you remember too, maybe you'll see what was always in front of your face… and then we can move on."

"God," shudders out on my breath. My eyes slip shut, unable to fathom where to begin. "How do we start?" When I open my eyes, Willa's gazing at me with an expression that petrifies me. The same expression every Gillette gets just before they steal something from you. In Kade's and my case, Wynn and Willa usually steal our minds because they already own our hearts. "Oh, fuck!" I scramble backward, my ass hitting a log.

This girl– this *woman* only turns into this creature around me. Even when she was broken, screaming when anyone came near her, high out of her mind, I'd wake in the middle of the night to her crawling in my bed, getting on top of me to ride my dick, and she'd steal my mind, my heart, and my seed.

Terrified.

Since Willa returned from rehab, this side of her has laid dormant. Prowling toward me, Willa swings her leg over my hip, sitting astride my lap. "Remember the first time I ever sat in your lap?" She wiggles her little, tight ass right on my crotch, just like she did the first time. Groaning, my fists clench and my toes curl against the need rising in me.

Swiveling her hips in my lap again, "Oh, Jesus. Fuck!" My head jackknifes backward into the log and I see bursts of starlight. "That ain't a memory I ever forgot. You turned me into a sinner that day, and I haven't stopped sinning with you ever since."

ஒ9 years ago஧

It's been three months since I had the freedom to ride around the dirt roads with my music blaring and the windows rolled down. I don't even care that it's freezing outside. After a bunch of failed playdates, where someone was always getting sick or Brennan was calling me back immediately because he missed me, I'm free.

I waited four hours to make sure the little feller didn't call me right up, begging to come home and snuggle on the couch with me. Donny's been pestering me just as much as Brennan has, getting clingy and visiting constantly but never bringing his new bride. *"Come up to the house,"* he'd say. *"You forsaking Kennedy land?"*

With my son at Francis Parker's house reluctantly being painted up like a baby drag queen, I take my time driving all over the hills. The binds of being a daddy slowly unravel so I can enjoy being a man with my brother.

I crank the wheel to turn into Donny's driveway, belting out the wrong lyrics to Mudvayne. Movement catches my eye and has me reaching for the baseball bat I keep tucked behind the seat. I'm out of my truck in a split-second and tearing across the yard.

"Hey!" I shout, swinging my bat in the air to catch their attention. I want to say more, but terror has taken possession of my tongue.

Willa's on the ground, slowly crab-walking backward, her hands getting caught on the hem of her dress. My brother is shielding his wife with his body, and Sean is towering over them both with rage pouring off of him in visible waves.

My brother's a small guy, nary a strong muscle on him. Whereas Corbin and I are short but stocky. We can give and take a lot of damage. But Sean– Sean is tall and thin with muscles built from steel pipes. It would take all three of us to bring him to the ground.

Either not hearing me or ignoring me because I'm no threat, "Hit her, Donald!" Sean bellows into Donny's face with his fists clenched at the ready at his sides. "Hit her, or I will!"

"I can't!" Donny cries, hands coming up to cover his face like he fears being hit instead. "I can't do it. Willa ain't done nothing wrong."

"You lied to me!" Sean's words are violent and fierce, ringing in my ears. His hand flings back to land a slap, but Donny's quicker. I miss a step when my brother's open palm connects with his wife's face– the force whipping Willa's head so far to the side her chin passes her shoulder.

My heart beats out of my chest, rage and confusion fueling it. I can't get to them in time to stop it. Willa's to her feet in an instant, glaring up at Donny. She sees me, a split-second later she's spitting blood in Sean's face, and then she drops to the ground as I swing.

"Get the fuck off my land, and don't come back," I snarl, giving Sean a warning tap to the back. "Go!"

"Your precious brother is a fucking liar." Sean holds his ground, eyeing the bat clutched in both my hands. "I bet I know him better than you do, Roy."

"Just go, Sean," Donny grumbles, looking defeated and exhausted. "Just go."

"I'll go, but I'll be back," Sean threatens. "And you better get your ass in gear, darlin'. If Don's not up to it, you best make him get it up."

In a silent tableau, Donny, Willa, and I stare after Sean as he crosses the yard, gets in his car, and speeds down the dirt road, rocks spitting and a plume of dust in his wake.

"Donny?" My eyes flick everywhere but see nothing. I'm so utterly confused that I don't know how to fix this. "Donny? Look at me," I command my older brother. "What happened?"

Donny doesn't look at me or answer me, but Willa does. "That was round three." Enraged, she wipes a fingertip across her bottom lip, smearing a drop of blood clinging to the corner of her mouth. "Round one, I just took it. Round two, I called my daddy and he did what you just did, Royce. Round three... well—" she points her bloody fingertip at her husband. "There ya go. I don't think I'm ready for round four."

"Is this the first time Donny has ever hit you like that?" Willa shakes her head in assent. "What about Sean?"

"That would be round one and two... when Donny refused to 'teach' me how to be a proper wife. I promised I'd never call my daddy for nothing, but Sean changed my mind. It took both Warren and Daddy to take him down. Then, after seeing them get beat up, I promised myself I'd never call again, 'cuz I worried they'd have to bring Wynn next time."

"Christ." I rub my palm over the top of my hair, trying to think. "How old are your brothers anyway?"

"Sixteen and ten," Willa blurts, flabbergasted.

"DONNY!" I reach down to drag my brother upright, but instantly drop him. "What the fuck happened to your face?" Half of Donny's face is black and blue, with open sores from the force of the impact with a fist. His cheek looks like squashed, over-ripened fruit.

"That's a little gift from Sean. Donny needed a lesson on how to be a proper husband, so he was smart enough to teach me how to be a proper wife."

"And what business is this of Sean's?" Is directed at my brother, but Willa answers.

"Fuck if I know." Willa yanks the collar of her dress, wiping the fabric across her bleeding lip. "All I know is— is that Sean's the one in charge 'round here, and when he comes 'round I hide. Don't ask where, 'cuz I ain't giving up my location for nothing."

Kneeling on the ground, I cup my brother's face. I'm furious at him for hitting his wife, but Willa seems more frustrated with Donny than anything. "What happened?"

"I lied to Sean." Donny refuses to look at me, eyes darting away every time I try to connect with him. "I deserved what he did to me, but Willa didn't. It's all my fault."

"Lied about what?" I demand, shaking my brother. He yanks away from me, looking like a trapped wild animal.

"I've gotta go." Trying to run to his truck, Donny limps and hops. "I've gotta apologize."

Mystified, I watch as my brother climbs into his truck, face contorted in agony and fear. He takes off at a clip, nearly wiping out my front bumper on his way down the driveway.

"What the fuck?" I mutter to myself...

But as usual, Willa answers me. "Yer brotha's a coward." Furious, she stomps to the house, making more noise than a person twice her size. I follow behind, hoping for answers but fearing what I'll find.

Willa's easy enough to locate, seeing as how she sounds like a wildebeest as she ruts around in the freezer. I make myself at home at the table we've had in my family since my granddaddy was still alive. I place my bat in the center of the table, noticing that Willa's been getting the care-packages I sent with Donny.

I flip through the textbooks, checking to see if they've been opened recently. I'm shocked to note how she's been highlighting passages she wanted to remember. I'd bought all the subjects she'd need to hone in order to get her GED, if she ever decided to get it.

Willa pulls out a bag of ice, wrapping it in a dishtowel, with one eye trained on me at all times. "You and I are gonna have words."

I'm taken aback. "Does that mean something else where you come from, girl? Because from where I come from, that means we meet in the bar parking lot and settle our differences with our fists."

She grabs the back of a chair, spins it around, and sits on it backward. She rests her forearms on the backrest, holding the bag of ice to her cheek. Her dress rides up, showing off her pink panties, and I gaze to ceiling.

Lord, help me. Why did I have to notice that?

Now that I have, my eyes keep straying down, checking out her smooth thighs– a strawberry birthmark rides high, nestled right up to her panty line. I lick my lips, suddenly starving for a bite of strawberry.

"I'm going to Hell," I croak out.

Willa looks at me, and in a very serious tone, she says, "Royce, we were all born sinners." I blink, and notice my bat is now in her hand, dangling at her side. "Have words," she reminds me. "Means I'ma talk. Yer gonna listen. And if you don't, I'ma hit a homerun with this here bat of yours against that stiff willy you got swelling in your jeans."

"I... I–I–" I swallow thickly, scrubbing at my face with my palms to clear away my impure thoughts. My eyes can't help themselves. Willa's a child, but right now she's wearing a thin cotton dress hiked up her thighs. Her hair is a wild mess around her head, like she just got done getting fucked good and rough. It's sick, but my dick is getting harder the longer I stare at the blood on her lip. Seeing it makes me feel violent, but the rage fuels my lust. "I'm sorry. I seem to have forgotten what I was gonna say."

"That's what I thought." Willa swings the bat around in her hand, flexing her wrist like it's a baton. "I'ma keep this here bat as a gift from you. I'ma place it in my hidey-hole and call it Sean-Away."

"I'll buy you more." I gulp a dozen times. "I'll make sure they're made of Birch. Light and strong. It will flex but not break. I'll toss in a wooden truncheon my daddy whittled years ago– it has a leather strap that goes around your wrist."

"Perfect," she drawls while gently placing the bat on the table between us. "I'm still figuring out your brother. Donny ain't much of a talker. He goes about his business, leaving me to mine. But his bubby's got some notion that I ought to be knocked up by now."

"Why?" My face twists up in confusion, trying to work that out.

"I ain't got no idea." Willa drops the cold compress on her forearm, and then rests her cheek on it. "Donny and me, every night for the first few weeks of our matrimony, he'd come to my room for our two minutes of coupling." Words dry, she looks less than impressed. "When I started my monthly, he left me alone. 'Bout a week later, Sean found out. He beat the piss out of Donny, furious that Donny and I weren't doing our duty."

Mulling that over, I get up from the table and make my way to the refrigerator. I grab two bottles of beer in each hand, and retake my seat. In a practiced move, I use the lip of the table to pop the bottle cap off. I toss the cap into the sink, and then hand Willa a beer. "I think you've earned this." I repeat the process, and drain my bottle dry in seconds.

"Y'all might think us women are ignorant, but we've got our little secrets." Willa takes a long sip of her beer, then licks the dang neck of the bottle. I shake my head, trying to get rid of the sight. "I gotta get knocked up, see? I'm sick of my husband getting beaten half to death every time I have my monthly because he won't hit me because it's my fault." Willa rolls her eyes at the ridiculousness. "Ain't my fault Donny don't visit my bed much."

"What the fuck?" I grab another beer, pop the cap, and drain in in a few gulps. I slam the empty on the table. "I've got to be drunk before this makes a lick of sense."

"I can't handle a fourth time. Sean might kill me next time. I went to my momma." Willa looks me straight in the eye, and I'm the one to flinch. Twenty-nine-year-old man being taken down by a hillbilly child-bride. "Momma said it's about certain times of the month, and making sure I'm getting off when he does. See, I remember the neighbor girls loving what Warren was giving 'em, but I've never felt that. But Momma couldn't explain how that works. You gotta kid, tell me how?"

"Willa, this is not an appropriate conversation." My voice dips, almost pleading because my cock likes this topic but my mind can't take it.

Pushing her bottle at me, "Have another beer."

"Willa." I sigh, leaning farther away from her.

"Drink it." She pushes it closer to me. "I ain't asking you to stick yer willy to me. I'm asking you how I can get it done with Donny. If you love your brother, you'll help us survive."

"How about I figure out what the hell Sean has on Donny and eliminate it?" Logic wins over lust.

"I wish you luck with that." The beer gets closer to me, a tiny fingertip pushing it inch by inch across the table. "But in the meantime, ya wanna explain the birds and the bees to me in greater detail, 'cuz if it takes you another two weeks to get Sean outta our hair, I'ma get my ass beat again."

"Two weeks?" twists out, confused.

"Donny held Sean off for a bit, that's why he was hooting and hollering about Donny being a fucking liar."

"What's actually going on with my brother?" I demand.

"Sean's got some weird hold over Donny." She's truthful but skirting around it. "I have my theories, but I don't know for sure. If you want to know why, ask yer brother. But know that he comes home beaten a couple times a week, and he's always groveling about how it was his fault. Since I'm that coward's wife and he does what Sean tells him to do, I gotta put up with Sean."

"Christ." I reach for the beer, draining it. I haven't had three beers in the last six months. An hour with Willa will drive a man to drink. "Get me some more beer. I'll need it to lubricate my tongue."

"Sure thing, boss." Willa backbends while sitting astride her chair. Her thighs spread wider, the seat of her pink panties pulling to the side to show off a bit of blonde fuzz. I will my eyes to shut but they won't obey. Willa's long hair dangles to brush the floor as she leans backward. She flicks the refrigerator door open and grabs a handful of beers by their necks. Leaning back up, she plops them on the table, then reaches back to slam the refrigerator door shut without looking.

"Goddamn flexible," I mutter underneath my breath as I pop the caps off three beers. "You better keep that–" using the bottle, I point at her panties. "–away from Sean."

"No fear, Royce-baby," Willa purrs, flexing her thighs. Then she winks. "Sean ain't hungry for what I'm selling."

"What's he buying then?" I grumble, and Willa laughs like I'm the ignorant one. "What do you want to know?"

"How to make a kid." She reaches over, snags the beer out of my hand, takes a dainty sip, and then licks the opening. My hand is still frozen open, as if I am holding a beer. With a giggle, Willa puts the bottle back in my palm.

My fingers wrap tightly around my beer, realizing this is a dangerous road I'm heading down. "I'm not gonna fuck my brother's wife," I warn, and all Willa does is flash a sinful smirk my way. "Sex. I'm positive you know what that is. Dick in pussy. Thrusting until the man spills his seed. It's gotta reach its intended target, so no pulling out and no washing it out when you go to the bathroom."

"Yeah, I got that part down pat." Willa's all proud of herself, and I feel like I've entered the Twilight Zone.

After suffering through being *'tickled'* by my funny uncle, I was sex-charged early. I lost my virginity to Annie a week after I turned fourteen. She was sixteen. Knowing she had me trapped, she made me wait and wait and wait. Years. I waited until our wedding night for a second taste. Annie led me around by my dick, making sure I met all of her daddy's demands. After that, sex with Annie was always a sensual affair about making love in our bed. Annie was my best friend, and our sex life was loving but not filled with any heat.

I'd bet my considerable wealth that Willa would be dangerous like riding a bronc in a rodeo. Wild and unbridled. Straight fucking. Rough, raw, and dirty. Something tells me Willa would ride me hard, get what she wanted, and then she'd tear my dick off for safekeeping just so no one else but her could ever use it.

"Yer wantin' me again," Willa whispers like it's a secret, wiggling a bit in her seat. "Yer willy is leaving a itty bitty wet spot on yer jeans."

"Stop it," I snap, cock jerking in my pants. "I'm not a pervert. Not only are you a child, you're my brother's wife."

"If it makes you feel any better, I'm certain ol' Donny's been fucking someone else– I'm the other woman." Fingertips run up and down her neck, drawing my eye. When Willa's positive she holds my undivided attention, those sneaky fingertips slip beneath the bodice of her dress.

My eyes snap shut, but I can still see her tiny nipples beading beneath her dress. My tongue curls in my mouth in anticipation.

Voice rough, I bark out, "What Donny does is on Donny. What you do is on you, and you're not drawing me into your insanity. As soon as I'm done telling you how to get pregnant, I'm outta here."

Voice husky, a throaty purr, Willa turns into my worst nightmare. "Have some more…" An open beer gets closer to my hand. "Drink up."

"Good God, you're evil incarnate." My hand snatches up the bottle and I drain it. My fourth? No, fifth. "Mid-cycle from one monthly to the next. Ya gotta have a lot of sex in that time frame, at least a couple times a day."

"Well, that's right now." Willa feigns surprise, suddenly an innocent girl.

"You already knew that," I growl. I tip my head backward and take gulp after gulp of beer. "You're using your feminine wiles on me." I grab another. "I'm not gonna fuck you tonight."

"Oh, I know." Willa gathers all the beer bottles and puts them in a tidy row. "But yer gonna show me how to get off, so when my husband is done fucking around on me, I'll take a turn. Momma says if we come together, his seed'll take."

"Willa, no," the words sound more like '*yes, I'll do whatever you want.*'

"*One. Two. Three. Four. Five. Six. Seven.*" Willa counts silently, fingertip touching the top of every empty beer. "I suspect yer feeling a bit tipsy by now. Did you know men get women loosened up with booze so they can have their wicked way with 'em?"

"I've never done that," I mutter– slur. Testing Willa's theory, I lean left then right and find myself woozy and dizzy.

I'm well on my way past drunk.

"Liar," Willa purrs in a voice too deep for a girl her age. "I bet there were nights Bren slept up here with his Uncle Donny, and you'd get your Annie to drink a bit too much wine so she'd finally suck your dick."

"You're waiting me out, aren't you?" The words slur together slightly. "What are you up to, little girl?"

"Mmm… Momma wasn't sure about this plan, thinking yer willy wouldn't stay stiff if yous was drunk. Donny's dick got as limp as an overcooked noodle last night. I didn't have to trick him, though. He was fortifying himself with beer. My husband is scared to death of me."

"Me too," rumbles from my lips. "My eyes are floating in my head. Why is that?"

"You're not much of a drinker, that's why." Willa stands from her chair, and my eyes take in her movements as if she's moving in slow-motion. She weaves around the table. I blink to find her slowly lifting her leg, dress bunching up, and then she sits directly on my lap. "Mmm… you feel good." She wiggles a bit, grinding my dick against what's hidden beneath her pink panties.

"Willa," I protest, but not very hard. "I can't do this."

"I hope you don't remember this when you wake up tomorrow morning, because I do like you a lot, Royce. I want you to be able to trust me. So I promise I'm not gonna steal yer seed. *Tonight*," she stresses. "When yer finally with me, I'll be the last woman you ever fuck."

"So sure of yourself, aren't you?"

"Yes," she says without a lick arrogance. "Why is it important to get off together?"

"It feels incredible," slurs quickly from my lips. My head is foggy and words just stumble out without a filter. "Moving together." My hips lift and lower, lift and lower as I speak. "If you know your partner's body good enough, you can time it just right. Annie would only let me come if she was– yeah, I had to get her drunk to get blown. That's a married man's trick."

Face sincere, voice serious, "I'd blow you sober." Then she bites her bottom lip as if she's envisioning what it would be like with my cock buried to the hilt in the back of her throat… or maybe I'm envisioning it right now.

"Fuck," I hiss, hating myself for reacting like I am. I reach around Willa, digging my fingernails into the edge of the wooden table, trying with everything I have not to touch her hips and grind up into her. "Have you ever given a blowjob?"

"No, you'll be my first," Willa says without question, and I whimper. "So it feels good? I don't get it but I do, never having come myself. But why does it help with the baby-making?"

"You've never come before?" Willa shakes her head, still gnawing on her lip. "No wonder you're so fucking horny." I grab her hand, wrapping my fingers around her thumb. "You're the boy in this scenario. Your thumb is the cock. My fingers are the pussy."

"Okay." Willa is an apt pupil, making her thumb as stiff as the dick in my pants. "Ride me. Ride me good, Royce-baby."

Chuckling underneath my breath, I rub her thumb a bit, getting into it. "Feel this?" I clench my fingers as I slide up and down. "Now imagine your thumb-cock is spurting inside my finger-pussy." I squeeze her tighter and tighter, trying not to moan as if I'm actually coming. "The waves of spasms in the pussy suck the seed up into the womb. Like an express lane to the egg."

"Ohhh…" Willa moans, counterthrusting with her thumb. I pull away quickly, getting too into our sex-ed session.

"Okay, so Donny comes to me pretty much prepped and ready to go. I'm sure he jerks his willy before he crawls in my bed and spoons my back. So what do I do? There's no way I can match him if he's done in less than two minutes."

I shut my mind off, pretending we're not talking about my brother, trying to remember this is his wife sitting in my lap and I shouldn't be jealous and coveting her. "Well, you gotta do what he's doing." Even drunk, I can hear the *duh* in my voice. "Get yourself off before he gets in bed with ya."

"How?"

"What?" I sputter, exasperated. "Touch yourself."

"I don't know how!" Willa's shout warps into a pout. "I had to share a bedroom with my baby brother. And it's not like anyone was around worth getting off on. Until you showed up, I ain't really wanted anyone."

"You want me?" I blurt out and wish I could take it back.

"My panties are wet." She leans back against the table to show me, but I squeeze my eyes shut. "I ain't that stupid. I know what that means. Momma was telling me a bit about that too. How I ain't wet for Donny, so that ain't helping the baby-making business."

"What do you want me to do?" grits through my clenched teeth.

"Show me," Willa demands.

"There ain't enough beer in the world–" Tiny, strong fingers wrap around my wrist and yank. "Oh, fuck me. I'm going to jail. You're underage. Hell, I mean. Being my brother's wife cancels out the jail term but sentences me to eternal damnation."

Not giving a damn for my drunk ramblings. "I'm wet. For *you*." Willa puts my hand on the seat of her panties. Soaked. She's soaked. I did that to her. Me. Her brother-in-law. Going to Hell, I am. "Yer so goddamned hard I can feel your heart beating in your dick." The little minx grinds her tight ass against me so hard I nearly pop my cork. "Show me."

"Fine," snarls past my lips. "Take me somewhere my brother will never go, and I'll *show* you. Since you said he always does it the same way, I'll be Donny. But I'm only *showing* you how to do it. Got it?"

"Thanks, you're a lifesaver!"

"A lifesaver? You make this sound like I'm doing you a favor… we're about to commit borderline adultery, and my brother will never forgive me."

"Knowing your spineless coward of a brother like I do, I'd say there is a good chance you could fuck me in front of him and he'd thank you," Willa says dryly as she climbs off my lap.

"That ain't happening, little girl," I warn as I get to my feet, only to sway side-to-side.

"Not tonight, no." Willa wraps her arm around my waist, supporting me as she walks me to the couch.

"My brother sits on this couch," I remind her.

"No, he doesn't. Sean does." Willa flashes me the evilest smirk I've ever encountered. "Seems fitting, doesn't it?"

"You are a depraved, little creature, aren't you?" I don't put up any sort of challenge. I drop to the couch when she shoves me.

Looking me dead in the eyes, Willa turns serious. "I'm only depraved with you."

I'm about to say, "*I highly doubt that*," but then I realize it's the truth. I'm different with Willa, and I bet she's different with me.

Body lax and rubbery, I allow Willa to tug on my hands and feet, moving me where she wants me. Until I'm on my side like we're getting ready to snuggle on the couch and watch a movie.

"What was this business about a dog?" Words slurring, my mind blanks for a moment. Willa just stares down at me, smirking like she knows what I want to say but she's waiting for me to finish. "Oh, yeah… this ain't how we do doggie-style from where I come from."

"I'm well aware." Willa rolls her eyes. "I lost my virginity bent over my footboard. But Donny felt bad about that, like it was dirty somehow. So he picked an even more boring way."

"How?" An arched brow betrays my interest. "Show me."

Willa crawls onto the couch, wiggling her ass in front of me. My arm automatically curls around her belly, tugging her closer so she doesn't fall off the cushion. Nose nuzzling the top of her hair, a sigh of contentment flows from me.

"This is nice. If only we had SportsCenter on, I could go nighty-night like this." My body ruts around, getting more comfortable. "Good night, Willamina."

"Hey!" Willa swats my hand. "You've got something to show me, remember?"

Propping my head up on my elbow, I look down at the side of her face. "You have sex like this?" My voice is drier than a popcorn fart. "My brother spoon-fucks you? Is this even a sex position?"

"I regret saying how I wasn't a dog," Willa grumbles. "I'd take dog over this anytime."

"Great position for snuggling and sleeping." I drop back down into position, trying to figure out how one thrusts while lying on their side. "Fucking? Not so much."

"I told you Donny's locked and loaded before he comes to me. When he's done, he stays where he is and goes to sleep."

"My left hand fucks me better than Donny does you," I whisper into Willa's ear, and a miracle happens. She goes completely lax and releases the dirtiest moan I've ever heard. I press my lips to her ear and she groans for me. "Are you wet for me, Willa," I flutter against her ear. "Do you want me to show you what to do with your sweet honey?"

"Yes," comes in a breathy moan. "Please," she begs. and I really, *really* like the sounds of that.

"Don't judge me if I spontaneously erupt in my pants." In my drunken haze, not only do I experience a total lack of inhibitions, I experience verbal diarrhea too. "It's been years since a woman has come apart in my arms, and I'm not going to be able to handle it. But I'll try to behave myself."

Arching her back, rubbing her tight ass against my stiffy, Willa moans like she's already coming. "Don't." Shimmy of her hips. "Bother." My hands grip her hips to stop her, but end up controlling the rock of her ass against me. "Misbehave with me," she pleads, and I lose my shit.

Gripping Willa's hips hard enough to leave fingertip bruises, I shift her around until my bulge is cradled in the curve of her ass. "This is how you fuck in this position." My hand slides up her inner thigh, raising her dress as I go. A hiss is torn from both our throats at the feel of my bare skin touching hers. Fingertips dimpling in, I grip her thigh to prop it over my hip. Then I dip my hips, getting right up in her, grinding my cock against the saturated seat of her panties.

"This is how sex should be." I pant, thrusting and rolling my hips against hers. "Arch your back more, tilt your hips, spread your thighs farther apart, and grind into me like you're desperate for a baby in your belly."

Voice forced from a craned neck, "Royce!" Willa shouts, so fucking close to coming that I can scent it in the air. This girl's got a hair-trigger. I bet I could force five or six orgasms out of her if she was mine.

Snapping, I doubt I could even stop if Donny was standing over the sofa threatening to kill us. "I'm gonna make you feel like a woman, little girl."

My hands seek Willa's, palms resting over the backs of her hands. Fingers woven together, I direct her how to touch herself. Starting at her neck, I force her to arch so I have better access to her ear. I suck on her lobe while our hands explore. Willa's keening by the time I reach her breasts, so tiny they fit into her palms. I run our fingertips over and over her nipples until she's writhing so hard we almost fall off the cushions.

"Imagine my cock is buried inside you as deep as it will go," I breathe into Willa's ear, driving her wild. Bucking her hips into me, I almost blow the top off my cock. "You'd like that, wouldn't you, you dirty girly?"

"Y–e–s…" rolls out her throat, vibrating against my lips. Clenching my hands, I clench hers around her small tits, gripping tight enough to hurt but she thrives on it.

Hands roving down her belly, we dip beneath her dress. Together, our fingertips slip beneath the waistband of her panties, going lower and lower until springy curls tickle our skin and moist heat beckons us forward.

"Christ." A shudder rolls up my spine at the first touch– scorching hot and smooth, Willa's so damn wet her cream is dripping off our fingertips. "This is why you wanna be wet." Without thinking through the ramifications of my actions, we slide silky smooth down her slit, and then press our fingers inside her narrow pussy.

"Deep?" We press in to the first knuckle. "Deeper?" We press in to the second knuckle. "Deeper?" We press in until we bottom out. "Promise land?" We curl our fingers forward, and then pull down sharply, fingertips hooking on her g-spot.

With a low grunt, Willa jackknifes in my arms, quivering and shuddering, spasms rolling through every muscle in her body. I slip our fingers free from her body, moving upward. "Willamina," I purr into her ear, lips wrapping around the lobe. "Meet your clit– the instant orgasm spot."

We roll our fingertips across the swollen bud, all that dampness paving our way, and Willa screams my name so loud she wakes the dead. Laughing, I can't believe I'm doing this. So depraved. So wrong. But it feels so fucking good.

Seductive mews still bubbling from her lips, Willa wrecks me. Her fingers slip free of mine and take me with her. Moving so fast I can't react, Willa's hand is shoved down my pants, gripping my dick, and she's jerking me off in an instant.

"That's crossing too many lines," I shout at the ceiling, jets of cum shooting all over the inside of my pants. "Don't fucking stop!"

Flipping around, hand still working me until I'm flaccid, Willa curls around me, and then she kisses me. All I can do is ride out my orgasm in her hand while she licks and nips at my lips.

"I've never touched a willy before– hard or soft," Willa reminds me, fingertips still playing along my softening flesh. "I've never kissed no one before neither."

"Oh, Willamina." My lips seek hers, kissing her softly the way a first kiss should be. "We shouldn't–"

"No–" she stops me. "Ask yourself this, Royce. Do you really think any of the three of us wanted Donny to be my first anything? Donny?"

"Willa." *I'm going to hell and loving every second of it.* "No, you should get to choose, husband or not. But don't make me betray my brother like that. My soul won't be able to take it."

"When Donny gets home, take one look at him and ask yourself whether or not he just got good and fucked. Ask yourself if a husband lets another man tell him to beat his wife, then does it. Then leaves his brother to pick up the pieces. Donny didn't even see if I was okay before he ran off groveling after the same man who has beat us twice before. Who exactly is betraying who?"

"Shh..." I hit Willa's off switch by breathing into her ear, and she falls silent. "I get it. I do. But I can't let Donny's actions change mine. I can't fuck around with my sister-in-law. No matter how alive she makes me feel, okay?"

"Okay," Willa agrees, finally getting it. "Thank you," she whispers shyly. "Thank you for teaching me how good sex can be, how I can pleasure myself. I'll try to use that with Donny, but I know it won't be the same."

"It won't be the same," I mutter through a vicious stab of possessive jealousy. "*I hope it won't be the same*," I whisper for only my ears to hear. "Do you need anything? How's your cheek and lip?"

"It was just a slap." I can hear the eye roll in Willa's voice. "My momma hits harder than Donny. Now, Sean, he hits harder than a hammer."

"Keep that baseball bat with you at all times," I order her. "And never let anyone know where your hiding space is. Ever... I'll get my brother to tell me what's going down with Sean. Somehow."

"Good luck," Willa mutters, not believing me. "I need something from you, and you can say no if you want."

"Anything." Part guilt. Part regret. Part need to be Willa's hero. I'd agree to anything she wanted.

"My baby brother, Wynn, he's a real sweet boy. He's gonna be a big'un, but not mean. He's not like the rest of us Gillettes. He's smart, kind– helpful. A hard-worker. He could have a future if only someone would show him the way."

"Done," I promise, and I promise myself never to break a promise to Willa.

❧Present❧

Willa leans forward, pressing her lips to mine. "Thank you, Royce. Thank you for remembering with me. Since the moment I met you, you looked at me like I was worth something, even when I didn't believe it myself. You didn't tell me I was too stupid; you bought me textbooks. You thought I was beautiful, desirable, smart, and worthy, and you made me believe it too."

My fingertips curl in the back of Willa's hair, wrapping around tightly. I give a tug, drawing her face away from mine. In the waning firelight, I really, *really* look at her. "Walking down memory lane is helping me rediscover who we both were, who we are, and why I fell in love with you in the first place."

"Me too," Willa releases with a smile. "Did Donny ever tell you why? Tell you about Sean?"

"No, there was nothing I could do to get him to spill. The guiltier I felt over touching you, the more at ease Donny became. I tried for four years to get rid of Sean… obviously that didn't work out too well."

"You should ask Donny again," Willa suggests, but I can see a silent horror moving beneath her eyes.

"You know, don't you?" I don't press; it's just a statement of fact. "You know all the whys to all the questions, and you're walking me through it, hoping I'll finally see it along the way?"

Willa just shakes her head yes, unable to speak.

Hands sliding down her back, I pull her forward into my arms. "You're the smartest, most loyal person I know. It's taken me a long time to realize just because something is moral doesn't make it right."

Willa and I have our own sleepover in the backyard next to the fire pit, just as innocent as the one Hayley and Hayden are having, and it's one of the most fulfilling nights of my life.

•AUGUST•

"Okay, so now that that is settled…" Amery Smythe, Donny's and my attorney, moves all of the **Community Growth: Life Skills Center**'s paperwork off the conference table. He grabs a box from the floor and places it on the table next to him. "Time to move on to the Trusts."

"I thought?" Wynn looks at me, confused all of the sudden. "I thought we were meeting with the lawyer to get everything for the non-profit ironed out. And I've just sat here for three hours since I have nothing to do with that. Bren too."

"I'm finally eighteen!" Bren makes a squee sound while rubbing his palms together in anticipation. "I get to sit at the adults' table."

"I meet with Amery twice a week, but once a year everyone has to go over the Trusts." I reach forward, grabbing files out of the box. I can feel confusion and frustration wafting from Wynn, but I ignore him as I put the files in order.

Willa's arm hooks the folders, drawing them in front of her. Having been through this with me a couple times a week for the past year, she takes over. "Talk to Wynn. Explain."

"I'm the trustee of six Trusts because their beneficiaries are not of age or otherwise incapacitated." I grab the main files, and spread them out across the table. "When Daddy and Annie passed, several Trusts were created from the large settlements, paying the beneficiaries for the loss of life."

Amery takes over from there. "With Donald Kennedy Sr. being the patriarch of two grown sons, the settlement was broken into three Trusts. A quarter each going to each Donald Jr. and Royce, and fifty percent to any grandchildren born of Donald Sr. At the time, all fifty percent belonged to Bren, with Royce as the trustee."

"So Bren has more money than Royce?" Wynn's head flips around like the demonic little girl in the Exorcist. I swallow back a laugh, noticing Kade 'coughing' into the crook of his arm.

With a shrug, Bren mutters, "*Had.* The grandkids split the pot. Hayley and Hayden came along, and now I only have sixteen percent." Smirking, he points at Willa. "Keep them legs shut,

Momma. Or at least wait until I'm twenty-five, so your little brood can share what's left after I take my third of our pot."

"You've got plenty," Willa volleys back, playing with Bren. She rolls her eyes so far in the back of her head I fear I'll never see the blue of her eyes again. "You can share."

"Bren, Hayley, and Hayden don't have access to these funds until their twenty-fifth birthdays. As the trustee, it's essentially Royce's money to do as he sees fit," Amery explains. "That's why it's best to appoint someone who has your best interests and won't drain your Trust."

"Dad's stingy," Bren grumbles, and Wynn finally catches on to why my son isn't rolling in dough.

"It was a terrifying few years when Donny was the trustee." I shudder, remembering how he would buy all sorts of unnecessary things, a substantial amount of money disappeared with no paper trail, and I had no way of stopping him. I feared my children's money would be gone before they could ever use it.

"Uncle Donny was the trustee?" Bren glares at me, hands clenched into fists on the tabletop. "Of *my* money?"

"Yes, that was the provision set by the judge so Donny and I couldn't fight over control. We each had a Trust of twenty-five percent, combined with this Trust, the trustee controlled seventy-five percent of my father's settlement. Assuming a father would act in the best interests of their children, the trustee was appointed by the majority. Two-to-one: Hayden and Hayley versus Bren. Donny took over the day of their birth. Then money started flowing like water. The day Sean pulled up in a brand new truck was the only time I'd ever hit my brother."

Willa's stare burns a hole in the side of my face… waiting. "Oh, fuck!" I slump to the table, arms wrapping around my head. I peek at Willa. "That's why? And you knew and didn't tell me?"

"We discussed divided loyalties at our last session, remember." Willa points at Amery Smythe.

"I was bound by Attorney Client Privilege, Royce." Amery looks about ready to burst from his skin. "I learned the details when I vetted Donny's defense team. Donny wouldn't speak to them unless I was present. There are things I wish you knew, but I cannot speak of them. I apologize for both Willa and myself, as she had to sign a gag order. The only person who can tell you is Donny himself, or if you figure it out on your own. But Willa and I can't speak of it."

"Well… no harm, no foul." A bitter laugh is torn from my chest, and a table-full of my family looks at me like they're worried for my mental health. "Okay, so a *lot* of harm and foul. But the good news is that I am now the trustee of one-hundred-percent of Dad's settlement. When Donny is released, I'm hoping to put a cap on the amount he can draw off his Trust at any given time, as he *obviously* isn't fit to manage his own money."

"That has already been written up and put into place after I learned the nature of the attack and the events leading up to it. Donny himself specifically asked for it, and appointed you as his trustee for life."

"Donny's forty-four years old?" Bren looks around. "So he's gonna have to beg for his money from you like I have to? An allowance? God, that would suck ass."

"Bren?" Willa gains my son's attention. "The grandchildren are down nearly three million dollars by Donny's misappropriation of funds– *your* funds, not his own. With more than half of his Trust gone." Willa opens her hands and mouths, *"Poof!"*

"To Sean," I whisper underneath my breath, ready to curl around the nearest trash basket and empty my gut.

"What–if–how–why–" Wynn stammers, trying to wrap his head around something, getting angrier by the second. "If Hayden and Hayley have money to their name, then why the fuck was Willa on welfare?"

"I was *not* on welfare," Willa snarls at her brother. The Gillette erupts in both of them. "Not that there is anything wrong with welfare if you need it. But I'll have you know, child support was taken from the Trust on a monthly basis for Hayden and Hayley's welfare based on our living situation. I gave that money to you to pay the bills because you were the only person I could depend on. It came straight from Royce."

"Why live in that shithole, Willa?" Wynn's rage lessens the more distraught Willa gets. "Why do that to yourself?"

I rest my hand on Willa's back to soothe her, but she flings me off. "Don't touch me when I'm angry," Willa bites out between gritted teeth. "I don't want to associate your touch with anger."

"I understand," and I do.

"You don't get it." Willa sits up straighter, eyes narrowed at Wynn. "You remember who I used to be and how I am now, and have glossed over who I was for nearly four years. When I got out of the hospital, Royce wasn't fit to help me, and I wasn't selfish enough to take his time from Bren and Kaden."

"But why come home to Momma and Daddy." Wynn's voice warps into a whine as he tries to understand. "Why, Willa?"

"I was safer there. There are things I can't discuss. But no one was going to target toddler millionaires in the hollers. No scam-artist drifters were gonna cross our daddy's boundary line and survive. I know there's more out there," she says cryptically. I freeze, realizing Sean didn't live to spend that stolen money yet it's still gone.

"I do and I don't get that, Sis. But–"

"Did you forget how I was catatonic? They wanted to commit me but Daddy wouldn't let 'em. Worthless drunk or not, Daddy was protecting me and my children the only way he knew how. Have you not noticed how the only people I interact with are people I've known my entire life." Willa taps Kade on the tip of his nose. "I've known him longer than I've known you. Got it? Even when I volunteer, I've got to take Royce with me. I trust y'all because I knew you from before, before when I was able to think straight. Now I doubt strangers, and want to crawl underneath the table and hide."

"Willa?" Wynn reaches out, trying to grab his sister's hand, but she won't let him have it. "I remember your screams. Nobody can fake that."

Wiping tears of frustration off her face, Willa pours it all out. "I was on so many drugs– prescription drugs, not the kind you assumed I was on. Even today, when I see a Seroquel commercial, I want to pass out. My choice was zombie or horrific nightmares where I saw Hayley in my place and Hayden in Royce's, and I couldn't survive it. Warren would get me– get me *stuff* he shouldn't have so I could feel alive for all of five minutes before my psychotropics took over and zombiefied me."

Willa rolls into me, resting her head on my chest and wrapping her arms around me. I allow her to hide. My arms automatically secure around her so she feels safe. I nuzzle her hair with the tip of my nose and squeeze her.

"*I'm sorry*," Wynn mouths, looking on the verge of tears. "I didn't know."

"It's not your fault, son," I murmur gently. "It just is what it is."

"Do we need to change anything on Brennan, Hayden, and Hayley's Trust?" Ignoring our emotional breakdown, Amery gets us back on track, bless his heart.

"No." I shake my head against the top of Willa's. "The twins are getting an allowance like the rest of their peers for doing chores and whatnot. Bren's share isn't to be touched until it matures. He has his own we use for his expenses."

"As I thought," Amery mutters absentmindedly, reaching for another file. I place the kids' files into the box. Done. "Now on to Donny… do you wish to decrease, increase, or stay the same on his commissary funds?"

"Increase by three hundred. Last month when I visited, Donny was very depressed." I blink away the vision of my brother's devastated face. Seeming to not age, my brother reminds me of a small boy begging me to help him because he has lost his way and can't see in the dark. Gaunt and thinner than I remember, it hurts to look at him.

"Is Donny speaking with you?" Amery sounds surprised.

"No, we do our thing where I ramble about whatever's happening, show him pictures, and he just watches me. I can tell he wants to hug me but is ashamed of himself."

"Maybe the anniversary will be different," Willa whispers against my chest. I know she writes Donny and he writes her back. But it's none of my business. Sometimes you've got to let go of control if it heals.

"I know this is an odd request, but I'd like you to petition for a private visit on the eighth. They allow conjugal visits for spouses, so maybe you can swing something where we only have a guard in a small room instead of a packed visitors' center."

"I'll do my best, Royce," Amery vows. "Donny's defense team is still working on an appeal at best, or a shortened sentence for good behavior at worst. They've passed Willa's and your statements around so much, I think our justice system knows the words by heart."

Wynn's face scrunches up, staring at Bren to see if he understands what's going on. When Wynn begins to question us, Amery shuts him down. "So, Royce…" My lawyer slides the final folder from my daddy's Trust in the box, and then places it on the floor. He grabs a single folder for Bren from his momma. "Any changes with Brennan's Trust?"

"You have more money?" Wynn turns on his brother, looking flabbergasted.

"God, the irony is gonna kill Wynn." Kade laughs into the crook of his elbow again, and Willa starts giggling against my chest.

Bren goes from depressed to sheepish in an instant. "Dad, I need a new car and I need monthly funds for an apartment and living expenses."

"What? I thought you were staying at home and commuting to school?" My eyes seek Kade for his counsel, and he shakes his head slightly to the left and then the right. "Okay, we can negotiate on that after we've spoken about it in private. Car? You have a newer car?"

"Remember how I said Dad is stingy?" Bren bumps Wynn in the arm with his shoulder. "I have all this money, and that dang man made me save up from the age of fifteen to sixteen to buy my first car. I worked for a year, and the engine blew up after two weeks. He learned his lesson about letting me buy something reliable." Bren looks me in the eyes for the first time in weeks. "My car is only two and a half years old for *me*, but it's fourteen years old now and I don't trust it."

"What car do you have in mind?" I blurt out without thinking.

"Land Rover."

"No, too ridiculously expensive for someone your age. Pick again. American-made."

"Jeep?"

"Jeep what?"

"Rubicon?"

"Fine. I'll release the funds into your bank account. You have exactly two weeks to make a responsible purchase. If you try to buy something else, something less and keep the difference, I'll jerk the funds right back out of your account. Trade-in on the old car?"

"No, I'm keeping it."

"Why?"

"None of your business."

"Fair enough."

Amery's amused laughter fills the boardroom. "That, my friends, is why Royce is the trustee. My god, you are a born negotiator."

"I'm a daddy. Every day is a negotiation," I mutter dryly. Laughs, giggles, and snickers flow around the room.

"Any more changes involving Brennan's Trust?" Amery is slowly shutting the file, but I stop him.

"Yes, I will be changing the automatic deposit into his account for living expenses, but I'll have to give you a number after my son and I speak in private." Amery nods his head in assent. "I also have another request, but it ties into Kaden's Trust."

"You have a Trust?" Wynn's head jerks around so quickly I fear he tore a tendon in his neck.

Eyes shuttered, voice even, "I went to college for four years, to a not-so cheap school, and I was as dumb as a box of rocks. I've now applied for grad school so I can be certified as a counselor… I have a mortgage and didn't have a job for seven months. What do you think?"

"No shit," Wynn sputters, looking ready to punch his boyfriend like he did just last week. "I knew Royce was floating you. But where did your Trust Fund come from?"

"From me." I shrug. "You asked if Brennan had more than me. No. When my wife died, I also lost something precious to me." Sympathy pains, Willa quivers in my arms. "I received a settlement from my wife and my portion from my father. I started a nest egg for Kaden, with his living expenses coming out of his wages. But we all know what happened to his wages." I eye both of the horny fools. "The Center isn't up and running yet, and we can't afford to pay the directors much. So Kaden's bank account has been slowly draining his fund. When he turns twenty-five, I'll have no say in how he spends it."

"I live simply." Kaden pouts, thinking I'm making fun of him after how Wynn rides his ass for not pulling his own weight. "I behave. A house and tuition isn't frivolity."

"I trust you." I grip Kade's shoulder, squeezing to hammer it home. "I trust you so much that I've made a big change." I turn to Amery. "In eight months, Kade will be twenty-five. On that date, I want you to transfer the trusteeship to Kaden for both Brennan's and Wynn's Trusts."

"Holy fuck!" Bren gasps, clutching his chest. "I'll have to ask Kade for my allowance? I should hold out for that Land Rover."

Kade slumps to the table like he's fainted dead away.

"I trust you, Kade. Bren's right." I turn to my ecstatic son—happy that Bren's not despondent for a change. "Some things are not my business. I think back to my daddy, and there was no way I'd want him to know certain things. So I understand why you've been freezing me out and confiding in Kaden. It hurt me a bit, but it also makes me feel good that you have someone you can count on. I trust you both to be responsible."

"You're seriously gonna put Wynn's money in my hands?" Kade looks like I've lost my mind. "What if we break up? If he cheats on me, I might drain his account into mine out of spite."

"Wait– what?" Wynn's looking around at all of us like we're strangers. "My money? I ain't got any."

"Here comes the irony," Kade sings underneath his breath.

"I set you up with a fund the same as Kade's, for the same purposes. It's not that large. A nest egg to get you on your feet. If used responsibly, you shouldn't have to struggle. But I know how you operate, so I'm not worried."

"I don't like this." Wynn glares at me. The insanely happy kid turning back into Teenage Asshole Wynn. "I don't like this at all. I won't touch the money."

"Where do you think your room and board came from, you little shit." Kade shoves Wynn almost out of his chair. "Don't be an asshole. Look at it this way, if you wanted into someone's pants bad enough, you'd do whatever it took."

"What?" Wynn and I say at the same time. Willa pulls away from me, laughing quietly.

"Dad already gave Penny a car and gave the deed to their house to Warren," Kade spills my dirty secrets. "And he'll tell you this long song and dance about why he did it. But truth be told, he did it for her." He points at a blushing Willa. "So get with the program and say thank you, ya little shit-ass."

Wynn's glare promises Kaden a whole world of hurt when they leave here. "Why not just give Willa the money?"

"Willa's name is on everything I own," I admit matter-of-factly.

"And with that," Amery stands from his seat to shut up my squawking children. "My work here is done." My attorney flashes me a waning smile that says, *"Good luck, buddy."*

"Call me as soon as you know about my visitation with Donny," my voice dips down into pleading territory.

"I'll make the request as soon as I get back to my office." Amery looks down at all the boxes. "You two are strapping lads. How about you help me carry all this to my car."

Wynn, given the chance to help anyone, jumps right up to assist. His mood lightens remarkably from just this little gesture. Kade, not so much. He taunts Amery and Wynn about how he's going to be the stingiest trustee they've ever seen.

Willa leans into me, pecking me quickly on the lips. "I'm gonna pick up the coffee cups and shut this room down. Why don't you two have words?"

"Dad?" Bren squints his eyes while drawling my name. "You gonna go beat me up in the parking lot? Is this a shakedown? What the fuck, Willa?"

Huffing a laugh, I lean down to kiss the hell out of Willa, and she giggles into my mouth. Standing back up, shaking my head left and right. "Damn woman ain't never figured out what that saying means. But gotta say, I miss the homerun threat."

"Son?" I gaze over my shoulder at Bren as we leave the meeting room– which used to be a print shop thirty years ago and has laid dormant until now. As the smallest building on my side of Main Street, I chose it to house our offices and meeting room. "We're just going to do a walk-through and see how everything is coming along for next week's unveiling. No talking. Promise."

"No talking?" Bren snorts, but he follows after me like a silent cloud of misery. "I'm positive I'm in for a lecture."

"Is that your guilt speaking?" I guess, knowing I'm right. "I've been there– I'm still there. Ya gotta let that shit go. It'll eat you from the inside out."

"Let it go?" he scoffs, yet his brown eyes hold a wealth of guilt and shame. "You ain't having much luck with that."

"I'm trying at least… and Dr. Cassidy would agree that I'm succeeding." I head out the front door, stepping onto the sidewalk. I stride backward to the curb, eyes on the Life Skills Center.

"So much for not talking," Bren grumbles passive-aggressively underneath his breath. If he's going to act like a kid, I'm going to treat him like one. I ignore him, knowing eventually it will break him.

"This–" I gesture to the block of buildings in front of me "–is letting go."

The five buildings that house the Life Skills Center loom overhead, a silent promise of Rusty Knob's positive future. With the inception of Rusty Knob, these buildings started out as a bank, a pharmacy, an insurance office, a diner, and a printer.

Over the years, businesses closed and others pulled in. But the sense of community was lost when a tanning salon took over a four-generation pharmacy, only to last three months because Rusty Knob's denizens got their tans out of doors for free while doing manual labor. Or how the printers, which was supplemental to our dying newspaper, was seventy years old before it went out of business. It became a video store until VHS and DVD rentals became obsolete. Then it was a touristy t-shirt shop that flopped immediately. After that, it became a place to buy fish and small furry animals we didn't need when they were overflowing our creeks and yards already. Advantageously, it changed hands with a tattoo artist, which was a big hit until the owner pulled up his roots and left for the nearest city. Last it sat empty for five years because no one could afford the rent on the building and we were out of ideas on how to yank money out of our neighbors' pockets in the quest to earn a buck and survive.

Until today, Rusty Knob was dying along with its elder citizens, leaving its rich traditions and its sense of community to be forgotten by the generations to come. In the quest to see the bigger picture, embrace technological advancements and the changes to our country, our vision has become peripheral. As we advocate saving an entire world, we no longer see what's right in front of our face.

As our elders would say, *"any animal knows, you don't shit where you eat and sleep."* If Bren heard my thoughts, he'd laugh right now. But these sayings hold greater meaning. In order to be selfless, we've spread ourselves too thin. We've shit on our town, where we live, sleep, and eat, by taking away the very things we need in order to survive. We worry so much about the greater good, we forget that we have to be strong in order to help others. In our weakened state, even Child Protective Services isn't capable of helping kids who are growing up just like Wynn had.

Those children are being raised by castrated men and beaten women, just as they were raised. The need to provide is ingrained in a man's DNA, just as the need to nurture is in a woman's. When the ability is taken away, the structure of humanity falls. Many spout, *"Well, don't have kids if you can't afford them!"* when that is at the very core of human nature.

If I hadn't been blessed with blood money, I don't know where I'd be today. I'd love to think my ideology would have saved me. But you don't know what you're capable of until your family is starving, and all the pride you possess is torn away from you because you have no means of providing any of your family's needs. Whether it be the government or a helping hand from a neighbor or family member, the man will think, *"Sorry, Bobby, but Uncle Sam is your daddy now."* It's no different than castrating a man, and then wondering why he turns to drugs to cope because his family no longer needs him.

"Just seeing this…" I'm rendered speechless, overcome with a billion emotions at once. I rest my hand over my heart as I speak to my son, but my eyes never leave the sight before me. "I've spent my entire life watching this town crumble, hearing the old-timers tell stories of how it used to be a thriving town, and wishing I could go back in time to when Rusty Knob wasn't just a shell of what it once was. Now–"

The impressive stone building on the end of the block, with its large entryway carved out of the corner of the building, welcomes members of our community. It was the perfect, historical location, long ago being a bank which relocated to a more central location. A small plaque rests above the keystone.

"You can paint a building, but you've got to teach its owner how to maintain it." I grab for my son's hand. "Let's spread some knowledge, shall we?" Striding up the stone steps, I pull Bren into the welcome center, seeing it with fresh eyes.

"This is my favorite off all the renovations." Awe laces Bren's voice as he pulls away from me to gaze at the walls. "It's like a time capsule..." His fingertips reverently linger on the Plexiglas protecting the black and white images of our history.

Rusty Knob from the mid-nineteenth century until present time, with before and after images of the same locations. Our town was built on the backs of the hardworking coal miners and loggers, and out of respect, they are represented on these walls. Along with the hills, showing the trees in every season, and the progress and passage of time on not only our town but its citizens too.

"I thought it wise to remind everyone why we're doing this– that protecting something built to last hundreds of years is more important than the next, big new fad that will die out in a year or two."

"I get it..." Bren's turned away from me, fingertip following the railroad line. "You always said that I needed to listen when the old-timers spoke, because if I didn't hear them, important knowledge would be lost." Bren looks at me over his shoulder, grinning. "I just pretended they were telling me bedtime stories so I wouldn't get bored."

"And rolling your eyes the entire time..." I grin back. "I know. Me too. Most of the stories were told on repeat, sometimes in the same conversation." Commiserating, Bren and I share a groan. "C'mon, let's wander through, making sure it's how we want it."

I know Willa wishes for Bren and me to 'have words' but I'm waiting my son out. He'll talk to me when he's ready. I'm hoping the final walk-through of the center will put him in the right frame of mind.

The bank was turned into a welcome center, with images on the greeting room's walls and a few chairs by the front desk. The only rooms not closed off to the public consist of the bathrooms and a small sitting room playing historical videos of West Virginia on a constant loop.

One of the hardest parts of the renovations was connecting the inside of the buildings to walk freely from one to the next without having to go outside. The bank connects directly to the pharmacy, with the entry behind the front desk for ease of flow. All visitors have to enter the bank to proceed to the other spaces.

Warren is hard at work, making sure the automotive work stations are set up correctly, after apprenticing beneath his father-in-law for the past few months. The pharmacy was the largest of the buildings, also housing a loading dock in the rear that was perfect for working on cars and bringing in oversized furniture for repair. We turned the pharmacy into the hands-on areas, where repairs of all kinds will be taught as well as put into practical use. Wynn oversaw everything dealing with carpentry, and Warren's finishing up the automotive.

Penny's father will be teaching mechanics classes one night a week. On the other nights, we have a contractor teaching home repairs, an electrician for the simple things, and a plumber to teach all the things that don't require a professional.

Nodding to Warren, I quicken my step to catch up to Bren. My boy hates anything where his hands would get dirty. I'm not going to lie– I'm the same way.

The insurance office is next, and Bren slows, simply because he likes the looks of the place. The narrow building still has its original wallpaper and the tin ceiling, completely contrasting with the computer desks with their shiny laptops, the printer station, and the large desks and sofas for studying.

Wynn, Bren, and Kade set this building up to suit the requirements of those who needed a comfortable place to study for their GEDs or gain knowledge in specific areas to get a higher-paying job. The Jacobs sisters will be teaching specific computer programs to pad a résumé, as well as hosting workshops for household budgeting and balancing checkbooks. Willa and Penny's coupon clipping will take place in this same space.

"God, I'm waiting for him to start making out with them." Bren's lips curl into a genuine smile, the first in a long time, while he watches Wynn buff the laptop screens.

"The boy sure does have a hard-on for technology," I mutter in wry amusement as we walk by. Tall, lithe body curled protectively around a laptop, Wynn doesn't even notice us because he's so absorbed in his task.

"Color me shocked that you agreed with Kade, Mr. Technophobe," Bren teases me, giving me a glimpse into the facets of his personality I've missed so much over the past few months of angst. "Thought for sure you'd have us in here carving wheels from stone and making paint out of horseshit for hieroglyphics."

"Ahahahaha," I mock laugh in my son's face while curling my arm around his shoulders to shove him out of the space. "It's about balance, dumbass. We need both skill sets. I'm all for higher education and technology, but even a doctor needs to know how to change a flat or how to wash his dirty undershorts."

Dragging my son, "Well, what do we have here?" I drawl, eyes instantly lighting on Willa when we enter the kitchen.

"Git off me," Bren struggles to toss my arm off his shoulder. "I can feel your heartbeat speed up. Eww…"

I swallow my laughter, not bothering to hide how Willa affects me. "You should see your face around certain individuals– that ain't something a father ought to ever see," I taunt Bren back."

Obviously the diner was turned into a large kitchen that is Willa and Penny's domain, much to Willa's annoyance. Beautiful face twisted with impatience, she's yanking a large glass jar from Penny's grasp.

"Penny!" Willa's exasperated tone causes both Bren and me to snort. "You will not be teaching any classes until you get the basics down. You just refilled the sugar canister with salt."

"It's not *that* big of a deal," Penny whines better than her son does, who's hanging out in a playpen in the center of the space. I make a beeline for the cute, little feller.

The baby is reaching out for me before I can get to him, squawking and babbling in delight. The girls know we're in here, but keep on bitching at each other just the same. Oil and water, Penny and Willa, with poor Warren stuck in the middle.

Copper settles in my arms easy enough, happy to be liberated from baby jail. "You don't go listening to them none." I nuzzle the top of his head, pleased to see his red curls have lightened a bit– now copper like his name, instead of the bright red hair he was born with. "Oh, do you want Bren to give you attention? Do you?"

"There is too a difference between corn starch, baking powder, and baking soda," Willa's gearing up. "You're the one who graduated. Didn't they teach you this shit in chemistry class?"

"I didn't take chemistry!" Penny shouts back.

"We're gonna kidnap you while your momma and aunt get their disagreement settled," I murmur to Copper as I stride through the kitchen area with Bren laughing loudly behind me.

"Maybe you should have. Just like earlier when you put the wrong fertilizer on the garden plants. Tomatoes need acid– cucumbers need alkaline."

"I don't know what the fuck you're saying," Penny's nearing tears.

"I'm trying to teach you. Stop being a blockhead!"

"Well, if you weren't so goddamned pushy!" Penny strikes hard. "I liked zombie Willa better."

"Well, aren't you a little cunt?" Willa's irate voice follows me. "It's no wonder Warren picked you– you act just like my momma. Stupid on purpose 'cuz she's too lazy to learn. Your momma needs her ass kicked for not teaching you a goddamned thing about being a woman."

"Well, how the fuck did you learn anything with Cora's lazy, fat ass raising ya? Explain why you knows better than me?"

"Easy," Willa says low and slow in a cold, calculating voice that is the Gillette in her erupting. "I did the complete opposite of anything my momma would have done. That's how. Now open your ears and follow directions, and you and I won't be having any more problems from here on out."

Walking back into the printers, the last building on our route, I pause in the area used for group therapy sessions. "If we could choose…" I whisper against Copper's wispy hair. "I'd be rethinking wanting a lady in my life. They seem more work than they should, especially when they travel in packs. I could see how being gay would be nice. Hanging around the bonfire, watching sports together, never being nagged. Sex and sleeping… I'd miss a lady then, though."

"Being bi means I can choose," Bren reminds me, slipping into one of the chairs set in a circle in the center of the room. "It ain't no easier, because you have no choice in who you fall in love with."

Taking my son's words as his way of opening up to me, I slide into a chair opposite him so we can look one another in the eye. I hold Copper underneath the armpits with his tiny sneakers on my thighs, and play bouncy bounce to occupy him.

The old printer building is Kade's domain, with a meeting room, our shared office, and space for group therapy and refreshments. I glance up, baby babbling to me in my lap, to meet

Kade's eyes across the expanse as he sits behind his desk in the office. He gets up silently, deciding it's high-time the three of us have *words*.

"Willa'd probably stop biting Penny's head off if you'd diddle her already," Bren taunts me just as Kade settles down several seats away from me. "I mean, when was the last time either one of you got laid?"

"You know?" I gasp, shocked.

Brennan rolls his eyes, but it's Kade who looks furious. "Of course he knows. Bren's not a moron. We were both home that one time Willa snuck in in the middle of the night, and we woke to Corbin dragging her crying ass out of our house at breakfast."

Wincing, "I was under the impression we were here for Bren…" I trail off, not looking forward to this impromptu therapy/intervention session. "Dr. Cassidy has everything well in hand when it comes to Willa and me."

"Dad!" Bren loses his patience with me.

"Fine," I mutter begrudgingly. I flip Copper around so his back rests on my belly and his hiney is on my thighs with his little legs kicking me in the knees. He goes to work gnawing on his thumb, looking at Bren and Kade like they are interesting. "A year and a half ago was the last time– approximately three months before I sent Willa and Warren to rehab. Dr. Cassidy said to wait on sexual intimacy until after we've exorcised our history."

"At least you were honest for once," Bren mutters to himself. "I don't want details or anything. But it hurts when you lie to cover up the truth."

I shift around, suddenly uncomfortable. "About exorcising our history. It's already penciled in– the truth. Prepare yourselves, because it's happening just before Wynn goes off to school in a few weeks."

"Shit!" Kade scrubs at his face with the back of his hands. "So much shit is going down, I can't keep track anymore. You know it's bad when I'm not the cause."

"I'm sorry." I squeeze Copper in my arms, needing the comfort. "I can't give details– I refuse. But I won't lie anymore. You're grown men now, and I can't expect you to clean up your own messes if I don't fix mine first. I'm trying to help this town, but as Willa keeps saying… help starts at home. I've got to help myself first." I take a deep breath. "So I am."

Little blue sneakers hold my undivided attention as I pretend two sets of eyes aren't boring into my face. I can't look at my sons, but I can put them at ease. "Kade, I think you get why I was keeping you and Wynn apart. The first time I was with Willa, she was only fifteen and I regret that that's how it went down. Yeah, she stalked me, pretty much assaulted the willing, but it doesn't make it right. I was only trying to keep you from a lifetime of regret."

"Thank you." Kade's voice breaks, and I chance a glance at him. His manly features are twisted in indecision. "I knew that already– I was just waiting for you to actually say it out loud. When I was younger, I didn't understand. You made me feel like a pervert. But when I found out the truth from Warren, I figured you were trying to help me and Wynn."

"I was," I breathe. "I knew you could handle the guilt and shame. Wynn can't handle stuff like that, but he's old enough to decide what he wants to do now…" I trail off, unable to voice giving my foster son permission to screw my adopted son. I just can't say those words out loud.

"I'm waiting," Kade admits, shocking me. "If Wynn can't wait with me, then that proves he wasn't ready in the first place. I can't… I can't do that with someone unless I know they're with me forever. I just can't."

"Sons," I start hesitantly. "I'm sorry my past has colored my feeling on men being with men. I know you know what I mean. Deep down, I realize it's no different than me being with a woman. How you won't hurt each other. I *know* this, but my terror feels very real to me when I think about it. So leave my issues out of your bedrooms."

"Wynn just graduated from high school," Kade reminds me. "I want him to experience college without our relationship holding him back. Trust me when I say your issues are *not* in my bedroom."

"Good," spills from my lips in relief. "I'm happy to see you have a good head on your shoulders." My eyes flick up to connect with my first born. Bren looks terrified and lost. "Forget about me, son. If you want to be with Jack, be with Jack."

Vulnerable, "I can't," Bren whispers, but then his resolve hardens. "I'm *not* gay. I'm not in denial. I totally get off on girls, and I'm not gay-for-Jack. Yeah, I ain't gonna lie… I have nightmares I wish I didn't have, and they affect me when I think about being with a guy. But that doesn't change the fact that I've never denied wanting to be with one. And I agree with how carefree being in a relationship with a guy versus a girl would be. But I know until I fall in love with someone and make a commitment, part of me is always going to be roaming around, craving whatever I'm not getting. It's something a bi person has to deal with."

"Do you need to talk to someone? I'm sure Dr. Cassidy could find a colleague so you didn't feel uncomfortable speaking with her."

"I know who I am," Bren says firmly. "I love Jack. I might even be in love with him a little bit. But just as Kade feels about Wynn, Jack isn't ready for that. I want Jack and Wynn to go off to school and experience everything, and I won't hold either one of them back."

"But that doesn't mean you can't too." My voice warps, nearly whining. "I want you to be a kid, Bren. We still have time to find you a spot in the dorms–"

"I don't want that," my son cuts me off. "I'm not great at anything in particular. I can't even tell you what I want to major in. But I do know that way of life isn't for me. I want to live on my own. I've already found a job near campus at a health club. Soccer moms will be paying me to push them to exercise harder." A pained expression crosses Bren's face. "God, Franny would get a kick out of that."

"If you're in love with Franny–"

"Royce," Kade is groaning at the same time Bren is calling out, "Dad, no. Franny's my best friend, and I miss him. He'd totally go nuts to hear torrid tales from the gym, and that makes me sad. But that's not what's going on. Okay?"

"Okay, I won't push," I promise.

Bren looks relieved, but then terror washes over his features. "I found out you can be in love with one person, but love someone else so much more that you'll do anything to keep them– no matter what."

"Like the shit I pulled with Willa?" I admit for the first time. "That wasn't just for Donny, no matter how much I try to tell myself it was."

"Kinda..." Bren looks decidedly uncomfortable all of the sudden. "More like in spite of how much you were in love with Willa, I would have come first. Like how it took you seven years to adopt Hayden and Hayley. Nothing and no one was going to get in your way."

"I-I-I... what?" I gasp, confused.

"Don't demand any answers until I'm ready to give them," Bren reprimands me, sounding like a grown man. "I'm going to be working, using my wages and tips for my living expenses. But I need enough to get started. Deposits for the apartment and utilities. Furniture. That sort of thing. After a few months, I should be on my feet."

Feeling suspicious, I ask, "You're still enrolled in school, right?"

"Yes, Dad. I might not know what I want to do as a career, but I do know I'm going to need a degree for whatever I decide. I'm not going to live off my trust fund– you don't. You have more money now than what you initially started with, and I want to be like you."

"Don't butter me up so I can't reason out what's actually going on." I warn, but I'm blushing from my son's praise.

"Don't even bother trying to figure it out," Bren warns back. "The day you tell everyone the truth, is the same day I'll tell you what's going on. So be patient. But I'll need that deposit in the next few days so I can secure an apartment."

"Fine. But I don't know if I like this commanding side of you," I mutter to Bren with my eyes narrowed.

"You lie," Kade taunts me. "You secretly love it." He gets up from his seat, striding over to Bren. Kade grips Bren's shoulders, laughing at some joke only he can hear. "Hot damn, my baby brother is acting like a *man!*"

Out of the corner of my eye, I catch Penny and Willa leaning against the threshold between the kitchen area and where we're sitting. I should have known better once their catfight ended. Acknowledged, they both step forward, looking perfectly content around one another after their confrontation.

"My baby doesn't know how to walk yet, so I figured he must be with you." Penny approaches me cautiously– the only member in this fucked up family who sees me as an authority figure.

"Copper loves his Uncle Royce," I use baby-talk as I pick him up to hand him off to his momma. "But he loves you more."

"Uh-huh… he only loves me 'cuz I'm the food source." Walking toward the office, Penny controls Copper's milk-seeking mouth and grasping hands before he gives us a show. "Time for some grub…" flows as she shuts the door behind her.

Resting a hand on my shoulder, "My nephew is such a guy," Willa teases. "Already going nuts over tits."

Chuckling, I want to show Willa what a guy I am. "Copper'll never grow out of it. Hayden was a fat little fucker, always suckling.

Arms flying everywhere, trying to knock his sister off your other boob."

"What started our bitch-fest in the kitchen is when I told Penny how she couldn't complain about Copper biting down during a feeding because she didn't have two of the leeches stuck to her tits at the same time." Willa shrugs, completely unrepentant. "I might have insulted her… oh, well."

"I've got somewhere I need to be," Bren mutters, fleeing the room in a mad dash to get away from all the woman talk.

"Me too, I guess." Kade shrugs at us, then stares at his closed office door with great longing. Sighing, "Well, my paperwork will have to wait. This gay man does not want to know what an enlarged nipple looks like, especially when it's shoved in his godson's mouth." With a visible shudder rolling up his spine, Kade walks into the kitchen, no doubt with Wynn as his destination.

"Now that that's over…" Willa tugs me from my seat, and then wraps her arm around my waist. "Time to see a real therapist."

"Ugh," I grunt, but then my voice twists up into a whine mimicking the kids. "Do we have to?"

"We have less than a week before we have our family session," Willa reminds me. "So I'd say we have to."

Being tugged out the front door, I mutter, "You're so smart. I'm glad you chose me."

"You have a lot of new developments culminating at once, Royce. The Life Skills Center opening. The anniversary of your wife and father's passing, as well as the anniversary of your attack. Your visit with Donny. The group session. Your sons going off to college, moving away from home. How are you coping with all of this?"

"Dr. Cassidy, I–" leaning forward, I grab the pillow from behind my back, and the good doctor misses nothing. Hugging the pillow to my chest, I eye the teddy bears hanging out near her desk.

Eyes twinkling behind her bifocals, "Not well, I take it," she mutters wryly.

"You are very sarcastic for a doctor," I drawl, causing Willa to giggle into her hand next to me– she's not hugging a pillow today. "Good actually. I'm hitting this shit head-on, knowing once it passes it's done and over with. I'm actually thrilled that all of this happens in less than a week."

"You'll feel a bit lost without all of this stress hanging over your head," Dr. Cassidy predicts. "So you'll need to find something else to draw your attention."

"I own a dozen businesses that I need to run, and I'm going to focus my energy on the center. My brother's appeal is always on my mind. I also have two eight-year-old kids who might be pissed at me after our group session. So there is that… and I whole-heartedly plan on focusing on Willa."

Dr. Cassidy's lips quirk up slightly at the corners, but it might as well be her version of beaming brightly. "How do you feel about cementing your relationship with your brother's wife?" she baits me.

"*Ex*-wife," I snarl.

"Ex-wife," the doctor allows. "How do you feel about that?"

"I feel nothing," I get defensive. "If you're wanting me to get down on my knees and grovel, that ain't happening. I don't feel any regret or shame when it comes to Donny over this– not anymore. Willa's marriage to my brother meant nothing. I belonged to her, and Donny knew it."

"What changed? Why did you go from the loyal widower, who wanted nothing more than to protect his big brother, to the adulterer who was having sexual intercourse with his very young sister-in-law? What happened to that Royce?"

"I'm still him. He's still me. I was him then, just as I am now. Nothing changed. *Nothing*," I bite out between gritted teeth. "*Nothing*."

❧9 years ago❧

Donny begged me to visit this time. For obvious reasons– mainly my dick seeking my brother's child-bride –I've avoided stepping foot on Kennedy land. For almost two months, he's been visiting me, never bringing Willa with him. But tonight he begged knowing I'd fold and give in.

I was going to bring the kid with me as a buffer, but Bren wandered off to a sleepover with his little friends, leaving me utterly defenseless against that innocent-looking, foul-mouthed succubus.

Gripping my steering wheel tighter, my hands are sweating from the nerves. My heart is joining the party, beating a wicked tattoo inside my chest. I can't put words to how I feel. Maybe this is that wild sensation teenagers go through when they meet someone who lights their asses on fire for the first time.

I never experienced that as a kid. I met Annie when I was a little guy, and she befriended me– was my only friend. I wasn't much of a joiner. Baseball came to me naturally, but I would have only played catch with my old man if he hadn't forced T-ball all the way through varsity softball on me.

Annie was my best friend, a few years ahead of me in school. She would come to my softball games because her daddy was the coach. Coach thought I was a hard-worker and going places. Reflecting back, that's probably why shortly after I turned fourteen, in celebration for earning a write-up in Kentwood County's newspaper, Annie said it was time to lose our virginity.

My Annie trapped me, but I loved her like a best friend anyway. So through courting her, meeting my father-in-law's demands, marriage, babies, and faulty ignition switches, I never got to be a young man. So, as I'm closing in on thirty years old, I don't know why I feel a bit crazy as I park my truck on Kennedy land, just because a wildling is waiting inside the house.

With a hitch in my step and a tune whistling between my lips, I act like I'm not freaking the fuck out. I take the front stairs two at a time, wishing my brother would have come to my house and sat around the bonfire with me instead.

The door is swinging open just as my hand reaches to turn the knob. Donny's hands are tugging me inside, like he can sense I'm about to bolt for my truck and hightail it out of here. "Royce." My brother's voice holds pure pleasure for being in my company as he pulls me into a back-slapping hug.

"You could have come to me," I mutter begrudgingly as I pull away. "The guilt-trips involving Kennedy land don't hold the same weight now that it's just a prefab modular, not the house Granddaddy built."

"The land's the same and I'm still standing on it." Donny flashes me a bright grin, like he's the luckiest bastard in the whole wide world because he has me. Guilt seeps in, twisting my guts over what happened during my last visit.

"I'm glad to see Sean isn't here." My words seem innocent enough, but the tone accompanying them is pure rage. I step farther into the house, the sound of the game filtering from the television set.

Donny ignores my Sean dig after refusing to explain himself last I asked. "C'mon, bud. Let's watch the game, have a few beers, and eat the junk food Willa's cooked up for us."

Self-preservation kicking in, "I best hold off on the beer." As I settle onto the adultery couch, I ask about the booze-peddler herself. "How's your bride of five months?"

Jesus, could I sound any guiltier?

I should have asked where Willa was, so I could keep an eye out for her. She might pop out of nowhere asking for my dick… and I'd probably put it in her hand.

I'm going to Hell.

My brother drops into his recliner with a deep sigh of contentment. "Good. She's prettying herself up."

Suspicious, I grunt, "Why?"

For me?

"Willa's a woman… they don't need a reason for anything they do." Donny hits the volume up on the remote, filling the living room with the echo of commentators and riotous fans. He reaches forward, grabbing his beer off the coffee table. His behavior is the usual, but there's an odd air floating about that I don't like one bit. Something's off.

"What's up?" I try to be heard over the TV, which I can only assume was the point of jacking it up so high in the first place. "You're gonna need hearing aids if you don't turn it down."

"Huh? What'd you say?" Donny goes back to ignoring me on purpose.

"Exactly," I mutter sarcastically. My eyes flick about, noting how the house appears to be the same as last I was here. Only now, Willa's books are spread across the top of Donny's desk on the far wall. At least she's still studying.

Knowledge in that woman's mind is a scary thing. She's already too smart and cunning for my own good. I ought to stop giving her textbooks, or maybe I ought to get her more advanced books.

Pretending to watch the game, cheering when Donny does, I can't tell which teams are playing against one another because I don't even know what sport is on TV. That's how insane Willa is making me feel.

Where in tarnation is that dang woman? I need to see Willa so I'll calm down.

"What the hell, Roy?" Donny calls me out. "Why would you cheer when the ref made a piss-poor call?" I blush bright red, thankful for the darkened living room. When I don't answer, my brother stares me down with eyes crinkling at the corners, laughing. "Boo! The right response is boo."

"Boo..." I rumble lamely, and Donny chuckles at me.

Antsy, I can't sit still. "Dude, if you wipe your hands on your jeans one more time..." Donny warns me, flashing me an odd look. "Go get a fucking dishtowel and hit the thermostat if you're so hot. What is your malfunction tonight?"

"Shit!" I jack-rabbit off the couch cushion, head toward the kitchen, and when I get there I forget why I went there in the first place. I end up back on the adultery couch, rubbing my sweaty palms on my thighs. "I-I-I I–"

"You look like you could use this," Willa's raspy voice has me shrieking in surprise. I'm so off my game that I take the beer from her hand and drain the bitch in a few swallows. "Thought so."

Willa's in yet another virginal white sundress, even though it's autumn now, and it's so transparent I can tell that she's not wearing a lick of clothing beneath. I can even see the soft fuzz between her thighs and the points of her nipples.

I'm using an express pass to Hell.

After passing her smirking husband another beer, Willa settles on cushion next to me, offering me another cold one. "Are you trying to get me drunk again?" I meep when I realize what I implied. "Not that you ever got me drunk before." I eye my brother, but he looks like he could give two shits about anything but the game.

"Calm down, Royce-baby," Willa breathes into my ear. Then the minx wraps herself around my arm, cuddling into my side like *I'm* her husband, and my brother doesn't say a goddamned word.

Frozen stock-still, I stare straight ahead at nothing. My heart is beating out of my chest, supplying the blood flow to my greedy dick. Every nerve in my skin is alive and quivering to get closer to Willa, and I don't understand what's going on with them or with me.

"Jesus! Really?" Willa shouts at the TV, sounding like a surly pirate. "Making bad calls against one team is rotten... making them against both teams? Get a new job, asshole!"

"Where do they find these morons?" Donny and Willa engage in a referee bashing session, both of them looking at each other, the game, and directly at me, and neither acknowledging the fact that Willa is wrapped around me like an afghan.

"What the hell?" lunging to my feet, I jump off the couch, tumbling Willa to the side. "Did I enter the Twilight Zone?" I charge out of the room, down the hallway, and straight into the safety of the bathroom.

Secure in the bathroom, I turn the taps on full-bore to block out the noise of the game. Toed up to the toilet, I unzip my jeans. Hand wrapped around cock, I try to take a piss with a hard-on. "Go down, you dumb bastard. What is wrong with you?" I stare down at my dick, getting angry with it. I choke it a bit, causing me to wince. "Go down!"

Stepping side-to-side, hoping that will help, I reason with my penis. "Why won't you go down, you perverted sister-in-law fucker? If you don't, I'ma cut you clean off at the nutsack. Eh? That doesn't sound fun, does it?" Through gritted teeth, I hiss, "Go down!" while squeezing my dick out of frustration.

"Yer doing it wrong if yer trying to jerk off." Willa has me jumping so far out of my skin, I almost tear my own dick off at the root. "Unless yer into hurting yer willy."

Wrapping herself around my back, nestling her tiny breasts against me, both of Willa's hands latch onto my dick and start stroking.

"Stop it!" I whisper-shout at her, yet I can't seem to get my hands to yank her off of me. "Donny will wonder what the fuck is up!"

"Don't *you* wonder what's up?" Willa sounds incredulous, even as she's giving me a handy jay. Fist squeezing so tight my cockhead almost pops off... "'Cuz I know what's up."

"You have to stop," I plead. My thighs start to give out from the pleasure of it, body sagging forward. Automatically my arms reach out to the back of the toilet tank to hold myself upright. "This is so wrong. Bad, Willa. Bad. No. Naughty."

"Depraved?" Willa whispers against my ear in the seductive voice of the devil. "I've missed you, Royce. You've been avoiding me."

"I wonder why, you succubus," I gasp out, panting like I'm running a marathon. My traitorous hips start weaving back and forth, causing my cock to slide in Willa's tiny palms.

The friction feels so fucking good... or maybe it's the sin that's wrecking me.

"Please," I beg... to come.

My eyes snap shut against the need to marvel over how huge my cock looks in her tiny hands, and to pretend I'm not so into it that I'm drenching her skin in my pre-cum.

"Please lie to me and say I'm hallucinating."

"Yer not." Willa's as blunt as ever. "We're standing in my bathroom, while yer brother is in the living room, and I'm jerking ya off... and yer lovin' it."

"Something is wrong with me. Very wrong with me." My hips jerk forward like I'm thrusting home. All it takes is the pinprick of a fingernail digging into my cockhead to set me off.

Forehead resting against the bathroom wall, hands clenching the back of the toilet tank, teeth drawing blood to keep the scream at bay, I ejaculate a lifetime worth of seed. "My God..." My neck arches from the pleasurable pain. "Forgive me." Quivering, it hurts so good I fear my nuts shoot out the tip of my dick.

Exhausted, I just fought a battle– with myself –and lost. My eyes slip shut, only to pop back open at the sound of Willa's voice. "Now you can take yer piss."

Head whipping to the side, "What? Is your head cracked?" I take one look at Willa and go ballistic, not caring if my brother overhears me. "Oh! No, you fucking didn't! Say you didn't?"

Willa runs around the small bathroom, avoiding my reaching hand. She hops into the shower and I follow, and the little minx hops right back out. "Oh, fuck no... no.... no... no. no. no. no." In denial, I mutter on repeat as I try to grab at Willa's moving parts. "You get back here! Get your hand out from beneath your dress. WILLAMINA KENNEDY!"

"Like you didn't know it was coming," Willa taunts me, looking flushed from evading my swinging arms. "I only promised not to do it the first time, and I waited until you were sober. Fair's fair."

"Fair?" A high-pitched shriek spills from my throat like I'm a teenage girl. "Fair?" I manage to grab ahold of her wrist. Hauling her up against my chest so I can get a better grip on her, "You stole my seed, you thieving hillbilly bitch!"

I toss Willa onto the vanity top, none too kindly, and then wrench her legs apart. "You didn't, did you? You're just playing with me? I mean, nobody would ever do this to someone. Would they?"

Acting like I'm the one in the wrong, Willa turns surly. "I don't know what fantasy land yer living in, buddy boy. But it ain't mine…"

My fingers wrap around Willa's slender thighs, widening them. Eyes on the prize, I notice how damp her girly curls are, and it strikes terror throughout my body. "There's no way…" Involuntary, my fingertips dip into her pink snatch, sliding easily inside. Silky, hot, and pillowy, her flesh sucks at mine. "Fuck," I snarl as the scent of my seed wafts up.

Leaving my fingers inside Willa, I reach with my other hand to grab a washcloth to clean her inside and out. The intense waves rolling against my fingers are undeniable, followed by Willa convulsing around on the vanity top like she's having a seizure.

"You cunt!" My words are harsh, but they're filled with awe as this wild young woman breaks apart against my hand.

"It's mine," Willa mutters belligerently, tearing my hand away from her pussy. Then snapping her thighs shut like the bars on a prison cell– or the gates to Hell. "I worked for it. I'm keeping it."

"You are seriously psychotic!" I step away, walking in a tight circle while yanking at my own hair. "Knowing you, it's your fertile time, you hillbilly bitch." I stop, stepping right up into her face. Pointing toward the living room, "That's my goddamned brother, you cunt! Do you have any idea how violated I feel right now? Do you?"

Hands folded protectively over her lap, "I reckon I might understand," Willa says all prim and proper, voice filled with false innocence.

"Why didn't you just get it from my brother?" I bellow into her face, not giving a shit if Donny hears me or not. "Your HUSBAND?"

"You want me," Willa challenges. "Don't deny it."

"I haven't denied that… but this?!?" I throw my hands up in the air, completely at a loss of what to do.

"Donny shoots blanks," Willa interrupts my freak-out. "His previous wives left because they wanted children. I've had five monthlies," she reminds me, looking at me like I'm the one who betrayed her. "You tucked tail and ran away after you saw me last, and you never finished yer end of the bargain."

Head cocked sideways, eyes narrowed, "What are you talking about?"

"Sean. You promised to take care of Sean. But Donny wouldn't tell you, would he?" she accuses. "I held up my end, using the knowledge you gave me. But two seconds after I started touching myself, Donny yanked out and hasn't touched me since. I keep getting beat because I'm not pregnant, and Donny keeps getting beat because he won't touch me."

"I-I-I-I…"

"Momma said if Donny couldn't get me with child, and if I wanted to protect myself and my husband at the same time, I best find somebody that no one would question once the kid popped out."

"I get why me." I raise my arms, shaking my head left and right in exasperation. "I'm the schmuck who obviously has a hard-on for you and looks almost identical to your husband."

"Yer manlier than Donny." Willa's tone screams how much she likes that fact, and I ignore the effect it has on me.

I mutter underneath my breath, "*Why do the women in my life always drag me around by my balls*?" My mind clears, and I get to the heart of the issue. "Why the fuck are either one of you allowing Sean to control you like this?"

"Ask yer brother," Willa mutters defiantly. "I don't know. No matter how snoopy I am, I can't figure it out." Silently crying, she stares down at her hands clasped in her lap. "I'm sorry." Her voice breaks, and it kills me. "I do like you, Royce. I want you bad for some reason. I have no control over what's going on in my life, but this I had control over. Choosing you."

"Christ, girl." My hand seeks the back of Willa's neck. I slowly draw her closer to me until her forehead is resting against my chest. "I'm the one who's insane. Somehow you managed to make me feel sorry for you, even after you stole from me."

Sounding pitiful, Willa whimpers as she pulls away. Arm reaching backward, she pulls her frothy blonde hair to the side, and then dips the back of her dress down, exposing her back.

Faint lash marks have me seeing red. Violent rage comes to a boil in my blood. My fists clench at my sides. "Why?" I cry out, voice breaking.

"Yer brother's back looks worse. But Donny promises Sean will leave me alone as soon as I get pregnant. So that's the only *why* I give a shit about, Royce."

Seething, I stomp from the bathroom, leaving Willa behind. The first thing I see is my brother's face wearing a goddamned satisfied smirk. I tear the remote out of his hand, silencing the deafening game, and then I toss it to the coffee table with a clack.

"Why?" I demand, pulling no punches. "You set me up. You called me up here to fuck your wife. Why?" I demand again while leaning over his recliner.

"Don't ask why; just do it," Donny challenges me back. "Do it for Willa and me *and* you. Do it because you want to fuck her. Do it because you didn't see the look on your face when you met her. Do it because you'd get off on knowing you put a kid in her gut. I don't give a fuck why you do it, but you *have* to," he pleads.

"I'm not a prostitute!" I bellow. "I'm not your wife's studhorse. I'm not going to bring a kid into this world and allow you to raise it."

"*Your* kid," Donny promises. "Sean just has to think it's mine. That's it."

"WHY?" I scream so loudly the vein in my forehead threatens to burst. "Goddammit, why?"

Lunging from his recliner, Donny pushes me backward out of his space. Hands tearing at his t-shirt, my brother strips himself from the waist up. "This good enough of a reason for ya?" he demands, facing away from me. "There's your why. I'm protecting you, you fucking idiot!"

"Donny... no..." My fingertips reach out to light on the lash marks marring my brother's back. Raw, puckered, and angry looking, he has to be in immeasurable pain.

My brother is one of the softest people I've ever met. So small and harmless– helpless. Why would anyone ever want to injure him?

"Get Sean out of our lives," I demand, voice hoarse and raspy. "Corbin would gladly do it, I bet. What hold does he have over you?"

Ignoring my questions and the pain in my eyes, my brother pulls his t-shirt back over his head, covering up the evidence. "Make a kid, say it's mine, but it being yours protects us all. Just do it, and enjoy it." Suddenly chipper, yawning widely while stretching, "I think I better hit the hay, brother. Don't go driving home– you've had too much to drink. Stay up, watch the game. Willa will keep you company."

Playing pretend, my brother acts like he didn't just order me to spend the night because I had one beer over an hour ago, all because he wants me to impregnate his wife for him.

I drop onto the adultery couch. Head in my hands, my mind mulls over the biggest decision of my entire life.

❧Present❧

"I gather you decided to do as your brother bid," Dr. Cassidy states the obvious. "Did you ever regret it?"

Mind and body experiencing the same conflicting, disorienting emotions as I did way back then, "No– never," I answer honestly. "Only now have I realized why Sean wanted Donny to procreate so badly, yet I still don't know why Donny went along with it."

"But you did it for your brother, no questions answered?" the doctor fishes for answers of her own.

"Donny's my brother. I wasn't the same man I am today. I was lonely. A bit lost without Annie tugging me around by the balls. It was the blind leading the blind. I did it for a million reasons that don't matter."

"Did you ever blame Willa for essentially raping you?" Dr. Cassidy crosses a line.

"Don't!" I threaten, causing Willa to grab a pillow and clutch it for dear life. "Don't ever categorize what happened in that bathroom to rape. I wanted Willa; she wanted me. If I didn't want her hands on my spunk, then I shouldn't have allowed her to milk it out of me. I know rape," I fiercely bit out. "And that wasn't it."

Trying to calm myself while reassuring Willa, I reach over to take her hand in mine. Dr. Cassidy misses nothing. "There was never a kernel of blame you felt for Willa? None at all? Even when you were calling her a thieving hillbilly bitch?"

"Truth be told, I was furious with her. But more so with Donny. I was frustrated. Lost. Helpless. Feeling out of control. All of it made me hate Sean. But I never blamed Willa, not one iota. She was a young woman in an impossible position. No one should be beaten. Ever." I squeeze her hand. "Willa did what she had to do in order to survive."

"Are you saying neither one of you enjoyed it?" Dr. Cassidy sounds incredulous as all get out. "That it didn't take more than once to create the twins? That some part of you didn't get high off the thrill of something so… what was the word Willa used? Depraved?"

⇾9 years ago↤

"We don't have to," Willa's voice is solid, resolved– more mature than her few years. She settles in Donny's recliner. "I don't want to do to you what everyone has been doing to me. I'm not a monster."

Leaning forward on the couch cushion, elbows on my knees, head in my hands, my eyes peer up to connect with Willa's. Swallowing thickly, I can't get my tongue to release the words I haven't thought yet… I just…

"Sean was here a few minutes before you showed up, that's what had Donny and me acting like we were losing our minds. I was wrong, and I'll admit it."

Whispering, unable to speak with any volume at all, "I'm terrified you'll go find some man and he'll hurt you, and you'll regret it for the rest of your life."

"I won't– I promise." Willa wrings her hands together in her lap, skin turning white from blood loss. "It was you or no one for me. Even if Donny had demanded someone else, I would've kick him in the nuts and ran back to Gillette Holler."

Head cocked to the side, I try to reason that out. "Why haven't you, then?"

"Daddy's loyal to Donny," Willa explains color to the blind. "I'm guessing they're close like brothers. So I can't do that to Donny, 'cuz Daddy wouldn't let me live it down." She gazes up, staring me dead-on. "I care about Donny, Royce. He's a real sweet man, and I don't want to see him get hurt, either. I know I'm strong enough to take it– he ain't."

Leaning forward, my palm glides across my neck to rub at my hair. "Shit," I hiss. "I don't know what to do here, Willa. If we were just talking sex... If I'd met you under different circumstances, I doubt I could have stopped myself from being with you. But you're my brother's wife– his buddy's daughter. But even with all that, I could survive the guilt of sex... but kids? Kids are a whole 'nother ballgame, and I don't think I can handle that shit."

Willa releases a bizarre laugh– sardonic, dark, and filled with agony. "I don't think I'm capable of making a decision here, Royce. My instincts are telling me to take you on the sofa. Just hold you down and ride you until you give me what I want. But then I think of what might come next... and I'm terrified."

"Forget the sex... that's the easy part." I get down to the real matter at hand. "Why kids? Do you even like kids?"

"I always wanted kids," Willa says without a lick of hesitation. "I guess now's as good a time as any."

"You've met my son... Christ!" My hands have a mind of their own, almost rubbing the hair off the top of my skull in a mix of indecision and frustration. "Does Donny even get what he's asking of me? To make a kid with you, and pass it off as his? To not raise it myself? To not allow my son to have his brother or sister? I don't think I can do that, Willa. I just can't."

Back straightening, looking like she doesn't need anyone to protect her, and it's so far from the truth. "Okay," Willa relents in a voice filled with strength and resolve. "I get it, and I respect it."

"What does Sean want with Donny's kid? I mean... if I do this, I can't have some man who's whipping my brother and sister-in-law getting his hands on my child. I would kill a man over that shit. The thought..." Bile rises in my throat. "The thought of some asshole touching Bren the way my uncle touched me and Donny, or the violent way your daddy touched you."

"I know why Sean wants the kid, and I know what hold he has over Donny," Willa finally admits. "And you best not try to get your brother to tell ya, 'cuz he's incapable right now. It's why it's me talking with ya and not him. But I can assure you, Sean won't ever touch the baby once it's born. It's just the fact that it exists."

"Tell me," I beg, practically beseeching. "Tell me why so I can fix it."

"There's no fixing it," Willa utters, sounding as if she wishes it wasn't the case. "It's something Donny has to work through himself. So we're gonna let him while we try to protect him from himself, while he protects us from Sean."

My head darts up, baffled. "A kid, though?"

"I might be a hillbilly bitch, but I knows me some things." The hurt in Willa's voice has me flinching in shame for ever calling her that. "I ain't ignorant. I learn quick. How I grew up taught me shit most will never learn. So if you consider this, we're gonna iron out the details now, and Donny will stick with 'em."

Smirking in the face of what's going down, I feel ridiculous. "You have my brother by the balls, dontcha?"

"No, not me." Willa shakes her head back and forth, left to right, muttering *no* underneath her breath. "Donny's prey, and I ain't. So I'm taking care of some things for him because I'm his wife."

"I have the oddest urge to thank you for that... insanity. I feel jealous, too." Gulping for air, I finally realize I'm going to go through with this, no matter what Willa proposes, and it's not entirely for altruistic reasons. I love my brother, but not *that* much. "This gives a whole new meaning to the word unconditional. Hit me with these details, Willa."

"You sure?" Willa's being cautious, and it comforts me some. "You seem like the uptight, holier than thou citizen. I just don't see you handling this well." I nod my head quickly, before I can back out. "The kid'll be yers. I'll know it. You'll know it. Donny'll know it. We'll do some type of bullshit that those rich yuppie folks use when they get a divorce. After it's no longer on my teat, we'll split its time equally."

"What about Brennan? What about the kid? Am I supposed to be Uncle Royce for life? I can't handle that." High wearing off, my voice breaks. "I can't suffer with that."

"Once the threat passes..." Willa looks away from me, but before she turned, I saw her wheels spinning. If Donny doesn't fix his shit, Willa will make sure somebody does. "I don't know what'll happen in the future, Royce. But I know if you want something, you have the brains and the means to get it. So don't worry about a little, ignorant hillbilly bitch. I know in the end, if the shit splatters, I'ma be the mother without a kid."

"Willa," I whisper softly. "Willa, don't cry. Please," I beg, voice dipping low. "We won't do this."

"We have to," Willa pleads, leaning forward, voice reaching out to me. "We *have* to. Donny's my husband– my daddy's buddy. He's yer brother. And right now some asshole is controlling him, and controlling us through him. So if Donny wants something, we've got to do it. Because just like you, he's smart and he's got a lot of money, but he's older and easily misled. I ain't got no power here, and you've got a lot to lose. Trust me on that, Royce. *You* have the most to lose."

Willa's cryptic words trickle into my mind, confusing me yet giving me the courage to do what I do next. I lean back on the couch, shuffling down until my ass is at the edge of the cushion. Comfortable with my lap exposed, I open my arms in invitation.

When she hesitates, with my eyebrow raised, I mutter wryly, "Thought you said something about holding me down on this here adultery couch and riding me."

"Adultery couch?" Willa's snort is feminine and cute, and it makes me laugh at how fucked up we both are. "That'll work. I've been imagining this moment since I met ya."

Sashaying toward me, Willa makes the ten foot span feel like a mile. Nervous, I lean back, rubbing sweaty palms on my jeans. Until the day I die, maybe even from the grave, nothing will ever be sexier yet more terrifying than Willa Kennedy in a virginal white dress. Nothing.

Moving quickly, Willa straddles me on the couch, sitting astride my thighs. In thickening silence, we stare at one another in challenge. My heart is beating in my throat, deafening me to everything but the steady rhythm of my blood gushing through my veins.

Light-headed, feeling foggy, I experience a high like no other. In the face of making the worst mistake in my life, I feel invigorated and alive.

Eyes locked, neither one of us moving, we're competing in a standoff. Who will make the first move? Who wants it more? Who is terrified but not a coward? Who will flinch?

Blue eyes wide and wild, I can practically hear Willa's blood rushing through her body, eclipsing the sound of my own.

Time has reached a standstill. We lick our lips in mirrored unison, and it's almost laughable. Holding our breath…

There's no going back.

We collide like two forceful storm clouds creating a thunderhead, with violence and darkness, and bright flashes of angry electricity that will raze the land to the ground. But when the fire dies out, the land will be reborn.

Attacking me with ferocity, Willa tears my t-shirt from my back, fingernails scoring my skin with the painful bite of passion. There's no denying we both want this more for ourselves than to get Donny out of trouble.

Gasping for air, I grip Willa's hands before she can remove that white dress. "No, I want this on you," rasps from my throat in a voice I don't recognize. "This goddamned dress is a fantasy I didn't know I even had."

Naughty, Willa's lips curl into a smirk, like she caught on to that fact before I did. "Depraved," I drawl, leaning forward.

Wrapping my palm around the nape of Willa's neck, my fingers trailing around her throat, I yank her lips to mine. Mouths open, tongues fighting, I kiss her like I've kissed no other, cementing how she's just as much mine as I'm now hers.

"Now," Willa gasps against my lips, breath shuddering. "I can't wait any longer. I can't." With force, she shoves against my shoulders, pressing my back against the couch. Lifting up onto her knees, Willa shuffles backward on my thighs. Her fingers attack my jeans, tugging and tearing at my button and zipper.

Blown away, all I can do is sit back and watch in awe as Willa takes exactly what she wants from me. Releasing a sadistic chuckle, she reaches into my pants to free my cock. With a grunt, my hips buck off the cushion when her fingers wrap around my flesh and yank violently.

"Good God, woman! Don't unman me," I warn, shoving at my jeans until they're past my ass and to my knees. "Your hungry kitty can wait until I get my dick out."

"Fuck too, it can," flows in a throaty demand as I'm shoved firmly against the back of the couch. I'll surely have palm-shaped bruises to my shoulders come tomorrow morning. Hitching her leg, Willa reaches down to grip my cock and stand it upright. My eyes glue to the vision of her hand wrapped around my length. Sitting down hard, we both grunt in shock as her body swallows mine– ass meeting thighs.

Back arched, neck straining, fingertips clutching the cushion, my mind can't absorb all the stimuli. It's been so long since I've been inside a woman, and it was never this hot and tight. Offering me no comfort, Willa yanks my hair roughly to force my eyes open.

Demanding I maintain direct eye contact, a tiny palm clutches the front of my throat, fingernails digging into my flesh. Partially choking me, Willa uses my neck as leverage to roll her hips in a wave, riding me as promised.

My eyes venture downward, taking in how glossy my cock looks as Willa flows up and down my length. Disappearing and reappearing, I feel disconnected from my own dick, like this can't be happening but it's the wildest fucking thing I've ever experienced.

I'm being owned by my sister-in-law and reveling in the sin of it. When we reach the pearly gates, one can't say they've truly lived unless there's a bit of tarnish on their soul.

A strained sound gurgles from my lips just as fingertips clench so tightly I choke. "Eyes up here, Royce-baby," Willa not-so gently reprimands me.

Manhandling me, I return the favor by gripping her dress and tearing it down the front, buttons pop from the fabric to fly through the air and ping off flat surfaces. No amount of choking returns my eyes to Willa's. Exposed, framed by innocent white cotton, tiny tits so firm they barely shake, let alone jounce with her movement, hold my undivided attention.

Palm lying flat against Willa's back, my thumb rests on one side of her ribs and my fingertips splay on the other. She's a dinky little thing with the personality of a dictator, making her seem larger than life.

Leaning forward, I wrap my lips around the tight bud of her nipple, feeling it bead against the curl of my tongue. Purring in pleasure, Willa's movements falter. Opening my mouth wider, I suck her entire tit into my mouth, teeth clamping down to bruise her flesh. Pussy clenching in spasms, Willa's reaction proves she's a masochistic little bitch.

Mouth still latched, my hand slides to cup her ass, giving it a sharp smack. The girl in my arms shatters apart, nearly taking me with her. Holding her by the ass, fingertips accidently brushing her pucker, I pick her up, still attached at the cock and pussy. Flipping her to her back on the couch cushions, I show Willa the one position I know she's never been in.

Still coming, soaked pussy milking at my cock, I lie down on top of Willa and roll my hips in a slow yet deep wave, not wanting this to end for me too quickly. I want to make it last.

In juxtaposition of Willa violently fucking me, I make love to her like a husband ought to his wife. *Now* I hold her eyes, and she's the one having a difficult time connecting with me when the emotions are softer, more mature, less angry but no less intense.

Kissing her softly, I allow Willa to shut her eyes, to hide from me. But I draw her back to me with my kiss, with the rock of my hips grinding my pelvis against her clit, with the deep slide of my cock in and out of her body. Relenting. Give and take. Willa surrenders.

"Royce," Willa moans, voice awed with innocence. She's no longer calling me that derogatory endearment of Royce-baby in a patronizing tone. "Royce," she repeats over and over again with every thrust I take.

Instinct taking over, Willa spreads her legs wide, heels resting at the top of my ass. Her hands grip my shoulders, fingernails leaving their mark of possession. Losing the fight to last, I rest my lips against her ear, whispering the dirtiest, most depraved things I plan on doing to her for the rest of our lives, whether she likes it or not, because Willa promised that once I was inside her, she'd be the last woman I ever entered.

I always keep my promises.

"Willa," I gasp, unable to hold back. The muscles in my back and ass clench, causing Willa's fingertips to slide in my sweat. The thief takes from me, counterthrusting from beneath– one roll of her hips and I erupt, flooding her body with my release and changing the course of our lives forever.

❧Present❧

"How were you able to look your brother in the eye after you had sexual intercourse with his wife, in his living room, on his sofa?" Dr. Cassidy's question holds no judgement, just morbid curiosity and fascination.

Next to me, Willa has turned inconsolable, unable to handle reliving such a pivotal moment in our lives. As I shared our past sins with our therapist, I experienced every single emotion as though I was reliving them in the present.

Walking across the office, I grab a tan, chubby teddy bear from next to Dr. Cassidy's desk, and return to hand it to Willa. She immediately accepts my offering, cuddling it with her knees tucked against her chest. I don't move to comfort her, knowing she's too raw to accept my touch.

"After Willa fell asleep in my arms that night, I immediately got up to get dressed. My brother came out to the living room as I was lacing my boots. He couldn't look me in the eye, not the other way around."

Dr. Cassidy is fast to hide the shock written across her face, but not fast enough. "Was it awkward when you spoke of it?"

"No, because we never did. Not once," I say with conviction. "It was just one of those things that could be left unsaid. It was what it was, and it was done and over with and nothing was going to change it. Donny feared if we talked about it, he'd have to explain what the hell was going on with Sean... which I still don't know or understand."

"So, it was just a one-time proposition?" Dr. Cassidy asks, already knowing the answer.

Leaning forward, bending nearly in half, I wrap my arms around the back of my head like in a bomb drill. "One-time proposition..." Manic laughter flows from my mouth, bubbling up pure insanity. "One-time?" My laugh dies out. "I've had a nine-year affair with my sister-in-law. Fucking her countless times, but making love to her more often than that. We've created two incredible children together... my only regret is that Corbin didn't come to me, asking me to marry Willa."

"From what I've gathered, I doubt you would have taken Corbin Gillette up on his offer." Dr. Cassidy proves she knows me better than I know myself.

Smirking with disgust, I shake my head left and right as I put my thoughts into working order. "Everybody looking at me sees this great, honorable man..." I spread my arms like, '*look at me*' and then let them drop. "And I ain't saying I'm not him. *I am.* I wholeheartedly believe in the words I preach and the way of life I lead. But I'm also flawed. I'm human, and my sons take after me."

"Brennan and Hayden?" Dr. Cassidy fishes.

"No, *all* of my sons. I'm more than what I project. The only reason I can give advice is because I've fucked up royally and crawled my way out of the shit I've created." My eyes dart to the side, checking on Willa and finding her avidly listening to me. "Every morning I wake up and slap on this uniform, and I never take it off. I call it *Dad*."

"So you're saying the person everyone sees isn't really you?" Dr. Cassidy asks, already knowing the answer.

"I'm him. He's me," I repeat. "But I'm more than the sum of my parts. I'm not only what I project. Kade is the closest to my personality, equally dark and light. Brennan, he's like me in the way he pretends to be someone he's not. Wynn... Wynn's the goodness in me. Kade can handle the shit I've been through and no one would be the wiser. Bren would suffer with it, but he'd survive. Wynn is too kind, and it would murder his soul. Hayden, I'm raising him so this shit doesn't touch him."

"Speaking of the shit you crawled out of," Dr. Cassidy uses my own words against me. "How did it feel to have to adopt your own children? Did you resent Willa while going through that process? Did you feel helpless and out of control?"

Breaking the rules, I lunge from the couch to pace around the room. I can feel Dr. Cassidy's eyes boring into my back as I move about. "We need to get one thing clear," I grit out in a voice brooking no room for argument. "Not once have I ever blamed Willa for anything. Just like I might have been frustrated and angry with Donny, I've never blamed him."

"Royce," Dr. Cassidy stills me with her authoritative voice. "I ask the same question in different ways, not because I feel you should resent Willa, but because I need you to learn how you really feel about a certain situation. No one is more capable of lying than we are to ourselves." She turns around slowly in her chair because I'm standing behind her seat. "I believe you. Your actions have never contradicted your words. Please, go on."

Anger deflated, I make a few passes around the room, eyeing the big, black teddy bear who looks like he could give really good hugs. Dr. Cassidy misses nothing. "After the beginning, Donny treated Willa as if she was *my* wife. With respect, companionship, and space. Sean never laid another violent hand on her after she became pregnant. Bren and I spent a lot of time with them, and Donny seemed happier than ever."

Willa's nodding along as I speak. I pause, thinking she might like to add something, but she remains silent and watchful.

"There was never... how do I put this into words?" I stalk around Dr. Cassidy's chair and retake my seat on the couch. I try to get her to understand, even though I know that's not the point of therapy. *I* need to understand– Willa needs to understand. "There was never a sense of betrayal. It was something we kept behind closed doors, no one but the three of us knowing what was happening."

"So no one suspected?" Dr. Cassidy sounds incredulous. "Not Bren? Not Sean? What about Corbin and Cora, or Warren? Anyone close to you would have recognized how you looked at each other."

Laughing darkly, "I'm a saint, remember?" A blush creeps over my cheeks– part shame and all embarrassment. "No one would have ever believed me capable of the things I've done. That's part of the reason Corbin hated me for so long, thinking I thought myself better than him. That I was this moral man without sin."

"And you believe nothing could be farther from the truth?" Dr. Cassidy coaxes.

"No, I don't. I believe I'm human, just like everyone else." Lifting my hips slightly, I yank the pillow out from behind my back and grip it to my chest like armor against the painful truth. "I believe I'm a good person with flaws. Now that I'm older, more experienced, I do have regrets. I think Annie chose me because of the same thing Sean saw in Donny– prey. Easily manipulated. I still loved her in spite of it, and feel she was my best friend."

"Do you regret marrying Annalise?" Dr. Cassidy's question throws me, and I really have to think about it.

"Yes," flows without hesitation. "Wynn thought I was being a nosy dad and treating Kade with disrespect when I tried to put a stop to their relationship. I did it for Wynn, but not against Kade. I wished someone would have stepped in and stopped me. Annie got me when I was twelve and she was nearly fifteen. She picked me and shaped me into the husband she wanted, and I didn't want that to happen to Wynn. I wanted Wynn to be Wynn when he connected with Kade. Kade and Wynn, not Kade's version of who Wynn should be."

Shifting in her chair, Dr. Cassidy sets her pen down on her notepad. "Did Kaden understand that?"

"Yes, I believe he does now, but not at first he didn't." Sighing, I turn contemplative, thinking and speaking of the things I've long buried. "I loved Annie– I did. But after she died, I didn't know who the fuck Royce Kennedy was supposed to be without her. I was stunted. The only thing I knew how to be was a husband and father, but not an individual. I've spent the last eleven years finding that man, and I have few regrets even with all of my fuck-ups."

I turn to Willa, not sure if what I'm about to say will do more harm than good. "I regret that Willa was so young when I met her, when we started our relationship. But I was wiser after being married, and I knew the effects of pressing your will upon another person. Until I shipped Willa to rehab, I'd never *forced* anything upon her. Not once. That lively, crass girl was one-hundred percent unique and original, and allowed to grow on her own."

"Do you regret having children with a young woman who was essentially a child herself?" Dr. Cassidy pulls no punches.

"No," I answer without hesitation. "I regret Sean and Donny. If I had met Willa, connected with her, it would have been a different journey with the same destination. No, Willa didn't get to go to college, get a job, find a husband, and start her own life. But whether Donny intervened or I did, that wasn't the path a woman of her upbringing would have ever been on. I believe Willa being with me is what saved her, and I know that sounds like I have a god-complex. I don't. She would've gotten knocked up by some worthless asshole, and lived a life of domestic violence. I know it. Willa knows it. Dr. Cassidy, you know it."

Baiting, Dr. Cassidy rips a reaction out of us. "So you were the lesser of two evils?"

"No!" Willa speaks for the first time this session. "No. It wasn't like that with Royce and me. I ain't talking… shit," she hisses. "Don't get me upset because my diction shifts," Willa reprimands, the '*you bitch*' going unvoiced. "I'm not going to go all moony-eyed and say when we met worlds collided and it was love at first sight. Girls where I come from who think that bullshit get hurt. We're not like you," she points at Dr. Cassidy. "There is no teenage crush stage– it's the get hitched stage. Annie was doing to Royce what she was taught. We're taught from a young age to target a man to take care of us. But being young means we usually pick the wrong target."

"I wish that hadn't been the case," I mutter underneath my breath, feeling surer of the Life Skills Center by the second.

"Young or not, I wasn't stupid. I have a good sense of people when I meet them. With Royce, it's like we're connected somehow and we can communicate without speaking. We just feel how the other person is feeling, and have respect enough to leave them be."

"When I met Willa, I thought she was a little brat and she intrigued the hell out of me," I say with amused affection lacing my voice. "It was this uncontrollable need to be inside her." I blush bright red to the roots of my hair. "That was not a pun. Honest. I meant inside her *mind*. She is the oddest creature I've ever known, and to understand her is a gift– that's what I meant."

"That's what I meant about others not noticing the dark secret you kept hidden while Willa was still married to Donny," Dr. Cassidy brings us back full circle. "They had to have known on some level."

"They did," I finally admit. "At least not those so close to us they were blinded by it. I was in the delivery room when the twins were born, Donny saying he would faint at the sight of blood. But the doctors and nurses *knew* I was the father. I held my daughter first, then my son... and learning that I couldn't be on their birth certificate killed me."

"Royce." Willa's hand latches onto mine when a single tear slips free.

"By law, if a child is born in a marriage, the husband is the legal father, even if he is not the biological father. Donny was placed on the birth certificate, even with Willa and me fighting it. Donny begged me not to take it to court because of whatever the fuck was going on with Sean. So after I got Willa help, I was able to adopt my own children... *adopt my own children*." My head falls into my hands, Willa's still twined with mine. "I had to ask my brother's permission to adopt *my* own children. The court knew the twins were mine, but it didn't matter. Live in sin, get treated like a criminal. I own that."

"So now the proper names are on the birth certificates," Dr. Cassidy tries to comfort me, and on the heels of that, she sucker-punches me. "Which is why in a few days there will be no more secrets."

"No more secrets." Willa and I promise in unison. "No more secrets and lies."

Emotionally, physically, and mentally drained, Willa and I stroll hand-in-hand up the front walk to our house. I can feel her need to talk more hovering in the air, but neither one of us are up for the challenge.

"We'll get it all ironed out before the group session," I comfort Willa, giving her hand a gentle squeeze. "Dr. Cassidy is saving the worst for last."

She tugs me to a stop just before I open the screen door. "I'm thankful you don't blame me–" she stumbles over her words. "But what about all the time I was… *sick*? You should blame me for that at least. I know I do."

Using her hand to control her, I drag Willa against my chest. Only a few inches shy of my short height, I grip her chin in my fingertips. Smirking, I whisper, "Shut up," against her parted lips, words fraught with affection no matter how rude they may sound. Fluttering a kiss, "Only I get to decide what I regret and who I blame… and I don't even blame myself. So shut up."

"Yes, sir," Willa teases me, when we both know she doesn't take orders from anyone. "I know you get sick of pizza, but I'm too drained to cook tonight."

"Deal," I agree in a heartbeat as I yank our front door open. Half a dozen voices flow in from the kitchen, and I know it's not going to be a quiet evening at home. Eyes sorry, I try to apologize to Willa without words.

Moving into the living room ahead of me, Willa pats the center of my chest with her palm, silently telling me it's okay. She understands. "In less than a week, it will only be the four of us…" she trails off, eager excitement, sadness, and trepidation warring in her voice.

"Probably five," I mutter when Kade's voice reaches my ears, and I try to dampen how happy I am to have the guy to myself, even if it's only for half the week. We'll finally be able to connect like grown men, no longer butting heads and playing tug-of-war.

Looking over her shoulder, Willa smirks at me, reading me like an open book.

"Pickings are slim with all the college kids sucking up the apartments. Here's a cheap flat," Kade rambles as we enter the kitchen. "But you said you wanted a two or three bedroom."

"Why so large?" I ask, looking around at all the kids my kitchen seemed to have vomited since I was in my house last.

Kade is curled around Wynn's laptop at the center island, with Bren hovering over him. Wynn is at the stove, banging around the pots and pans, creating some concoction that smells like cumin and chili peppers. Jack is on the floor with my little ones, constructing a Lego town. Lastly is Jessica, sitting at the breakfast nook with a Kindle Fire in her hands.

Bren flashes me a guilty look over his shoulder, but doesn't answer me. Willa heads in Wynn's direction before he messes up her special-order cookery.

"I'm picking out Bren's housing and his new Jeep. My first attempt at being his trustee." Kade tries to comfort me, but knowing I'm out of the loop hurts. "Instead of renting for the next four years, I'd suggest buying a foreclosure. The rent on those apartments are jacked up high to drain parents' pockets dry. But a college town has a hard time keeping homeowners. The mortgage, or just buying it outright, would be cheaper. Then after you graduate and move back to Rusty Knob," Kade says with hope filling his voice, "You can rent the place out to college kids to pay the mortgage on your permanent home."

"Do whatever you think is best." I sigh, feeling even more depressed. "But Bren has to have a hand in it, or he won't learn anything." That comment earns me a snarl from my first born. "You have a steady job lined up and college courses scheduled. I trust you," I appease my son.

Jack flashes me a grin when I kneel on the floor next to him. The usually happy kid is hiding his sadness well, but it's twisting his smile to look dark and gloomy. I pat the kid on the shoulder, realizing I'm going to miss having him around after all these years. The specter of Francis Parker lurking has cast a shadow of sadness over all of us, but Jack's absence will be felt even stronger.

Going off to college should be an exciting time, and these kids act like they're being executed. They're terrified, and they act like the rug has been yanked out from beneath their feet. I thought only us old folks were supposed to experience Empty Nest Syndrome. I seem to be handling this better than I thought, and they aren't handling it at all.

Except Wynn. He would have left yesterday if his dorm room was ready. The kid is vibrating with excitement, and I'm happy for him.

Sitting against the wall, I ask, "How ya doing today, Jackson?"

"Good," he lies. "Glad I'm in a dorm room and don't have to worry about all this shit," he tells the truth. "Jesse is making us up a list of stuff Wynn and I will need for our room, and it's so much easier than what Bren needs to set up a house."

"Entering adulthood is rather terrifying... and expensive." I sigh. "Which is why the dorm room is the best avenue. It gives you a transition period. No 'out of the frying pan and into the fire' issues."

"True that," Jackson grunts, eyes flicking toward Bren with sadness, and then to Jessica with resentment. Realizing I saw, Jack shakes his head no to stop me from questioning him.

Hayden is absorbed in his building, not noticing I've arrived home yet. My heart beats out of whack a few times, both in pain and in happiness. I've come so close to losing my youngest time and time again, that I will never take a second with them for granted.

Organizing all the parts by color and size, Hayley looks up and smiles like I raise and set the Sun. "Hi, baby girl," I drawl, and receive a quick peck on the lips for it.

"Welcome home, Daddy," my daughter sings in a voice that's already more mature than it was a few months ago. She rises to her feet with grace, and then is skipping to her mother's side, latching onto Willa's waist and begging to try whatever's in the pot on the stove.

Leaning against the wall, I take over Hayley's job of organizing the bricks for Hayden and Jack. Tiny, deft fingertips keep snagging the pieces I set out. Always focused on the task at hand, coming into contact with my big palm, Hayden stills, confused, and then he realizes I've joined him.

"Dad!" Hayden grins, clutching at his chest like I would, like I scared the piss out of him.

My son looks like me but not as much as Bren does, so most people would never question whether Hayden was or wasn't my offspring. That difference is what made me love the Gillettes so much. Seeing Willa, Warren, and Wynn reflected on my son's face— seeing Corbin gazing at me from Hayden's eyes —it's a humbling experience.

"Did you have fun with Aunt Penny today?" I prompt, enjoying nothing more than chatting with my kids. "Have you held Copper yet?"

Hayden is terrified of his baby cousin for some reason, when Hayley has taken to the boy with a natural maternal instinct. "I helped Uncle Warren a bit, but then Aunt Penny snagged us and made us go back to her house, said we were getting in the way at the center. It was okay, I guess."

"Liar," Hayley says in her momma voice. She plops down next to me, forcing Jack out of our orbit. The young man chuckles as he gets to his feet, joining Jessica at the breakfast nook. "Hayden likes all of Aunt Penny's little sisters," Hayley announces with a wicked gleam in her eye.

Poor Hayden.

"Sis!" Hayden whines, batting her hands away from the Legos. "Do not!"

"Do too!"

"Do not!"

"Do too," is my cue to get up.

While the twins bicker, Jackson is lighting into Jessica. "Curtains? Really, Jesse? Curtains?" He points at her Kindle Fire with fury lacing his voice. "I'm gay, but that doesn't mean I've grown a vagina. Wynn and I don't need curtains."

"Let me see that," Wynn comes to the rescue, taking the tablet from Jessica's hands. "We're not allowed to have a microwave or hotplate, but we can use the ones they have in the student lounge. So yes to the popcorn. We'll need a mini-fridge for drinks, though." He passes the tablet to Jack instead of its owner. "No curtains. No bullshit we don't need."

"We do need extra pillows," Jack mutters as he changes the list. "And an air purifier."

The tiny blonde's ponytail is vibrating from the way she holds in the outburst readying itself to explode. I've heard Jesse cheer at all of the basketball games, and that girl has a set of lungs on her, so I have no idea why she's not lighting into Jack and Wynn.

"Fine," Jesse hisses from between clenched teeth as she retrieves her tablet. "I'll do the household list instead of your shitty dorm room bullshit. If you forget anything important, you get to live without it."

Wynn looks baffled, but Jackson is a breath away from launching himself over the table and choking the piss out of his childhood friend. I have no idea what's going on between Jack and Jesse, but Wynn's just as lost as I am.

Diffusing the situation, "You'll want blackout curtains, fuckfaces," Kade mutters as his fingers click away on Wynn's laptop. "Jesse ain't a prissy girl anyway, so you know damn well it wasn't for decoration. Rise and shine isn't always when the Sun decides. By the end of your afternoon classes, you'll hit your dorm room and drop dead on your beds. So stop pissing the girl off, or she might never help you again."

"*Thanks*," Bren mouths to Kade, confusing me more. Even Willa and Hayley are looking back and forth, trying to ferret out what's going down in our kitchen.

"I narrowed it down to three houses." Kade slides off his stool. "Bren can decide later. Git yer ass over here, Wynn." Still confused, Wynn shuffles over without complaint to sit on the stool Kade just vacated. "I need you to bring up that spreadsheet you keep with all the stuff in the storage units, and crosscheck it with the items on Jesse's lists. I trust you to not be wasteful."

"Aye! Aye!" Wynn says with a grin, but Kade doesn't smile back at him, which confuses both Wynn and me even more.

I slide up beside Willa at the stove, and whisper into her ear. "Maybe it wasn't such a good idea for those four to be at the same school for the next four years." I peek into the pot, surprised to see that Wynn had made us a batch of chili Willa's doctoring up with extra spices. "Smells pretty good."

"I'm taking three classes a week for my masters of education in school counseling, on Mondays and Thursdays," Kade is still in '*the man in charge*' mode, and it makes me grin with pride. "The house you pick better have a room for my ass to sleep twice a week so I don't have to drive back to Rusty Knob, and I'm too old to bunk in the twinky dinks' dorm room."

"I know." There's an obvious eye roll hidden in Bren's voice. "We've been over this all damn day. I just want to rest."

"You have five days to get this settled, sweetheart," Kade taunts his brother. "I suggest you sleep later."

"What about Perty?" Hayden asks, causing Willa to toss her hands up and point the wooden spoon at Kaden.

"Oh! No, you don't!" Willa pokes Kade in the chest. "Nope. You are not dropping that dog off here for me to clean up his shit piles off the floor."

"Perty's been going to obedience training." Kaden blushes, even the tips of his ears. "He hasn't had an accident all week."

"Accident?" Willa snorts, and then says firmly, "No."

"Yes," Kade says with a grin, realizing how they are bickering like the twins had earlier. "Your kids love my dog. They've always wanted a puppy."

Hayley's high-pitched squeal of excitement has us all flinching. "Yay! Perty can sleep in my room."

"Jesus Christ," Willa mutters, wishing she'd never met Kaden.

"Excuse me," Jesse tries to cut through the chaos to make it to the guest bathroom. I step to the side, but not before I notice how green around the gills she looks. "I don't do well with so much..." her hands gesture vaguely around the room. "I like quiet." Then she's locking herself in my bathroom.

"Where's Jesse staying?" I ask out of curiosity. "A dorm room?"

Slipping by me to go check on his friend, "With me," Bren shocks me senseless.

"Ah, three bedrooms? I get it," I mutter to myself, but the way Jackson looks ill yet furious has me rethinking my words. "I don't want to know, I take it."

Interpreting everyone's facial expressions, only Jack and Kade know what the hell is going on, with the rest of us in the dark.

Kade pushes me out of the room with a heavy palm on my chest. "No, you don't want to know," he whispers as he tugs me into the den. "I need to talk to you in private." Then I find myself behind the locked door to my office.

"What's going on?" My ass automatically finds my desk chair, with Kade sitting in the seat in front of my desk. "Is it about Brennan? He's not with Jessica, is he? How would that even work? He might be bi, but she's a lesbian."

"Forget their shit." Kade makes a hand motion like he's washing it away. "Just a bit before we headed home this evening, Warren was teaching me how to change the oil in my Durango out by the service bay to the shop."

"Yeah?" I mutter, suffering whiplash from having no segue from one topic to the next.

"Hayden was with us and Hayley had just left with Penny and Copper– Jeb came back for the kid about a half hour later because Penny's sisters were driving her nuts and only Hayden quiets them down." Kade laughs at the memory, but he looks sick to his stomach.

"Warren said if he could teach me anything, then he'd have no issue helping his father-in-law during the training sessions."

I don't say anything, but I'd agree with Warren. Kade is smart, but it takes a lot of patience to drill the knowledge into his brain.

A lot of patience.

"Hayden will be wanting to change the oil in your car, I suspect. He's a quick study, but I still have no clue." Kade shrugs self-deprecatingly, knowing I don't care because I'll love him no matter what. "We had a visitor," he finally gets to the point.

"Who?" is a breath on the wind.

"Warren acted like it was nothing, so I suspect he never cut off communication–"

"Corbin." Sighing, I look down at my hands folded on my desktop. "I see. Did he want to see Warren? Or was he checking up on Wynn again?"

"He wanted to see Hayden," Kade draws me up short.

"What?" I gasp. "Why?"

"I don't know," Kade's voice drops into whine. "The kid is his grandson."

"What'd you do?" I don't mean for my voice to sound like an accusation, but it does anyway.

"Royce–"

"I see," I say again, feeling helpless. Just hearing Corbin's name reminds me of a time I want to pretend never happened, much to Dr. Cassidy's regret. She says Corbin's name constantly to desensitize me.

"It was me and Warren. He's Hayden's uncle, and I'm just a foster-whatever, or the guy his uncle is dating. We're family, but not enough for me to be in charge."

"I understand," I whisper, hating how helpless I feel right now. "I trust you."

"Good." Kade chuckles, causing my eyes to snap up to connect with his. "What a ringing endorsement," he teases me. "Corbin looked uncomfortable and out of place, but completely sober."

"I saw him a few months ago at graduation," I finally admit. "He was sober then, too. Looked healthy." I try to hide my resentment.

"Warren and I just kind of looked at each other, both of us wanting the other to make the decision. Which is not how War operates. Ya know?"

"I know." This time I laugh, and it's genuine. "If it was anyone but you, Warren would have done whatever he wanted."

"True," Kade allows. "So we let the kid pick."

"What?" I gasp in surprise.

"Hayden's a big kid now, so we let him pick whether he wanted to see his grandfather or not. But we wouldn't let them be alone."

"Smart." I mull that over, nodding my head up and down. "Very smart. What'd my son decide?"

"Hayden is too much like Wynn–"

"I know, and I'm not sure if that's a good or bad thing." I lean back in my chair, sighing heavily. I fold my hands on my chest. "So what did Corbin do when Hayden decided to visit with him?"

"Cried."

"What?"

"Yeah..." Kade's voice is thick with emotion. "Corbin cupped the little guy's cheek, and kept saying how much he looked like Donny, and how he could see himself in the kid's eyes, which only seemed to make him sob more."

"I... You? What- huh?" I grunt, completely at a loss. "Corbin knows Hayden is my son."

"Everyone there knew," Kade agrees with me, but then kicks me in the teeth. "Hell, Warren and I think the kid even knows. So needless to say, it was an odd exchange. Corbin chatted with Hayden, asking about Hayley and Willa. He asked me about Wynn, and kept chattering with War about Penny and Copper like he saw them yesterday. I didn't recognize that man."

"Corbin's not *evil*," I twist out, wishing it wasn't the case. "I just don't like him. I spent my entire childhood dealing with Corbin taking my brother from me. The only time I liked the asshole was when Sean came to Rusty Knob and Corbin kept trying to run him out of town... then he–" I cut myself off. "I don't like him. He's violent when he's drunk, but that doesn't mean he's not human."

"Warren and I have always tried to figure out why you left your kids with him for three years."

"Good question," I mutter, not knowing myself. "You'll have to ask Willa. She said it was life or death and promised Corbin would keep my babies safe... and he kinda did. But he lost me my brother, and that I can never forgive."

With curiosity lacing his voice, Kade tries to get me to release secrets that aren't mine. "How?"

"I'm sorry, Kaden." I reach across the desk. "I'd tell you if I could. Corbin lost me my brother and I'll never forgive him for that, and that's all I can say."

"Then I guess you won't want his message, then?"

"Give it to me," I order, nearly begging.

"Corbin asked me if it was okay to visit the Life Skills Center, saying Donny would want that," Kaden relays, and I hiss sharply in pain. "Then he said to meet him in the usual place at the usual time, and he wanted to clear the air once and for all." Kade parts his hands in his lap, "That's it. What's it mean?"

"I know what it means," is all I can reply. "Thank you. Thank you for allowing me to keep this private, for not pushing for answers I can't give, and for taking care of Bren and whatever mistake he's making. I'm proud of you, son."

FREEDOM

It will be five years tomorrow since I've set foot on Kennedy land. In all of my years, I never missed more than a day or two without connecting to my roots. After Annie died, Bren and I spent nearly a month up here, grieving with Donny's support.

I've allowed the past to change me, to remove my lifeblood from my veins. I haven't felt right in the head, and I thought it was because of what had happened to me. Now, as I drive down the dusty backroads to Kennedy Holler, I realize my soul was weeping because I was neglecting who I am.

Kennedy Holler always represented home, solace- safety. Even after Daddy sold the land, he made sure we had a life lease on the deed so we could stay connected to our roots. Annie never questioned, somehow understanding, when Daddy, Donny, Bren, and I would squeeze in my pickup truck and drive home.

No matter the season, we'd open all the windows, crank the stereo, and drive like a bat out of hell on the rutty dirt roads. It was freedom, and it's been more than five years since I've experienced the sheer joy, and I've lost my soul in the process.

After Daddy died, we bought the land back, but it was still missing that essential spark only Granddaddy's house and Daddy brought to it. After Willa, I forgot our ritual because driving to Kennedy Holler meant something else entirely. With that, not only did I neglect myself, I neglected my daddy's memory.

Tomorrow marks twelve years since Daddy and Annie passed, and five years since our lives were rocked to the core. With Dr. Cassidy's help, knowing tomorrow morning, on the anniversary, I have to spill my soul, I decided it was now or never.

Windows down, humid summer air whipping me in the face, X Ambassadors' Jungle reverberating from the speakers, I drive with wild abandon. Trees zip by close to the shoulders of the road. Rocks spit out from beneath my tires around every bend and curve. Up and down I fly through the hills.

"Howdy, ya drunk bastard!" I shout at the top of my lungs as I pass the turn to Gillette Holler, surprised to see Corbin mending the fence. I flip him off, and he shocks me once again by smiling and laughing while shaking his head back and forth, looking decades younger like when we were teenagers.

I've been to Gillette Holler every few months or so for the past several years, but I never passed the turn off to go up home, some commanding force not allowing me to drive farther on.

Today, I succeed.

Cresting one last hill, my foot turns heavy on the gas pedal, and down I go as fast as the truck will allow. Hitting the bottom at seventy miles an hour, my stomach hits me in the throat from the G-force as the truck curves back up the next incline.

With a loud bellow of a whoop, I ride the road like a child does a roller coaster. Heart beating in my throat, it's not the excitement revving my system.

At the quarter mark up the hill, I crank the wheel hard, tires rumbling over a heavy rut from the creek water runoff. Nuts pounding into the seat, I don't slow until I pop out the tunnel of trees on either side of the drive.

Two decades ago, the view would have been a well-maintained tiny two-story shack, flowering shrubs and trees, and a woodshed that always needed a fresh coat of paint, even if it was just painted the season before. There was always smoke billowing from the chimney and Granddaddy sitting on the porch.

A decade ago, our roots were gone, and in their place was a cookie-cutter modular home, which sat nestled in a circular drive, with a pole barn on the side. There was no smoke because there was no chimney. There was no Granddaddy on the porch because there was no porch and Granddaddy and Daddy passed long ago.

Today... today sits an empty expanse of land as far as the eye can see, which isn't far because it's a flat nestled deep in the mountains, surrounded with lush green, wildlife, and history.

Emotions suffocating me, seeing is believing, reality hits me. Hard.

One of the storage units I own is filled with everything from Donny's house. Tucked safe and sound away from harm. They're our memories from generations ago until five years ago. Handmade furniture, my grandmother's quilts, our picture albums. I couldn't handle looking at them, sorting through them, knowing I'd tarnished our lineage.

My brother gave me everything he owned, knowing his sentence would be for most of his adult life. I couldn't bear it, knowing I was the reason he was in prison, no matter how many times I tried with all my might to get my brain to blame Corbin instead.

After the trial, the police even gave back my baseball bat and Granddaddy's truncheon, like I'd want a constant reminder of the suffering they caused. To this day, I've never been able to hold a bat, let alone watch America's favorite pastime.

Hands gripping my steering wheel, X Ambassadors singing about holding onto me because I'm a little unsteady, a wasp buzzing my face, I stare into oblivion with tears coursing down my cheeks.

With the house empty, Corbin took care of the rest at Donny's bidding.

The house where nightmares were made. The house, which stood on this piece of land for all of seven years, burned in the night, leaving nothing but ash to fertilize the ground.

With a fierce urge, the need to resurrect the past overpowers me. I remember every single knot in the wood of Granddaddy's house. I could have an architect recreate it on this very land.

But you can't recapture the past. You can't find comfort in what no longer exists. To hang onto the past is to ignore your present and stop your future.

The day Annie died, Daddy was taking her to the baby doctor in a nearby city. If tragedy hadn't struck, Annie and I would be living in town, Brennan would be going off to college the day after next if he'd done well in school, or he'd be in a dead-end job just like his father– me.

Our little girl would be eleven years old, with brown flowing hair and huge brown eyes and not much of a future unless she studied hard or married a man who studied harder. She'd be running around the yard while Annie was inside taking care of the chores. Carefree, trailing a girly giggle I'll never hear.

Our trailer had a porch, so depending on ailments, Daddy would have been sitting outside, watching the townsfolk walk by after working too hard at his dead-end job to put food in our bellies.

Donny would be married for the fourth or fifth time to some bar hog who hoped he'd take care of her. She'd sleep all day and carouse all night, and he'd make excuses for her treating him like shit, just like he did with wives one and two. They'd live in the side yard in Donny's trailer, just as it had been before Daddy and Annie passed.

Donny would sit on his porch with Daddy on ours, and they'd have a shouting match of a conversation across the lawn where my nameless daughter played.

We'd be poor. We'd struggle just to put food in our bellies and to take the chill from our bones, but we would've been happy because of the love we felt for one another.

That vision of the present burst in a ball of flames in the center of the interstate, killing my daddy, my wife, and my unborn daughter. But if it hadn't, so many things would be different. I wouldn't trade Hayden and Hayley for a child I never met. Nor would I trade Kaden, Warren, Penny, Copper, Willa, and Wynn, and all of Rusty Knob's futures to resurrect the dead.

Our lives are what they are because they are meant to be that way. We can't live in the past, and it's time for me to let it go. To release the truth so I can finally live in the here and now instead of being a ghost in the present.

With a deep breath, I release, "I'm ready," feeling fortified by Kennedy land.

❧Five Years Ago❧

"Are you doing good, bub?" I reach over to pat my son's leg as we drive up to Donny's place. "I know today is a difficult day for all of us."

"Dad, I'm fine." Brennan's voice is dry, almost bored sounding. "You've asked me that for the past few days straight. I-I… I've spent more time without Mom than I remember being with her. I miss her. But–"

"But this is our life now, right?" I coax. "We should be comfortable in the present, but don't ever lose what memories you do have. It's why on the anniversary, no matter what, we visit the cemetery, and then spend time together as a family."

"I know," Bren breathes out, no doubt wishing he was in town with his buddies where he could forget what today meant. "What I meant was… I don't know if I miss Mom, or if I miss not having a mom. If that makes any sense. So this just feels uncomfortable for me, because everyone's upset and I'm numb."

"You're almost fourteen, so I've got to start treating you like a young man now."

Bren bays a laugh, and it's jarring after a day of quiet reflection. "You mean how you treat Kade like a man?" Snorts bubble up, one right after the other. "He's nineteen, and you still make him call you from school every night before he goes to bed."

Suddenly furious, "Brennan Honor Kennedy, don't bait me into an argument just so you can hide outside with your cellphone instead of spending the day with family. We're not mourning their deaths anymore." I remind my son. "We're celebrating their lives by sharing memories. I know it hurts, but it's a good hurt."

"Good hurt?" Bren scoffs, and I have to remind myself for the billionth time that the teenage years only last until he goes to college. But then I remember how Kade is still a pain in the ass and decide that they will finally behave around age thirty. Which is a terrifying revelation since I'm only thirty-four myself.

It's a long road before we escape the asshole years, and I've got two more coming up the ranks behind him.

"Just suffer through today for me." I squeeze Bren's knee, and then put my hand back on the stick shift. "For me. *Please*. Your mother was my wife, remember that. I lost *my* life that day. A wife. A daughter. My father. You may not have had them in your life for long, but they were my life for twenty-six years, and now they're gone. So treat your uncle and me with respect and don't start fights to get out of suffering through this with us. You're a Kennedy."

"Guilt-trip level ten," Bren grumbles, and then releases a chuckle. "Mom would be proud of you."

I turn to share a grin with my son. "See? That's what I'm talking about. That's the kind of thing worth remembering. Then someday when you have kids, you'll see parts of your mother in them, whether it be how they smile, or the way they say a certain word. Then you will be thankful you were forced to remember, so that you could look your child in the eyes and see your mother shining back."

Face whipping to look out the passenger window, "I'm not feeling so numb anymore." Bren sniffles. "Thanks, Dad."

Bren doesn't sound too thankful to my ears, which makes my grin wider. "Anytime, kid," I mutter as we pull into Donny's driveway. "Anytime."

Before the tires roll to a complete stop, Brennan is slipping out the passenger door, trying to get away from me in a confined space. "Corbin's here," he points out. "This will be interesting."

"Fuck," I snarl as I get out of my truck.

Bren walks backward chattering at me, taunting like we're on the basketball court. "I'm waiting for you and Corbin to arm-wrestle over Uncle Donny, with Willa as the ref, and me and the twins as the spectators."

"Just you wait," I warn Bren. "Hayden will be jealous of your buddies, feeling left out, and then you'll understand."

"Nah," Bren shakes his head no. "We're too far apart in age. Plus, Hayden's uncle is one of my buddies. You are a freakin' weirdo, is what you are." Still walking backward, I don't warn Bren he's nearing the front steps because he's being a little asshole. "Let your brother have his own friends. You should get your–"

Clunk.

My lips twist. I try my damnedest not to laugh as Bren's arms pinwheel as he flounders to stay on his feet. "Karma," flows from my mouth when my boy lands on his ass on the bottom stair tread.

Laughing with me as I laugh at him, I offer Brennan a hand up. "You forgot something, son... You seemed to have forgotten how jealous you get when Kade or Wynn has friends who want nothing to do with you." I raise a knowing eyebrow and my boy looks away guiltily. "If you behave, I will."

"Pfft!" Bren dusts his behind off. "It took forever to get Wynn to like me." Stilling, my son implores me with huge brown eyes. "I won't make fun of you, and I'll even enlist Warren's help, but you've got to continue Wynn and Kade keep-away. 'Kay?"

"Sure, kid." I ruffle up his hair. "You're not at all jealous."

"If they become friends, Wynn won't have nothing to do with me anymore and Kade won't give you any attention, either. It's hard work keeping a brother."

"Fair enough," I allow, but that's not the real reason I'm playing keep-away with my foster son and Willa's baby brother. No sense in repeating history.

If Willa's my succubus, then Wynn would be Kade's incubus. Best not go down that particular road.

"Showtime," I mutter out the corner of my mouth to Bren as I open the front door. "Hello. Hello. Anybody home?"

We step in to find Corbin hanging out in the kitchen with my kids in his arms. I hate Corbin so much sometimes because he makes it hard to hate his guts. Like now, when he's obviously being a good grandfather, and it leaves me feeling confused.

I've never understood how such an ornery bastard can look so pretty when he's relaxed and happy. Obviously Willa gets her looks from her father, and that freaks me out some, too.

"Where's my brother? Willa?" I ask, not moving past the entrance, but Bren has no such qualms.

"Hey, Mr. Gillette." My son walks right up to the bastard with a smile on his face, and then lifts a wailing Hayley from his arms. My son has bigger balls than I do because he's not terrified of Corbin Gillette.

"Bren! BREN! BRENNAN!" Hayley is shouting her little head off, wiggling around to get into her brother's arms, and it makes me laugh. The twins just turned three, and their favorite pastime is screaming at us and running around like chickens with their heads cut off.

"Hayley?" Bren coos to soothe her. "I'm right here, girl." Settling her in his arms, he grunts, "You sure are a little chunk, aren't you?"

"Dad-dy! Dad-dy! Daddy!" Has my feet moving forward without thought. Raising an eyebrow in challenge, Corbin passes my little guy to me.

"I never told them to call me that." I blush bright red, loving the sound but fearing what will happen if Hayden says it around mixed company. The instant he settles in my arms, he quiets and my heart bursts with love. "I've missed you," I murmur against the top of his head, nuzzling his hair.

"You keeping my son in line?" Corbin chats softly with Bren while I get lost in my tiny children. Snuggling Hayden, his hands stretch out for his twin sister. Corbin helps to settle both kids in my arms so they can interlock like puzzle pieces. They simmer down the instant they're both cuddled in my arms– safe and sound where they belong.

"Sure am, Mr. Gillette," Bren chatters back. They have an odd rapport, Corbin and Brennan. It's the same as how easily Corbin and Donny get along, and it makes me feel left out all over again.

I can admit I'm jealous, seeing as how since Annie died the only friend I have is my brother, and he splits his time between Corbin and Sean. I hate Sean because he's a terrorist. But my issues with Corbin are of the green-eyed variety. Plus, he's a rotten bastard.

"Have you been enjoying your summer?" I roll my eyes at the man who treats his youngest like shit while talking my boy up. If my hands weren't full of cuddly toddlers, I'd punch the asshole.

"Brennan's summer is spent a lot different than Wynn's," spills out my mouth without a filter. "He doesn't have to work at the Circle K under the table to pay my tab, and he doesn't have to work for a relative to get his ass out of my house for the weekend."

"Huh?" Corbin grunts. "Here I thought my boy was pretending to work for you so it wouldn't look so fucking odd that your *brother's* children were spending every weekend with you. Between all that shit and Warren visiting when the cutter still lived in your house, it's like you're running a fucking summer camp."

"The cutter?" Bren snorts, loving Corbin's twisted sense of humor– the asshole knows exactly who Kaden is, seeing as how he's the originator of the Kade and Wynn keep-away. "I'ma start calling Kade that next time I see him."

"Explain to me why you know what Sean has over my brother and I don't?" Now I'm just being an asshole, but it rankles me that Corbin doesn't talk like a hillbilly when he's sober. When he's drunk, I can't even decipher what the hell he's saying.

Asshole.

"I just– Jesus Christ, sometimes I just want to punch you, you judgmental fuck," Corbin hisses into my face. "You're not ten years old anymore and annoying the piss out of Donny and me while we tried to get away from ya. We've been trying to include you, but you have a long memory and won't let the shit go."

"You used to beat me up," I grumble, squeezing my kids tighter.

"I'ma start it up again if you don't knock your shit off. Donny's having a hard time, and you acting like he can't have no friends besides you ain't helping none. I'm not trying to steal your brother from you– trust me on that."

"Trust you?" I gear up to say a few choice words, but that's when Willa and Donny walk into the kitchen from the hallway. All words dry up when I see how upset my brother is.

Shoulders hunched, eyes rimmed in red, tear-stained cheeks, I remember why I'm here today. "Donny," I go to support my brother, but my arms are filled with napping toddlers.

"I'm okay." He brushes me off, seeking Bren instead. "Hey, kid. How you holding up?"

"I'll be great when tomorrow comes so I don't have to answer that question again for another year."

Corbin barks a laugh at my surly teenager, but it dries up quickly. "I better git outta yer hair. See ya, daughter." He leans down to kiss Willa on the cheek, who is surprisingly sedate for once, which means Donny is bad off.

"Bye, Daddy," Willa barely breathes. "Tell Momma I said hi."

I pretend not to watch with one eye as Corbin comforts my brother, giving him a hearty hug and a deep squeeze before pulling away. He whispers something in Donny's ear that has my brother's tears renewing.

I hate that I can't hate Corbin Gillette, no matter what foulness he commits.

Willa smiles at me through her tears, both of us pretending we're not trying our hardest to listen in on Donny and Corbin's whispered conversation. It takes her a few seconds to get the courage, but she eventually finds her way to me, pecking me on the lips.

Ordinarily when we greet each other, Donny keeps Bren and the twins occupied, and we do everything in private. Which is another reason I suspect Willa has had to be Donny's shoulder to cry on all afternoon, and Donny can be downright overemotional at times.

"You doing okay?" I whisper to Willa, and she just offers me a wane smile in return.

"I'm off," Corbin announces, striding through the house to the front door.

Sobbing, Donny walks into the living room and falls into his recliner.

Willa, Brennan, and I share a look. *"What do we do?"*

"So much for walking down memory lane," Bren mutters sarcastically, reaching for whichever twin he can tug free of my arms. "I'll go in their room with them and–"

"Hide?" Willa smirks, but it's pale compared to her usual spunk. "I don't blame ya."

Hayden is easy to dislodge and wake up. He leans against his big brother's thigh, scrubbing at his sleepy eyes with pudgy fists. Then Bren reaches for Hayley, and all hell breaks loose.

"Daddy! No!" Hayley's high-pitched shriek has us all wincing. "I want my daddy! No!" She struggles with me as I try to set her on her feet. "Daddy, no."

"Hayley, honey…" I realize I'm trying to reason with a toddler. "Uncle Donny needs Daddy right now. Your brother will read you a story."

"Daddy!" Hayley's still shouting, causing such a distraction we don't hear the front door opening.

"Bren!" Donny is on his feet, charging into the kitchen before I even know what's happening. Hayley is still screaming bloody murder, not wanting to be out of my arms. "Get the twins in their room and lock the door. Don't open it for nothing. If someone tries to get in, go out the window and get your asses out of here."

Heart pounding out of my chest, the tension in the air is suffocating. I look up to assess the situation, and my eyes connect with an enraged Sean. Hayley is out of my arms and thrust in Brennan's in an instant, with him tearing down the hallway before I can even blink.

I reach for my cellphone and lob it, and it's hitting my son in the back as I'm shouting, "Call 9-1-1." I pray the phone didn't break when it landed on the carpeting. Bren reaches down to pick it up just as Donny bellows in the silence, "Call Corbin back here. Now!"

Sean is standing taller than ever, with his left fist tightening and loosening in time with his molars grinding together. I have no idea what's going on, but I know I'm about to find out. Judging by Willa and Donny's petrified reactions, I might not survive to learn the truth.

I was so distracted by Sean's left fist, I didn't pay attention to his right. The click of a hammer being pulled back is deafening. We all freeze, turning immobile with terror. "I warned you," Sean says low and slow to Donny, but his eyes are trained on me, as is the revolver in his hand. "I warned you, didn't I?"

"Sean," Donny's voice is pleading, but I can't tear my eyes away from the 357 Magnum to look at him. Turning cross-eyed, I stare down the barrel of the gun. One slip of a fingertip and my brains will be splattered all over the kitchen cabinets. "This is all my fault."

"I know it is," Sean's voice rolls over me. "Which is why your brother will pay the price. I warned you, but you didn't listen."

"I've done everything you asked of me." Donny doesn't move but his voice warbles. "It doesn't matter that the twins aren't my kids; the law says they are."

"It matters. Now it's three to zero in Royce's favor." Sean's fingertip twitches and I piss my pants. "And we both know Royce will never do what I say."

Heart beating in my throat, blood surging in my veins, hot humiliation streams down my thigh, proving I still breathe. No amount of willpower could stop it. An involuntary reaction to facing Death. The trigger didn't pull, but my body doesn't realize that. Urine soaking into my jeans, the steam of it wafting up to rankle my nose, I'm rendered powerless to protect my family.

"It was a godsend when I thought you had twins, you fucking moron, and I don't mean so for me." Sean is still running off at the mouth, causing him to be careless– fingertip twitching as he turns more and more enraged with every word he speaks.

The barrel of the gun is four feet from my forehead, not far enough to miss but close enough to blow my brains out the back of my skull. There is nothing I can do but turn into a statue and pray to God as piss streams down my leg.

"Your two kids meant I didn't have to murder an innocent kid. Now that there's three of them, Royce is the liability. So I just went from minding my own business to being a serial murderer because you couldn't stick your dick in your own wife."

My hand is nudged. Instead of flinching in reaction, I freeze in shock. My fingertips are pried apart, and then smooth wood is settled into my palm. I recognize the shape immediately– my granddaddy's truncheon, which I gave to Willa for protection against Sean.

The weapon is six inches long, made of hardwood with a leather wrist strap. Instead of skinny and shaped like a baton, my granddaddy carved it to be bulbous on the end. A blunt-force weapon meant to stun and incapacitate, leaving the person unconscious so you can get away to safety.

As sweet as it feels in my palm, it's doing me no good. If I breathe too deeply I'm dead. There is no way I can swing the truncheon before the trigger pulls.

"You're such a spineless coward." Sean sneers at Donny, too incensed to notice Willa arming herself with my baseball bat. I close my eyes, always knowing that woman would be the death of me.

"Do you think I want to be here? Do you?" Sean has one eye trained on Willa now, with the other on Donny. He doesn't have to look at me because his gun is doing a mighty fine job of keeping me in his line of sight. "I've had to stay in this bum-fuck town for the past five years, doing a job I can't stand, having to deal with your sniveling ass nonstop. I'd shoot you all if it didn't mean I'd be executed the second I did so."

My mind spins, trying to find a reason why Sean is doing any of this and drawing a complete blank thanks to the gun trained on my forehead. I grip the truncheon tighter, using it to anchor me.

"This is what we're going to do, boys and hillbilly skank," Sean says sweetly in a phony voice. "We're going to put our weapons down, or I'm going to shoot Royce in the forehead. Keep in mind, I never miss."

Fingers relaxing, a solid thud reverberates near my foot, and it's echoed a split-second later with the louder sound of a baseball bat hitting the floor.

The sickening sound of defeat.

Whether Sean shoots me because we didn't drop our weapons, or because of some other infraction he comes up with, he's going to shoot me before the night ends, and I'm terrified of what comes before the end.

Just as long as my children survive, I don't care what happens to me, and that includes Willa and Donny.

Only the children matter.

This is the first time in my life I regret being on Kennedy land. Even if Brennan gets through to 9-1-1, it will take them time to dispatch a car, and then at least fifteen minutes to get from Rusty Knob proper.

There is a reason crime happens in the hollers instead of in town, and that is the exact reason my late father-in-law demanded Annie and any of our children were to live in town.

We're dead, and I won't even get the chance to hear the answer as to why.

"Good," Sean says patronizingly. "So glad two of you have the comprehension skills of a toddler. At this point I can't figure out how Donny survives everyday life."

"What do you want from me?" I growl, teeth not even moving as I speak in fear any movement on my part will give Sean a twitchy trigger finger.

"We'll all survive another day, going on our merry way until I find a way to fix this horrendous fuckup of Donny's. So we're going to learn our lessons tonight. Eh? I think we should teach your baby brother what it's like to be in your shoes."

"No!" Donny gasps, lunging forward.

It only takes a split-second for my life to flash through my eyes. Donny jumps forward to stop Sean, who has the presence of mind to jerk his finger off the trigger. If he hadn't, I would have been shot by accident– my brother's fault.

With a sharp crack of a backhand, "Ah… such a fucking idiot," Sean is snarling at Donny. My brother's face whips to the side, so far backward that his cheek is meeting his shoulder. "I don't plan on killing anyone tonight if I don't have to, so don't make me shoot your brother by accident."

"Don't," Donny pleads, getting onto his knees before Sean. Helpless, my brother leans his chest against the floor at Sean's feet, abasing himself. I choke on vomit, recognizing what this position means for my brother. "I'll do anything you ask, just let everyone else go."

"I've already broken this toy." Sean releases a sadistic laugh while kicking my brother directly in the face with a steel-toed boot. Blood arcs before the popping sound of broken cartilage reaches my ears.

Powerless to react, all I can do is stand frozen and watch my brother groan in misery, rolling around on the floor between me and the man who is holding me at gunpoint, my piss seeping into my brother's jeans. Blood pours out of Donny's broken nose, trailing down his neck to be absorbed by his t-shirt.

Besides actually cutting my balls off, I don't think there is a more emasculating thing you could do to a man. Isolated, locked in a house in the woods filled with my brother, my children, and my woman, and all I can do is stand and watch while soaked in my own piss.

Fists clenched at my sides, tears stinging my eyes, teeth gritted against the scream building in my throat, I take it like a man.

Muzzle grazing my forehead, the cool touch of metal branding me for life, Sean whispers in a menacing voice laced with rage. "Get on your knees and pray."

Slowly lowering myself to the floor, Willa senses Donny will be in my way– she yanks my brother a few feet toward the living room. The muzzle follows me down, never losing contact with my forehead. Bowing, pressing closer to the gun, I close my eyes and begin to pray to God.

"That's not what I meant, toy." Sean's sadistic laughter is thick with evil intent, sliding over my skin and taking root in the pit of my stomach. Guts twisting, bile rises in my throat when it clicks into place that there are much worse ways to ruin a man than pointing a loaded weapon at his forehead.

Sean didn't break my brother by beating and lashing him or threatening my life.

This is a threat all women have to live with on a daily basis, and it gives me new appreciation of their strength and will to survive. With a resigned sigh, I submit to my fate, knowing the quicker I get this over with, the faster I will die. Hope upon hope, I hope my prayers will be answered, that Sean will only have time to fire off one shot when the cops arrive, leaving my brother, his wife, and my children safe from harm.

Clenching my eyes tight, the sound of Sean lowering his zipper terrifies me to the point I almost faint. Light-headed because my breath seized in my lungs, I weave back and forth on my knees.

There is no comparison between Sean's dick and a loaded gun. I'd rather have the 357 Magnum shoved in my mouth and the trigger pulled than to submit to this degradation.

Laughing tauntingly, Sean is too distracted with the prospect of his own pleasure to keep an eye on Willa and Donny.

"I'm sorry, brother," Donny cries out as I peer up to look at him in wonder, realizing too late I'm his intended target, not the man preparing to violate me. The butt of my baseball bat flashes before my eyes. The sharp crack of it making contact is the last thing I feel as everything fades to black.

I suspend in the in-between state of consciousness and death, sights and sounds flashing at random, warping into madness.

"Donny! Stop hitting him," Willa screams so sharply it causes my eardrums to ache. "You're killing him. R-O-Y-C-E!!!"

My body is rocking as if I'm a capsized boat being beaten against the rocky shoreline. I'm wrenched forward, my clothing torn from my back, face-first into the tile floor. The scent of my own piss rankling my nostrils.

A grunt is torn from my throat– the pain excruciating and indescribable as I'm torn in two. Then the poundings begin anew. Sharp thwacks to my skull, causing strobes of light to eclipse my vision.

"Stop it," Donny bellows back. "He can't regain consciousness. Do you want him to remember this for the rest of his life?"

Roughly panting, voice raspy, "Knock your shit off, or I pull the trigger," Sean warns, metal branding the back of my neck. "Royce takes the punishment, you learn the lesson. I don't care if you beat each other to death in the process. I either do this or my boss executes me, then he'll come after everyone in this shitty fucking town. So have at it."

The rocking renews, tearing a death knell from my chest, then the pounding returns, causing me to see bursts of stars.

"Donny!" Willa screams shrilly, yanking me back from the darkness. "Stop it! Hit Sean instead!"

"You do get that Sean's finger is on the trigger of the gun pressing against the base of Royce's skull? Don't you think hitting Sean would make that finger pull?" Donny's voice cuts off the moment Willa gasps in pain. "God, why won't either one of you pass the fuck out?" My brother's voice warps, twisting with agony. "I haven't slept in years without waking to nightmares. Just let me do this for you– let me save you."

"No," Willa wails. "I'd rather know than not know."

The crack is deafening, the pain unlivable, followed by the bliss of utter darkness.

Seconds. Minutes. Lifetimes… moments warp into muddled confusion.

Lying on my belly, listening to Willa's screams of terror. Her fingernails cutting into my skin as she tries to shake me back to life. The deafening crack of a gun. The murmur of many voices filtering into my ears. First Corbin, then Bren, lastly the cavalry.

Sensing safety, I finally allow myself to drift away, knowing my family will be safe from the monster whose presence I no longer register.

TEDDY BEAR

ᔥPresentᔦ

Shivering, a quaking wracks my entire body from the soles of my feet to the top of my skull. My teeth rattle together, causing an ache in my jaw. Sweat slicks down my forehead, mixing with the tears of terror and shame running down my cheeks. Try as I might, I can't freeze my muscles from spasming.

Softness is clutched against my chest, my arms and legs wrapped around the comforting warmth as I rock back and forth while muttering nonsense.

Blinking tears away, I expect to see my mother's sweet face. "Roy, are you sorry for hitting your brother?"

"Yes, Momma." I sniffle, rubbing my cheek against the big teddy bear clutched to my chest. "I'm so sorry. I learned my lesson."

"You can come out of the corner then. Just don't hit Donny again. He might be older, but he's too small– fragile."

"Okay, Momma." My hand won't release its hold on the stuffed animal, and my body can't move except to shake uncontrollably. "Don't tell Daddy. Please. I don't want him to think poorly of me."

"There's nothing you could ever do to make yer daddy love ya any less, bub." Big brown eyes shine down at me with pride, but then they warp and shift to watery blue.

"Royce?" Willa calls to me but doesn't make a move to touch me. "You're gonna be okay. I promise you you're safe."

Anchored to the teddy bear, the corner of Dr. Cassidy's wall supporting and protecting me, with her desk acting as a shield, I crouch in shame.

"I can't... I can't... I can't. I can't. I can't," I mumble over and over again, unable to look Willa or Dr. Cassidy in the eye. I stare at the teddy bears lined up against the side of the desk. I'm holding Papa Bear– he's black and formidable and at least three feet long. There's a slightly smaller tan bear that I'll call Momma Bear. Then there's the Baby Bears– pink, blue, green, yellow, and purple.

"Those bears are us. Aren't they?" My accusation is launched at Dr. Cassidy.

"Yes. I've waited session after session for you to take the bear you've been eyeing since day one." Dr. Cassidy admits in a calm, professional voice, handing Willa the Momma Bear to hold. "The pink is Hayley. Blue for Hayden. Green for Brennan. Yellow for Wynn. The purple is for Kaden. Whether they ever see the bears or not is not the point. You needed to see that everyone is safe and happy, warm and cuddly, and perfectly healthy."

"But–" my question is cut off when Dr. Cassidy pulls something big and brown from beneath her desk. Her chair had been hiding it. It's an exact match to my bear, only lighter in color and trapped by the desk. "Donny."

"Your brother is safe, Royce." Dr. Cassidy hands me the bear, and I immediately latch onto it. "I speak with him twice a week for our sessions. You need to understand how some things are out of your control, and that's okay."

"No, it's not," I argue. "It's my fault he's locked up." Hugging the bear, I press my face into its fur. "I want my brother back. Right now."

"You feel helpless because you can't free Donny, I get that. We all do. Donny understands it more than any of us."

"It's not fair," I whine like a child, looking exactly like a child as I clutch two teddy bears to my chest. "He didn't do nothing. He doesn't deserve to be locked up while that monster rots in the ground. I hate Corbin. I hate him!" I bellow so loudly my eardrums vibrate and ache. "Hate him!"

"It's not Corbin Gillette's fault." Sitting in her chair, Dr. Cassidy tries to reason with me.

Turning feral, I scream, "YES! IT! IS!" at the top of my lungs, until the vein in my forehead throbs and my throat is dry and raw. "If he hadn't killed Sean, none of this would be happening!"

I hear my words– their insanity –but it doesn't change how irrational I feel. I know I'm hurting Willa by yelling about her daddy. But I can't stop once I start. Five years of hatred pours out of me, and decades of jealousy fuels it.

"It's his fault I lost my brother! I hate him!" Screaming so forcefully I break blood vessels in my eyeballs, "Donny rots behind bars because no one believed us– they thought Willa and I were lying to save Donny. Because the evidence was shot in the head in the woods."

"Is it Corbin's fault that you were assaulted? Held at gunpoint? Raped?" Dr. Cassidy pulls no punches– as blunt as the truncheon that left me with a colostomy bag for two months while I healed. "Is it Corbin's fault Donny beat you and Willa so badly that he almost killed you both?"

"Yessss," I hiss. "Because whatever is in Willa that made it so she wouldn't pass out came straight from her daddy. Pure Gillette stubbornness. Donny would have stopped hitting her if she would have gave in. So it's Corbin's fault."

"Royce," Willa snaps. "Listen to yourself."

I bellow, "I am!" right in her face.

"The part in me that wouldn't give up was my maternal instinct. Our children were in the house. Someone had to protect Donny from himself, and someone had to watch over you. Sean didn't want anything to do with me. You were always his target, using Donny to get to you. This has nothing to do with my daddy. You have to let it go."

"Donny's in jail for two counts of attempted murder, Willamina," I remind her like she could ever forget. "Against us! They thought he wanted our money, remember? But he wasn't the one— Sean was."

"I know," Willa murmurs patiently. "I know, Royce. *I know*."

"Without Sean, Donny looked guilty. If it wasn't for that sick gift Sean left inside of me, they would have pinned my rape on my brother too." Face buried in the fur of both teddy bears, I begin to sob and rock back and forth again. "I want my brother out of jail." Rocking back and forth, "It's my fault."

"Which is it, Royce?" Dr. Cassidy challenges me, stilling my frantic movements and gasping sobs. "Is it your fault, or is it Corbin Gillette's fault? Or perhaps, every person needs to take responsibility for their own actions and how they contributed to what happened."

"I am— we are."

"Not well, you aren't," Dr. Cassidy's sarcasm is not appreciated. "You're all the victims, and you've let it destroy your lives. You look like an upstanding citizen but inside you are pure chaos. Your brother is actually acclimating well and working through his part in all of this. Willa is at the end stages of acceptance. You are stuck. Corbin destroyed himself, blaming himself for not protecting Donny, protecting his daughter, protecting his grandchildren... protecting *you*."

"That wasn't his job— that was mine," I snarl.

"If it wasn't Corbin's job to take care of his family and friends," Dr. Cassidy traps me in my own words, "Then he can't be at fault for your brother being sent to prison for beating you. Because Donny *did* beat you, no matter how altruistic his reasons."

"But the jury couldn't hear the reasons because Sean was dead– killed by Corbin. So it is his fault." Eyes gleaming madness, I stare up at my doctor.

My face whips to the side, a palm print blooming on my cheek. Willa leans over me, glaring. "If Daddy hadn't taken Sean out, none of us would have survived long enough for the police to arrive." Willa finally tells the truth. "Sean was lost in the madness of violence, taking out whatever demons he had inside himself out on you. Nothing short of a bullet to the head would have stopped him from hurting you– it didn't happen in the woods."

"I– I can't remember because Donny wouldn't let me."

"You don't *need* to remember," Willa seethes. "I wish I didn't, and so does Donny. So does Daddy. You were the victim, and we didn't want you to remember. But your body does," Willa proves she knows me better than anyone. "For all this hate you preach– for someone not wanting to be beholden to my daddy, you sure do take care of him and his."

"I don't remember," I mutter again, then repeat Willa's words. "I don't remember but my body does. It's like a memory imprinted on my skin. My body will seize up for no reason. I can't remember my rape, but my ass does." I hide my face deeper into the teddy bear and whisper the truth. "Do you have any idea what it's like to be terrified to take a shit? Because my body remembers what I don't. I had a panic attack the first time I went to the bathroom after I healed up and the colostomy bag was removed. When I see a bat…"

"If the positions were reversed, I wouldn't want to know either," Willa says softly. Her anger has been replaced with compassion, and not an ounce of pity is shining through. "It's not so much what happened to you that is messing with your head, but your constant need to be in control of everything. It drives you insane to think that we know something you don't, especially when it's about you. You know what happened– no one needs the details. *Ever.*"

"What you must see when you look at me." I gaze up at Willa, pouring out my greatest fear. "You must be sickened at how weak I am. I'm the father of your children, and I couldn't even protect myself, let alone you and the kids."

Gripping my chin with ferocity, "Don't," Willa orders. "Don't go there. I see *you* when I look at you, and nothing else. Sean– or whoever the fuck he really was –was a madman. No amount of strength and manliness could have protected you or us from him.

We all have our fears, and I lived for three more years terrified of when the others would take you from me."

"Others?" Nothing could have broken through my bitter shame except for that. "Explain."

"I can't," Willa grits out, frustrated. "Gag order, remember?"

"Why can't I know?"

"Because you can't," Willa snaps, frustrated. "Do you honestly believe they didn't know what happened to Sean? The FBI *and* his associates? That Donny might be where he is as protection? That my daddy kept me and the kids in squalor to save us? That me going back to you was terrifying because it put us all in one spot as an easy target? There is more here than your assault, Royce."

"It's all about the money," I mumble, hating every last green cent of it.

"Of course it is," Willa snarls. "Isn't it always about money? Always?"

Scrabbling to my feet, I'm hard-pressed to let go of the teddy bears. "I need to see my brother. I'm going to be late for the visitation our attorney arranged."

Willa's to her feet in an instant. "I'm going with you."

"No!"

"Yes!"

"No! I'm going alone. I *need* to spend time with my brother, Willamina!"

"I'm driving you because you're not capable right now—" Willa growls at me, baring her front teeth. "Don't start that shit with me, mister. I don't want to hear any macho bullshit. You just suffered emotional trauma, and I'm not gonna play to your ego by letting you drive when you can't even think straight."

"You're such a pain in the ass." My eyes cut to the side, noticing Dr. Cassidy watching us intently with a slight curve to her lips.

"You wouldn't want me any other way." Willa flashes me a smirk, gripping my hand.

"True." I squeeze her hand. "But you're staying in the car."

BROTHER BEAR

Staring one another down in deafening silence, Donny and I are only separated by a metal table. My fingertips curl against the edge, resisting the urge to hold my brother, to make us both feel comforted and safe and secure.

I wish I had Brother Bear with me, because I know Donny won't allow me to hug him.

My brother always looks good– young for his age with something about him that will always feel childlike. He just turned forty-four last month, and no matter how hard I tried, he wouldn't see me on his birthday. His brown hair is a little shaggy, the tips of his ears sticking out from where his hair is tucked back. He's in need of a Kennedy brush cut and a clean shave. His scruff is starting to gray along his jawline, and tiny lines are bracketing the outside corners of his eyes.

Looking at my brother makes me sad, remembering him looking larger than life when I was a little guy. How I grew bigger, taller, and stronger and began protecting him. But Donny and Corbin wouldn't let me, saying I was just a kid– an annoying technique I pulled on Wynn decades later.

Where did our twenties and thirties go? I've yet to hit forty, but I feel ancient as I stare into my brother's eyes, finding that I'm the one who is lost, not him anymore.

Small at five and a half feet, Donny used to be really soft but he's been firming up his muscles here in jail. The revelation worries me, because who in here is protecting my brother? He has no Corbin or Royce to protect him from the Seans of the world when we're locked out of his life.

To me, it's not Donny locked in prison. It's me on the outside of the door, pounding and begging to be let in so I can keep him safe and save him. But that's not the real reason. It's because Kennedy land is not my home. My brother is.

For the past five years of silence, I've felt like my heart was hacked out of my chest. I can survive the nightmare, but I can't survive losing Donny.

That bond– that amazing bond I'm forging in my own children –is exactly what was exploited by the bad men.

We do our thing that we've been doing for the past five years, where I beg my brother to talk to me, and all he'll ever do is listen. He won't even communicate with his eyes anymore– totally shutting me out so I can't see the truth.

But today is different. Not because it's the anniversary of the attack or the loss of our family, or because I had a breakthrough with my therapist. Today is different because we're not sitting in the loud clamor of the visitation room with fifty-plus inmates and their family and friends, surrounded by ten guards with batons.

Money got us into this horrific situation, but it also bought Donny and me a bit a privacy for once. Alone in a small, dark room filled with a table and two chairs bolted to the floor, the only eyes on us are from the security camera overhead and the single guard leaning against the door, who appears to be mentally counting floor tiles.

Our guard is wearing a dark suit, and suspiciously looks like a federal agent. He might be obsessing about the one tile that doesn't follow the gray and white pattern, but his ears are open and avidly listening.

Agent OCD is not here to make sure Donny doesn't hurt me or that I don't give him contraband, like the guards in the visitation room are for. No, he's here to guard that gag order Willa keeps speaking about but never truly explains.

I start out with my spiel. "Tonight Bren and I will visit Daddy and Annie. We'll leave a bundle of daisies from you as usual." I wait for Donny to nod his head, but he never does.

My brother always joined Bren and me every year, where we'd talk to the dead, and not visit them until the following year on the anniversary. Donny would bring daisies and regale Daddy's tombstone with wild tales from throughout the year. Then he'd breakdown on the way home. Even five years ago we did this– the early morning because that was Daddy's favorite time of day, with the attack happening later that afternoon.

"We're doing it in the evening for Annie this year– it was her favorite time of day," I explain, but he already knows. "More to it, though. We have the grand opening for the Life Skills Center this afternoon." A spark of recognition lights in Donny's eyes, so I know someone's been talking to him.

"Willa? Corbin?" Donny doesn't even twitch to give me an answer. "The kids are going off to college the day after tomorrow. Bren's got himself into a pickle, but he won't tell me what." I silently think to myself, *no one ever tells me anything*. "But Kade is taking care of things, because apparently I'm incapable."

Donny flinches, hearing the underlying resentment in my words but he doesn't reply.

"Dr. Cassidy made me recall the attack early this morning." The words are out before I even think them. Stunned, my brother and I stare at each other. Begging is not beneath me. "Talk to me."

Donny's hair flops around his ears as he shakes his head left and right.

"Talk to me. Please," I plead in an aching tone. I reach across the tabletop for my brother's hand. But he snatches it away before I make contact. "Please, Donny. Let me touch you. Stop freezing me out."

A strange noise rumbles up my brother's throat. He keeps whipping his head side-to-side, and I can almost hear him say, "*I can't.*" Wet splotches dot the metal surface of the table, tearing my heart out and incinerating it.

"Brother," I beg, using the fact that I've finally got a reaction out of Donny for once, even if it's him crying. "Are you okay in here? Are you safe?"

Nodding up and down rapidly, he won't look me in the eyes.

"You haven't dropped the soap, have you?" The lame joke comes out of nowhere, causing Donny to choke on a laugh and a sob at the same time.

Covering his mouth with the back of his hand, Donny grants me the pleasure of his voice for the first time in five years. "No," he mutters wryly. "I shower alone. I'm fine. Safe. Don't worry about me, Roy."

"I do, though," I say hesitantly, scared he'll shut me down. "Worry about you."

"I know." His eyes flash up, connecting with Agent OCD at my back. "But you shouldn't. I'm fine. Let's just say it's a small group of us together. Like witness protection for convicts."

"Mr. Kennedy," Agent OCD warns in a gruff voice. "Younger Mr. Kennedy gets to talk, and you only listen. Remember?"

"Yes, sir." Donny sounds deflated, but there is rebellion lurking in the depths of his eyes. "I'm not supposed to talk to you or touch you, because they fear I'll say too much."

"Why can't you talk to me?" I ask again.

"Corbin was telling me–" Donny hesitates when the agent clears his throat. "How you didn't tell Wynn about the adoption until after the fact. Willa added more to it. How you wanted Wynn to have the summer to himself because it would give normalcy to the twins and Penny. Remember?"

"Of course I remember. It was only last year." I sound surly like Willa– defensive. "It was my responsibility to shoulder the burden. If Wynn knew, the kids would feel it, and it would upset the balance. In Wynn's case, ignorance was bliss."

Donny just stares at me for a long moment, and I stare back confused. It takes Agent OCD chuckling behind me before I get a clue.

"I'm not Wynn, goddammit!" Snarling, the side of my fist meets the metal table, causing Donny to jump out of his skin and the agent to laugh outright.

"Royce," Donny says in a calm voice that belies the way his eyes are narrowed. "Kaden. Wynn. Brennan. Hayden. Hayley. That is why you don't know. You have to live an everyday life for the children. Eh–" he puts a palm out to stop me from arguing. "Corbin couldn't handle looking over his shoulder because he murdered their inside man, and it cost him his family and sobriety. Willa couldn't handle the stress of always wondering who was going to come for her children and you and Bren, and she sought drugs for escape. Warren didn't know what was happening, but he could feel his family disintegrating before his very eyes, so he sought escape. Wynn… he tried to kill himself."

"I-I-I… I don't see what any of that had to do with this."

"It's because you're refusing to see what's before your face. You have all the answers; you just refuse to see the truth." Donny casts sad eyes behind me, looking defeated. "What you don't know can't hurt you. What we know makes us a threat. Willa said the fuck with it and decided to live her life. Corbin's trying to follow suit. I'm safer in here than at home. I miss you, but I'd rather remain breathing, so stop trying to repeal a conviction that is my version of witness protection. Just stop it."

"I want you home with me." Fists scrubbing at my damp eyes, I hate how desperate I sound. "I miss you so goddamn much I feel lost."

"If you love me…" Donny looks away, ignoring the tears washing down his cheeks. In a tight, strained voice, "Prove you love me by not making me feel guilty– and before you say you're not blaming me, that's not what I meant. Stop telling me how much you miss me when I can't get out of here to be with you. Like I don't miss you, miss Willa and the kids. Like I don't wish I could come home and sit around the bonfire with you and Corbin. But unlike you, Corbin knows that to tell me he misses me and his life sucks because I'm not around, is to rip my heart out. So just back off."

"I'm sorry." Leaning forward, I wrap my arms around my head, trying to comfort myself. "I'm being selfish. I'm sorry."

"You're not selfish," Donny says with conviction. "You don't have to take care of everything for everyone to be a man. You're a man because you're a man. You're a good father, husband, brother, and friend. You don't have to prove anything to anyone."

"I do to myself," I grumble, but he doesn't hear me.

"You can't fight my battles for me, Royce." Now it's Donny's time to beg and plead. "If you hate feeling like someone cut your balls off, then stop taking mine. I need this. I need to protect our family. I'm the oldest, and they aren't my kids. They *need* you, not me."

"I need you… After what happened, I have to prove myself worthy–"

"Royce!" Donny bellows, and he never yells– at least he didn't used to. "What happened to you was an assault. It had nothing to do with sex, and absolutely nothing to do with whether or not you're a man. When consensual, it's not like that. Sean wanted to harm you."

"Sean did that to you, too, didn't he?" My guts twist up, bile rising in my throat. "He made you do that all the time, didn't he? I'm sorry. I should have protected you better."

Donny's sharp laugh is sardonic and warped. "Royce, how do you think they targeted me in the first place?" His laugh gets more strained, like it's being pushed through a cocktail straw. "Sean found me in a gay bar up in Pittsburgh less than a week after we won the civil lawsuit. I was celebrating. I didn't know I was his mark– the rich hillbilly with an even richer brother. By the time I figured it out, it was too late, and I'd been fucked every which way, including sideways, and I loved it."

In deafening silence, my brother and I just stare at each other. I try to say something, anything, but my mouth can't form words my mind won't supply.

"Well, this thread of conversation is unexpected." Agent OCD breaks into the heavy silence. "I never thought Donny would get the balls to come out to you."

"You're gay?" rolls off my tongue, feeling funny and sticky, like it's all wrong somehow. "But you were married."

"Three times, yes." Donny snorts. "It's what men my age in a town like Rusty Knob do. You get hitched, pray like hell no one spots you in cities nowhere near your hometown, and that you don't pick up a disease in a club. But my wives weren't happy unknowingly being my beard."

"What's a beard?" I ask without hesitation. "I'll need to know what that means for the boys' sakes."

"That's what you pick up?" Donny's tone is incredulous. "Wanting to know what a beard is? Not the fact that I just told you Sean was my lover? You don't ask the specifics? You don't even mention the fact that he raped you to punish me?"

"It all kinda clicked into place when you said you were gay. I don't need details. I'm assuming after he hooked you, he started blackmailing you," I ramble, still shocked and more than confused. "But why not just tell me you were gay, then he wouldn't have anything over on you?"

"Gay?" Donny huffs a laugh, not sounding amused. "He didn't blackmail me over being gay. Two years into dating, after I'd given him gifts like buying vehicles and paying his bills, it wasn't enough. He needed money for–" Donny changes the course of his words when the agent coughs loudly. "–whoever sent him. He threatened to kill you first, so that your money would revert back to me and I'd get custody of Bren. He compromised because I told him with you dead, he'd have no hold over me. The compromise was for me to have a kid. I didn't realize he planned on killing Bren so I would be the trustee of the grandchildren's Trust. But we had the twins, which saved Bren's life. Two-to-one, me versus you. That's what was going down. Sean wasn't going to kill us that night– he was going to bring you into it and tap your Trusts next, until we were bled dry."

"That's enough!" The agent barks out, coming to stand at the side of the table, leaning down on his hands. "I thought it time Royce knew enough so he'd stop asking questions and leave it be. But if you go any further, Donald, you'll be dragging him into this and putting his life at risk. Understood?"

"Yes, sir," Donny replies immediately, properly cowed.

"You have exactly one minute to say your goodbyes," the agent commands, pointing in turn at each of our faces. "No more talking."

Eyes narrowed, I glare at the FBI guy, hating him having any sort of power over me but knowing he holds my brother's safety in his hands. "May I please give Donny a hug, just this once?" I turn to my brother. "If you want to, that is. I'm not gonna force myself on ya."

Snorting, eyes glittering with tears, "C'mere, dumbass." Donny stands up from the table and takes a step toward me. I stare at his outstretched arms for a nanosecond, and then I fly into them.

Emotions spiking and crashing, shaking uncontrollably over the fact that I'm granted permission after waiting for so long… Arms wrapped tightly around Donny's torso, the first thought I have is how shocked I am over the fact he's stockier than the last time I held him.

"This is so much better than Brother Bear," I murmur into the side of his neck, inhaling the scent of home.

"What?" He chuckles, clearly thinking I've lost my mind. "Royce, you've got to just live your life and don't stress out over me. I'm doing what I need to do, and you need to do what you're already doing. Trust me."

"I'll try." I sniffle, feeling like a little guy again. "I'm not very good at it, though."

Donny barks a sharp laugh, a glorious sound that I haven't heard in years. "Understatement of the century." He squeezes me so tightly I can't breathe, and then he's pulling away with a quick kiss to my throat. "I love you. I miss you. Blah. Blah. Blah." A brilliant blush is creeping up his pale skin. "Tell Willa and the kids I said hi–"

"And that you love 'em and miss 'em." I finish Donny's sentence like I did when I was the annoying little brother. "I will."

"Good." Grinning at me, feeling the chasm of separation disappearing, our silent communication skills are back online. With an eye-dart in Agent OCD's direction, Donny leans in to whisper into my ear. "You ever gonna marry the mother of your children, or are you gonna make her live in sin for another decade?"

Dumbfounded, I just openly gawk at my brother.

Laughing, patting the center of my chest with his palm, "In case you're wondering… that was me giving you my blessing."

"We will get hitched as soon as you can stand up with me and be my best man," flows from my lips with conviction, even before my mind had a chance to sort it out.

Donny fists his chest, then closes his eyes and bows his head like he's praying. "That's a promise," he vows to come home to me someday.

In slow motion, time stilling, Donny wraps his hand around the back of my neck, lowering my forehead to his lips. He places a press of a touch as a silent goodbye, and then he's out of the room with the FBI agent in tow.

Instinctively I know there will be no more monthly visitations in the main room with all the guards and inmates. These few moments were a gift from my brother, letting me go while simultaneously reassuring me he will be back.

No longer set adrift, I follow the path I would've chosen no matter what, with my destination as Willamina Kennedy.

"I can't believe you left the grand opening early for this," Bren's voice follows me as I walk down the dirt path toward the Kennedy plot in Rusty Knob's cemetery. I'd hoped as my son got older that he'd understand the ritual of remembrance.

"I'll spend ninety percent of my time at the Life Skills Center until the day that I die." My fingertips glide along the tops of the tombstones as I walk– my way of saying hello and goodbye, a comfort for those interred that they are not forgotten. "I won't be missed at the grand opening because this will always be more important."

"Visiting the dead?" Bren is so confused, I realize I hadn't been going about this the correct way.

"No, son. Family. Lineage. Never forgetting your roots. Taking a few moments out of your day to remember where you came from and those who helped you along the way, so you can appreciate where you are now, who you will become, and where you'll end up."

Money or not, for the same reason I never built the largest house in town, or bought an expensive vehicle, I live as the natives do because I am a native. We reach the Kennedy plot, only a simple six-foot-tall cross dominates the center with our family name etched into the black marble.

"Respect the sacrifices made." I kneel down before Annie's grave, placing Donny's daisies on top of the tombstone. "I'm not forcing you to grieve or to remember. This isn't a punishment we must go through yearly. This is a reward because we still breathe."

Annalise Payton Honor Kennedy
Daughter. Wife. Mother.
January 26th 1974 – August 8th 2003
Herein lies mother & unborn daughter. As in life, may they never be separated in the afterlife.

Removing a hanky from my back pocket, I begin the task of cleaning the face of Annie's tombstone. Bren is a silent shadow above me, no doubt mulling over the reasons I do this, and finding them a waste of time. I turn to my daddy's grave, and take as much care as I had with Annie's.

Donald Brennan Kennedy Senior
May 16th 1951 – August 8th 2003
Kennedy Patriarch.
Loyal Husband, Father, & Grandfather.

"A lot has changed in the past year," I say to Annie and Daddy, but it's more for Bren's benefit. "Yet it's still the same in most ways. I'm still proud of who my children have become, and even prouder as I watch Willa and Warren struggle to better themselves. It has inspired me to find myself instead of just putting on my daddy uniform and going through the motions.

"I've learned a lot this past year– I'm more than the sum of my parts. I have a lot to give, but I also deserve to take. I have people who will pick up the slack if I need to take a breather, and those same people deserve the same trust and respect I demand from them."

Bren's stillness overhead makes me wonder if he's finally getting it. Visiting the cemetery is a cathartic release– a type of therapy that can only be met head-on. You can't hide from your grief. You've got to plow right through it. Pretending they never existed isn't the answer. Celebrating their existence is.

Brennan is more like me than he realizes. Donny was the one who would chat for two hours, then spend another hour sobbing on their graves like a melodramatic wife. But I respected his form of grieving. I always said a few words, then looked after my brother. But the entire time I longed for privacy, because this is a very private agony.

"You know where I'll be," I whisper softly as I rise to my feet. Bren says nothing, but I know he will release a torrent of pent-up emotions the moment I'm out of ear-shot. He may or may not understand why we do this, but his subconscious does.

Drifting through the cemetery, taking a moment to glance and the names to pay my respects, I make my way to the tree-line. "Same time, same place," I mutter to Donny's replacement, never understanding why.

But then again, I've never understood a single thing Corbin Gillette has ever done.

Blond and blue-eyed, tall and strong, looking older than he should but better than he did, Corbin's narrowed stare freezes me mid-step. "You asked to see me– so talk," I demand none too kindly.

"I want a thank you," Corbin breathes so lightly I strain to register his words. "And an apology."

"For what?" I scoff, folding my arms over my chest in a defensive gesture.

Corbin mirrors me, only it's more intimidating. How a man who's never put in a solid day's work is corded with muscle defies logic. "Time and time again, I've ruined my entire life for you Kennedys, and you never say thank you."

"I'm not going to thank you for murdering Sean," I snarl. "Because of that, Donny went to prison."

"Don't," Corbin barks, and I listen. "Don't do that shit. You don't wanna know what Sean was doing when I pulled the trigger."

Raising my eyebrow, "Oh, I'm pretty sure I have a good idea."

"No, you don't." Corbin turns away from me, looking out into the distance. "You think you have to be the one to ride in and save the day, but sometimes it's not your job. Sometimes it's mine."

"Says the drunk bastard who sold his children–"

"Says the bastard who had to get drunk so he could stand to sell his children to protect a Kennedy." Corbin uses my words, but they take on an entirely new meaning. "From the outside looking in, it was heinous. But you weren't on the outside, Roy. You chose to make me out to look like a monster."

Exasperated, "You drank before you sold Willa, Corbin."

"I had my reasons," Corbin sneers. "Donny needed Willa, so I did what was best for everybody, and it didn't turn out too bad."

"Too bad?" I whisper-shout, sounding incredulous. "You sold your daughter against her will."

"She knew," Corbin shocks the hell out of me. "I didn't like it, but Willa knew her future was no different, no matter who she married. She fought me at first, but then I explained and she simmered down. You know how Willa can be, better than anyone."

"Explained? You beat her!" Uncontrollable, I pound the side of my fist against my thigh.

Holding his temper, Corbin surprises me yet again. "I've never hit a woman except for Cora, and that was because she was beating the piss out of my children." He looks away, mumbling, "I hate my wife. *Hate her*. We're toxic together. Cora moved in with her sister, and both of us are the better for it. Sometimes I snap, and I can't help myself. I like living alone. It's best not to have people around who make me snap."

"That's no excuse… What about Warren and Wynn?" I fling the accusation.

"Warren understands," Corbin whispers softly. "Wynn and I are oil and water. He's the most stubborn, judgmental child I've ever met. Just one look and I feel like God is casting me unto eternal damnation."

Snorting, I grumble beneath my breath, "I wonder why?"

"I heard that," Corbin spits. Arms folded over his chest, his palms curl into fists, then relax and loosen. "The tarnish on my soul belongs to *you*."

"Fine– whatever. You'll always spin it to make you out to be the good guy." I step side-to-side, staring at my feet, hating how Corbin always reduces me to feeling like a child. "So spin how you weren't treating my children like shit?"

Leaning into my face, seething, Corbin bites out the words. "I. Never. Laid. An. Angry. Hand. On. My. Grandchildren. *Never*. Not once. As for Wynn… I was dealing with a lot of heavy shit, and if there was ever a person on this planet that was judgmental, it's that little shithead. Looking into his eyes was like looking in the mirror and seeing how far I've fallen."

"You've fallen far," I mutter, snorting.

"For you, you ungrateful fucker." Losing his temper, Corbin stabs me in the chest with his fingertip. "*For. You*. For you I gave you my children– to protect you. I feel sick for what I've done to Wynn, how I made him feel. It's like I couldn't help myself. But I gave him up for you."

"How was giving up your son for me?" I bat his fingertip away, and then cross my arms back over my chest. "Explain that shit."

"Donny said to protect you, so I did." Fists balled, Corbin shoves them into his armpits to contain his rage. I take a step back, knowing how hard the bastard punches. "I hope you get that you had a target on your back and Bren had one on his forehead."

"It would have been nice for someone–" I glare at Corbin. "–to inform me my son and I were in danger."

"They leeched off Donny because he's weak, and that kept them occupied. If anything had happened to you, Kaden wouldn't have been able to keep the kids and Bren wasn't of age. So someone would have gotten the twins and would have controlled their money. All it would have taken was two bullets, and somebody out there would have been richer than a small nation."

"Yeah, so?" My eyebrows knit together, mulling over Corbin's words. "That's in the past."

"Is it now?" Corbin's glacier stare freezes me on the spot. "I gave you my son to protect Brennan– to protect my grandchildren. You needed an adult son, so I gave you one. Did it ever occur to you how odd it was that I allowed you to adopt my son a few months before he turned eighteen?"

"Wait– what?" Corbin stares me down as I try to work that out. "I took the kids because they weren't safe with you anymore. Wynn tried to kill himself."

"He did." Surprisingly, Corbin doesn't even flinch. "Willa chose to come back to you for a reason. With Donny secure in prison, what good would it be killing you off– killing Bren off –if they had Kade and Wynn to go through just to get their hands on the children and their legacy?"

"Are you saying there's a Kennedy out there who's behind this?" Baffled, my mind runs in circles. "There aren't any more."

"And you think *I'm* the fucking moron." Corbin sneers, upper lip curling. "I'd suggest you go out and adopt some more misfortunate children," he says none too kindly. "Use them as cannon fodder to protect my grandchildren. Spread all that money around so no one can ever get a big chunk." Knuckles cracking, he clenches his fists so tightly, I fear he'll break bone. "Your goddamned money is a curse, and I wish I'd never met you."

"Met me?" I point at my chest while glaring at Corbin. "You have no problem spending my goddamned money!"

"Let's see…" Corbin takes out his wallet, retrieving a twenty, a ten, and four ones. With his fingertips, he flicks them in my face. "Take it! I don't want it. It ain't done me no good."

"Pick your money up." I sigh in defeat. "You need it. Disability isn't enough to live off of." The look on Corbin's face makes me say something I regret instantly. "What exactly is the nature of your disability?"

Corbin murders me with his eyes. I've never seen such a look of hatred in my life. Startling, grabbing my wrist, he shoves my hands down his pants. "Clench your fist, goddamned you. Clench your fist and tear my nuts right outta their sack. Do it! You know you wanna."

Shocked, all I can do is suffer as Corbin shoves me away with disgust written across his face, but it's the look of betrayal that follows that draws me up short.

"It was never me taking your brother from you, you bastard. I was willing to get to know you, be your friend, but you always had to belittle me, make me feel small." Corbin turns his back to me, facing the trees. "If it wasn't for Wynn looking just like me, I'd swear he was yours… Even after I saved your life, you made me feel like scum."

"Why couldn't you work?" I murmur softly, curiosity finally winning out. A montage of fights between Wynn and Kaden play out in my mind. How I generally sided with Wynn, even when Kaden had good reasons why he wasn't working.

Back turned to me, Corbin mutters, "Imilliterate."

"What?" I lean in trying to hear him. "What did you say?"

"I'm illiterate." Corbin turns around quickly, glaring at me. "I said I can't read. Now you've got another reason to feel better than me."

"What– huh?" I'm not surprised, but I am. "That doesn't mean you can't work."

Shaking his head left and right, Corbin is dismembering me inside his mind. "It does when you get fired 'cuz of it, or when you fuckup and get someone hurt 'cuz you can't read." Like Willa, Corbin's diction shifts with great emotion, just like when he's drunk. "Or when the guys find out, and they beat the piss out of ya like in little school."

"So learn!" I nearly shout, flabbergasted. "You're the exact reason I opened the Life Skills Center."

"I tried!" He bellows back. "It was like reading gibberish. Nothing made sense." Corbin takes a few gulping breaths to calm down. "Until Wynn, no Gillette has ever graduated high school. They're real smart, but Warren and Willa only made it to eighth grade." Corbin turns his back to me again, unable to face me. "Warren was struggling, getting into fights. He beat up his English teacher because the asshole didn't believe that he couldn't read. The kids were picked up by a social worker, and it took two minutes for the lady to figure it out. They were sent home to us that same day, the teacher was suspended, and we learned Warren was dyslexic."

"Warren can read," I remind Corbin, refusing to bring it to his attention that I was the one who hired the tutor.

"I know– they taught him how." Large shoulders curving, head lowered, Corbin shrinks into himself. "But nobody ever taught me how."

"Jesus Christ!" I yank at my hair out of sheer frustration. "Stop making it impossible to hate you."

"I asked Kade to find someone to teach me," Corbin tugs my heartstrings. "I'm sure there's more people dotting the hillsides whose letters get jumbled up."

This time I breathe the benediction. "Jesus Christ, Corbin." I stomp around in a circle, thinking. "Being dyslexic, having a shitty life, that doesn't excuse the horrible things you've done. You're a drunk, a wife beater– eh!" I stop him. "Hitting Cora in retaliation for hitting your kids doesn't make it right. Selling your kids, no matter the reason is wrong. Murder–"

Gargling, words getting choked off by the hand squeezing my throat. My eyes flick up to see my son standing in the distance, but the traitor makes no move to help his father. Fingers tightening, spittle flying out between clenched teeth, Corbin tries to control himself as the Gillette in him erupts.

"You are *not* God." Firmly in control, fingers tighten against my throat but do no harm. "You don't get to pass judgement on me. You don't get to approve my reasons. You don't get to stand on your pedestal of self-righteous indignation when my sins were for *your* benefit." Abruptly I'm released, falling to my ass. My palms curl into the leaves and pine needles lining the ground. "I'm not a murderer– I protected you. I saved your life. I was exonerated, so stop making me feel like a monster when if it was anyone but me I'd be a hero."

"Corbin–"

"No! Shut up!" He points down at me, enraged. "You get to listen. I drank because I felt small, helpless. Powerless. I was terrified someone would come into my home and kill my family because of what I've done for you– *you* make me feel small," he drawls, voice thick with betrayal. "I couldn't work. My life was derailed by your brother. I thought you'd changed when you opened the Life Skills Center, but you're still calling me worthless for the same things you sympathize in others. Just like Wynn does!"

Speechless, I stammer nonsense. My eyes light on my son as he stands a few feet away, watching but doing nothing to help. "Just another kind of therapy," Brennan murmurs. "Willa thought it time you two cleared the air. Can't have you hating on your future father-in-law, now can we?"

"Brennan," I issue as a warning as I climb to my feet. Dusting my ass off, I'm at a loss of what to do or say. Nothing like being taken down a couple dozen pegs by your arch-nemesis and feeling guilty for being an asshole.

"I'm sorry," I mutter begrudgingly, words thick on my tongue, refusing to completely spill from my mouth. "That's all I got."

"Quit paying me off so you don't feel guilty." Corbin has my number. "All I want is some gratitude. The only Kennedy to ever thank me was Brennan."

"What?" I gasp, snapping my head to the side to look at my son, who is refusing to look at me.

"Donny didn't take none too kindly to me killing off the bastard who twisted up his head. He was in love with Sean. It took two years before he contacted me from prison... to apologize but never say thank you. Willa had to read me the letter."

Corbin's face twists up in agony, and I don't have the balls to speak just yet.

"Bren– Bren heard the shot, ran outta the twins' bedroom, and he didn't look horrified with what he saw. Donny was screaming at me about how much he hated my guts. Willa was busy helping you while your brother flipped his shit. Bren came right up to me and told me thanks for saving your ass, and then helped me drag Sean off ya."

My head whips around, eyes lighting on my son. "You only told me you saw– that was it."

"Don't!" Corbin orders, like he fears I'll harm my son. "Bren's a good kid, knows about loyalty. You leave him be." Stepping away from us, Corbin begins striding across the cemetery. "Gotta pay Donny's respects for him."

Gazing after Corbin's broad back, I flounder with something to say. "Thank you?"

Corbin flips around, fury etched across his features. "Don't say it again until you mean it," he warns. Then he's dropping down to his knees by my daddy's headstone, head bowed in silent prayer.

Brennan and I engage in a stare-off, neither one of us blinking. He's challenging me to speak so he can hand me my ass, same as Corbin Gillette just did. Emotions roiling, I've never been more confused in all of my life.

"I– I just don't understand," I mutter, gaze never breaking from my son's. "Why lie to me? Why not tell me the truth?"

Turning, Bren starts toward the truck. "Asks the man who keeps the biggest secrets."

"Touché." Feeling defeated but realizing I needed the ass-kicking, I follow my son. "I'll be clearing the air in two days... what about you?"

"You first." Bren slips into the truck cab, slamming the door behind him. I crawl in, feeling small and worthless. "As soon as you tell Wynn about the kids, I'll tell you what's going down with me, but not a moment sooner. You haven't earned my truth yet."

"Fair enough." I crank over the ignition. "Truce?"

"Dad." Bren's voice wavers with annoyance. He turns to face me while latching the seatbelt. "We're always in a truce. No secret is too big for us. You just have to let it go."

"Easier said than done."

"Ain't that the goddamn truth?" As I drive from the cemetery, Bren's eyes stay glued to Corbin praying over my daddy's grave. "Leave him alone– he's doing better without us in his life. Warren's been playing keep-away with you and Corbin for the past year while he got his shit together. He doesn't need your kind of help."

Flinching, "You make me sound like the bad guy."

Voice gruff, Bren stares at the side of my face. "There are two sides, and both sides think they're right. Neither one of you is a bad guy, but neither one of you is right."

THE POWER OF THE BONFIRE

Not saying another word on the drive home, Brennan allows me to contemplate all my wrongs. I realize for someone who loves to preach open-mindedness, my eyes sure have been squeezed shut to the things I didn't want to see.

Punching me in the arm, "Stop looking like I kicked your puppy." Bren teases me as I pull into the driveway. "Remember? We're to be thankful for the sacrifices others have made. It's not up to you to dictate whether or not they can make those sacrifices, so you can't feel guilty once they do. Just let it go."

"Easier said than done," I murmur again as I get out of my truck. Lost in thought, Bren grabs my wrist, yanking me toward the backyard, where three tents are erected a few feet from the roaring bonfire.

Backs resting against the logs, Willa's showing the kids how to start a fire by rubbing two sticks together, while Kade and Wynn chat animatedly with Jackson. No doubt they're making a game plan for once they get to West Virginia U.

Scrawny chest puffed out, "Behold–" Bren gestures wide with his hands, gaining everyone's undivided attention. "–the restorative powers of the almighty bonfire!"

Chuckling, I put my kid in a headlock, and then kiss his forehead. "Dumbass. Always picking on dear ol' dad."

Dropping to take a seat, Bren looks around with a huge smile on his face– the first real, genuine smile I've seen in months. "Dad got his ass handed to him by Corbin." With a wink in my direction, "He's a bit rubbed raw right now."

"My daddy?" Wynn's voice is thick with emotion, betrayal and sadness, and I realize he hasn't seen hide nor hair of his dad since he left Gillette Holler nearly sixteen months ago. "You didn't hurt each other, did ya?"

Face twisted with sadness, Willa looks concerned, but she doesn't meddle, leaving me and Wynn to work it out on our own.

"We had some stuff we had to talk about." I don't sit, not in the mood to socialize, even if it's with my children. "We had to clear the air, so to speak."

"I saw Papaw a few days ago," Hayden spills without thought. "He quit drinking."

Betrayal washes over Wynn's face, causing Kade to put a heavy palm on his chest. "Stay. Easy now." Kade talks him down, coaxing and soothing the Gillette temper. "I talked to your daddy, too. I was there. I think it best if you have a visit with him before you leave for school. Trust me. Maybe meet at the center or something."

"Daddy doesn't want a lick to do with me." Wynn turns away from us, hiding his face. "He sold me for a new roof and some windows."

In the past, I would have comforted Wynn, given him sage advice on how Corbin's behavior didn't have anything to do with Wynn. I hadn't realized my opinions were tinted with the color of jealousy. So instead of being selfish and solidifying Wynn's and my relationship, I do the only thing I should. I don't need to keep Wynn in my life by keeping him out of his daddy's. I need to trust Wynn's judgement.

"Wynn?" I call out, gaining his attention but he won't look at me. His shoulders are curled just as Corbin's had been earlier. "Corbin wants to see you– *needs* to see you. The decision's yours, but I think it'd be best if you'd see him."

I let Wynn feel what he's feeling with the only amount of privacy I can offer– I don't push.

Mentally, emotionally, and physically exhausted, just as Dr. Cassidy predicted, saying this would be the most trying week of my life, the only thing I want to do is sleep. Turning, I catch sight of Willa. She has tears glistening in her eyes as she mouths, "*Thank you,*" for only me to see.

"Well, I see you have everything you need out here," I say, pointing at the hotdogs and s'more fixings, then the tents beyond. "I'm hitting the hay. Have a good night. I love ya. Blah, blah, blah," I repeat Donny's words, feeling amused and comforted by the fact.

Every eye is on me, stunned that I'm denying the almighty power of the bonfire. Turning, "Willa?" I call as I stride across the yard. "Git your ass in our bedroom– the big shits can watch the little shits one last time before they run off to their college life."

Bren's, "Holy shit!" has me chuckling as I mount the back steps. "*Our* bedroom? Since when? Does that mean what I think that means?"

"We should hassle Royce like he does us." Kade's no doubt razing Wynn. "See how he likes it."

"Excuse me," Willa says demurely, voice getting closer. "Kids, you mind Uncle Kade."

"Where ya going, Momma?" Hayley's asking as I'm opening the screen door to the kitchen. I slip in, and then rest my back against the outer wall, curious to see what they say.

"Momma and Daddy are tired," Willa tells the truth, but then her voice switches over to a naughty giggle. "Nobody steps foot into this house until morning, or they will be dealing with me."

"Oooooo, scary," Kade taunts. "Royce better be relaxed in the morning, or I'm gonna doubt your feminine wiles!"

"You know nothing of feminine wiles," Willa taunts back. "I know how to work a D better than you do, and that's saying a lot since you have one."

"Oh!" "Burn!" Jack and Bren shout in unison, with Wynn snickering, "Them's fightin' words!"

Hayden's, "What's a D?" has me smothering a laugh. "Do I have one?"

"It's yer willy." Hayley sounds just like her momma.

"Oh!" Hayden's voice rises in pitch. "I got me one of those."

Willa's chuckling into the back of her hand when she steps into the house. My whispered words ring out in the deafening silence from the shadows of the kitchen. "Their questions will never end. You started a riot out there."

Jumping, "Royce!" puffs out from between Willa's lips at the same time her palm covers her heart. "You gave me a scare."

Eyeing Willa's face, I tug on her blouse, drawing her into my arms, and I instantly feel at peace. "That was very naughty of you. The boys won't get a lick of rest with the twins pestering them."

"Better to keep 'em out of our hair," Willa replies in a saucy tone. Blue eyes softening, "You doing okay?"

I think that over for a second to the background of my little ones driving the big kids nuts. "Yes? No? Maybe? I don't think so?" Brow raised, I wait for Willa to answer for me. "Do any of those answers fit?"

Raising her brow, mocking me, she supplies, "All of the above?" Tugging on my hand gripping her blouse, "Same here. C'mon." Curling her fingers through mine, Willa draws me up the stairs, down the hallway, and into my bedroom. "Did you really mean what you said?"

Standing in the middle of my bedroom, the room where Willa and I have shared my bed many times over the past five years when she was high out of her mind and I was emotionally distraught. But not once since she was sober, because I've been the one who was broken, lost– in denial.

"I thought I was waiting until you were ready," I whisper to Willa. I fight the urge to look away, but her strength fortifies me. "But it was me all along, wasn't it?"

Willa simply answers, "Yes," while slumping against the door in relief.

Walking backward, my ass lands on the edge of the mattress. "How did you survive looking over your shoulder for monsters you couldn't see?"

"By taking psychotropic drugs with a heroin chaser." Willa's as blunt as ever. "I'd suggest you don't go down that particularly destructive path."

Kicking off my sneakers, I snort.

"So, you could say, I didn't exactly succeed in surviving it. But seeing my momma smack Hayley for the first time– that flipped a switch I didn't know I had in me. I realized I was letting those motherfuckers win by tearing our family apart."

"That's why you came to me?"

"Yes," she bites out viciously. "Watching Wynn self-destruct. Putting up with Momma blowing a gasket for no reason and reaching out to whack whoever was in arm's reach, then Daddy beating the piss out of her for hitting me or Warren. I realized it didn't matter if there were people out there lying in wait to take my babies, because we were all tainting each other. So we all left."

Laughing at how odd it is to see things from a different perspective, "I didn't take you guys in. Y'all came to me."

Lips twitching at the corners, Willa tries not to laugh. "It was better if you thought it was your idea." Parting her hands, "You're a man. I knows me some things." She switches back into her hillbilly diction to make me smile. "I knows how y'all tick. Gotta make a man think it's his idea."

Widening my legs, I crook my finger in Willa's direction. "C'mere," I order, but it comes out as a soft breath.

Willa stands between my parted thighs, knees brushing the edge of the mattress. Her hands rest lightly on my shoulders, with my hands at her hips. Staring down at me with intense eyes, she whispers. "Ask."

"Is it because we're not married?" I ask the question she's not waiting to hear. "If we were married, would the the gag order still apply?"

Looking vaguely insulted that I'd suggest we marry for that reason, Willa bites out, "Ask."

Gazing up at Willa's face, eyes tracking her emotions. "Who? If it isn't some anonymous person you're looking over your shoulder for, then who is it?"

Fingertips clenching at my shoulders, nails slightly biting it, I can see Willa's wheels spinning. I fear she won't answer me. But what terrifies me most is the fact that my ignorance for the past twelve years could have gotten Bren and me killed. I'm not ignorant any longer, but I still don't know who to be on the lookout for.

"When Donny was dating Sean, we figured it out," Willa admits hesitantly, eyes never straying from mine. "It was after the kids were born, and Sean was getting more aggressive." An agony-filled laugh echoes around the room. "Understatement, that. I drugged Sean's beer, and he sang like a canary. But Donny didn't believe a word of it."

"Believe what?"

"After your momma died, your daddy was lonely. He was seeing a married woman who had a couple of kids. Her husband found out, so they moved out of state."

Eyes bugging out, "Come again?"

"As you've found out, that pesky law of any child born into a marriage by law belongs to the husband. The Probst family had a dark secret similar to our own, and that secret excluded them from your daddy's settlement."

Pushing Willa away from me, I launch across the room, terrified of harming her. "Sean was *not* my brother!" I rest my head against my bathroom door, feeling like I'm being flung down a long tunnel with no end in sight.

In a calm voice, "No," Willa comforts me some. "But Sean was Octavia Probst's big brother."

Turning to the side, forehead still pressed into the cool wood, "What? I have a sister?"

"The FBI are trying to figure out if Octavia has anything to do with any of this. When they first started, the civil lawsuit was on the national news, and their dark secret came to light. So Sean was just checking up on Donny, then he began begging money off him. Then the Probst brothers caught wind of what their big brother was doing and all hell broke loose."

"There's more of them?" Rolling, my back slides down the door until I land firmly on my ass– subconsciously protecting it, I think. "They're not related to me, are they?"

"No." Willa sits on the edge of the mattress, facing me. "Octavia is definitely your sister. She's thirty-one years old, living in Virginia. Sean was the oldest and not the brightest, but he felt your daddy owed their family."

"I have a sister." I taste the words on my tongue, and it feels strange but nice. "Sean's gone now, and if my sister isn't involved–"

"I didn't say she wasn't," Willa reminds me. "She's just living her life, but that's doesn't mean jackshit. See, she has two other brothers. One's a year younger than Sean named Damon. He's in jail for putting a hit out on you two years ago, thinking with Donny in jail and you and Bren dead and with my entire family high out of our minds, Octavia had a chance at getting your daddy's money, and Annie's through the kids."

"Shit."

"It gets worse, and this is where the FBI comes into it. They can't locate the youngest brother– Cain. We're positive he's the one who took control of Sean. He's a ghost. We don't even know what he looks like. But we do know that fucking with the Kennedys gave him a taste for extortion, and he's targeting families who receive large settlements."

Charging to my feet, I whisper-shout at Willa, "Why wasn't I told?"

"What good would it have done, Royce?" Willa's words stop me from committing something violent. "Your sister is trying to live her own life, and she knows where you are if she wants to introduce herself. We have no idea where Cain is, or when he'll crop up. We have a security system on the house. The kids were safe in Gillette Holler, with Octavia's brothers terrified of my daddy. What good would it have done making you a paranoid mess, when we needed you to take care of everyone and keep an eye on your money?"

Pacing, eyes darting all over the place as my mind reels, words tumble from my lips. "You mean like I did to Wynn– *am* still doing to Wynn."

An ironic, humorless laugh echoes around the bedroom. "You said it, not me." Willa falls backward to lie on the mattress. "Good grief, it's been a horrific day." Kicking her flip flops across the room, Willa makes herself comfortable. "It's days like today that make me want to reach for a bottle of pills or a syringe. Sorry if that freaks your ass out, but it doesn't make it any less true."

Terrified, voice breaking, "It's my fault for pressing you."

"Don't." Not only can I hear the eye roll in Willa's voice, I watch her do it. "I said *it makes me want…* not that I was actually gonna do it. I've worked too hard to go back down that road." Closing her naughty, rolling eyes, she purrs, "Distract me. Make it all go away. At least until tomorrow."

Standing over Willa, watching how peaceful she looks with her eyes closed. Only the throb in her neck and the steady rhythm of her chest rapidly rising and falling betrays the fact that she isn't as calm as she's trying to appear.

This is the first time in over a year that Willa has brought up using, so I know it's riding close to the surface, ready to pull her under.

After more than a year with no sex and a lot of family bonding, I tease her with, "Wanna play a board game?" I'm rewarded with her throaty laugh. Back arching off the bed, Willa clutches her chest as she giggles evilly. "We've got Operation out in the hallway. The dang kids refused to put it away."

"Royce," Willa chuckles my name, eyes dancing with delight. "A board game, really?"

"I could be the doctor," I offer, keeping a straight face. "I could keep poking at you to see if you'll squeal."

Humor fading away, Willa's face transforms from a happy young woman to that of my succubus. "You can poke me all night," comes in a throaty purr. Sneaky fingers hook into the front of my shirt, controlling me. "But I'm gonna be the doctor."

I squeal like a girl when Willa pounces.

Crouched with her knees on my thighs and her palms holding her weight on my chest, Willa grins down at me with eyes flickering depraved thoughts. "Are you going to be a good patient, Mr. Kennedy?" Her fingertip twitches, hitting my nipple, shooting sparks down my spine to take root in my cock.

Grunting, I shift on the bed to adjust myself. "Depends," I rasp roughly, amazed at how this vixen can make me go from terror to a heartbeat away from coming in my pants. "I have a feeling you're no Dr. Feelgood."

Arching her neck, Willa laughs at the ceiling. "The generational divide just widened, old man." Tweaking my nipple, she rights herself until she's straddling my hips. "Pretty sure Dr. Feelgood was before your time, and we both know I'm more into rough handling."

"You have a shitty bedside manner." With a firm swat, I time my words with my hand landing on her firm ass. "Slap-happy Willamina Kennedy." Groaning, rolling my hips up into her, I grip her ass and knead my fingertips into her flesh. "I've always loved calling you Willamina Kennedy because I could pretend it was me who had the honor of sharing my last name with you and the kids."

Flashing me a look loaded with annoyance and the threat of punishment, Willa points at the locked door behind her. "Regret stays out in the hallway tonight, mister. Tomorrow morning when we get up, we're gonna kick it down the stairs and out into the yard like a misbehaving pup. If you bring it up again. *Ever again*. I'ma punish you for it."

With a voice filled with need and urgency, I rasp out, "You promise?" causing Willa to look gobsmacked. Before she comes to her senses, I perform a wrestling maneuver to reverse our positions.

Glaring while laughing, Willa's fists of fury pound against my back and her heels dig into the mattress. "This is better," I murmur softly, palm brushing her blonde curls from her forehead. I kiss the tip of her nose to still her. "I have something for you. I-I-I..." stammering, I blush ten shade of Hades.

Hand reaching out blindly, my fingertips pull the drawer to my nightstand open. I fish around, trying to locate what I'm looking for. I grin in victory, palming the prize. "I know you're not a flashy girl.

You don't long for materialistic things. And I realize we both just accepted the fact that this is our fate." I gesture to us, around the room, to the house and beyond, and to our children out by the bonfire. "How about we scrub a little bit of the tarnish off our souls before we go any further tonight."

"Royce?" Willa's voice pitches high with fear, knowing exactly where I'm leading.

"Every time we've laid together, you were either my brother's wife, or high out of your mind, sneaking around with me. It wasn't right, and you deserved better."

Eyes scrunched tight against the threat of tears, "It's what I wanted," she breathes, choking on her words.

"I know. Me too." Unbiddenly, my cheek is rubbing against the tip of her nose, comforting the both of us. "I wanted you, consequences be damned. But it's time we do this right. From now on."

Shifting up onto my elbows, I make sure I'm not pressing down onto her. "Willamina *Gillette*, would you do me the honor of calling me your husband? Will you be my partner in crime, old man that I am? Will you take the name you already own? Will you drag me around Rusty Knob by the balls and tell me to knock my shit off when I start acting like a judgmental, self-righteous prick?"

Choking on a laugh and a sob, Willa's eyes are bright with wonder.

"What?" I tip my chin, trying hard not to laugh. "Did you expect a bunch of romantic bullshit? You're blunt like a ballpeen hammer, girl. I expected you'd appreciate the down and dirty of realism." I tilt my head to the side, taking in how beautiful this creature is, and I'm all hers. "I can do better, though."

Raising a blonde eyebrow in challenge, "Oh, yeah?"

"Oh. Yeah, I can." I nod my head rapidly, silent laughter flowing from between my lips. "How's this? You're a stubborn succubus who stole my soul the moment I looked at ya. In fact, I've sold my soul a dozen times since, and I'd do so again and again until the day I die."

"That's so much better." Willa snickers. "So flattering."

I grip her tiny chin with two fingertips. "How's this?" I lean down to steal a quick kiss, not even giving her time to pucker up. In a serious voice, I tell the God's honest truth. "Winding road of a journey or not. I've never wanted anything more than to be your husband, the father of your children. To protect, nurture, and teach you and yours, and have you protect, nurture, and teach me and mine. To walk this earth at your side. In our olden years, to sit in a pair of rocking chairs on the porch, shouting at the hoodlum grandchildren and great-grandchildren we created. And to share my last breath with you."

Eyes glued to the water blue gazing up at me, my fingertips flick the box open and fish out the ring. "Willamina Kennedy, would you do me the honor of becoming my wife, simply because I love you."

Nodding her head up and down rapidly, unable to speak, tears are splattering my cheeks from both her eyes and mine– tears of happiness. "I'll take that as a yes. Not that I'm surprised." I pluck the ring I bought her nearly a decade ago. "I was buying Donny a watch just a few weeks after I met you, and I saw this ring and some supernatural force compelled me to buy it."

"That long ago?" Willa draws out the words, awe lacing her voice. "The first thought in my head when you walked into Donny's house was that Daddy hitched me to the wrong Kennedy. I would have gladly taken it like a dog with you. Hell, I was going nuts over the thought."

Barking a sharp laugh, I drop the ring in the bedclothes. I have to rut around for it while bubbles of amusement make my movements jerky. "We'll be doing that later tonight– that's the one position we've never tried."

"Hurry up and get that ring on me, Royce-baby," Willa taunts me, fingers joining the search. "You're killing me."

"Woohoo!" I release a whoop in victory when my fingertips pluck the ring up from the quilt. With shaking hands I locate Willa's ring finger, and try several times unsuccessfully to slip the ring on her.

Being impatient, Willa sneaks in and slips it on herself. Without looking at the ring, because that's the type of woman she is– the type I need –Willa stares up at me with crystal clear eyes filled with clarity, no longer fogged by substance and fear.

"Do you know why I want to marry you?" She asks, waiting for me to respond before continuing, but all I can do is smile in reply. "I want to be your wife because living a life without you in it wouldn't be worth living at all."

Curling my palms against her cheeks, "Willa," I cry out, aching for her because the tone of her voice was pure agony.

"I've lived without you, needing you, wanting you, longing to be with you, and that made me appreciate how perfect it is now even if everything falls to shit. I'll always remember the pain of separation, and that will force me to never take anything for granted."

With surprising strength, Willa reverses our positions, always wanting to be on top. We're both panting softly from the struggle, but I never really put up much of a fight. Straddling my hips, finding her favorite place to sit– grinding my engorged dick in a painful way –Willa inspects the ring on her finger.

Expression blank, Willa stares at the ring. After a moment, she bites her lip and tries to stop her mouth from quirking up in confusion.

So I put her out of her misery. "You don't strike me as a girl who likes something flashy. I mean, obviously I could afford to buy you the biggest rock I could find, but it wouldn't mean anything."

Staring at the old, worn infinity band circling her ring finger, Willa contemplates my words, but she doesn't get it yet.

"Most baubles start out shiny and brand new, and they age with use and become worthless." I rub at the ring on Willa's dainty finger, showing her how it will shine brightly one day. "With this ring, the years will rub the tarnish away, leaving behind pristine metal. The longer we're together, the more valuable the ring becomes and the stronger we'll be."

Expecting an, "*Oh, Royce,*" in a girly voice filled with adoration, I get attacked instead. I laugh through the mauling, lips being pried open by a very demanding tongue. With inhuman strength, the woman pins my wrists to the bed so I can't retaliate without hurting her. Riding my hips, struggling to keep me pinned, Willa bites and nips and sucks at my face.

"Down, girl," I gasp into her mouth, surviving the attack. "Let me kiss ya back, for Christ's sake."

"Uh-huh," vibrates against my bottom lip, then teeth sink into my flesh, causing me to jackknife off the mattress. Willa head-butts me back down until I'm spread out flat on the mattress. "You be a good patient, and let Dr. Feelgood take care of ya."

"Oh, my God!" I shout against Willa's mouth, her teeth trying to latch onto my tongue. "You're fucking nuts." She captures my tongue and starts sucking it in a salacious manner, lips pulling in a rhythmic pattern. My cock starts to throb in time with the pull of her mouth. It's a move I know all too well from back when she'd wake me up on nights she snuck into my room for a rough ride. She always greeted me with a set of lips wrapped around my cock– either from her mouth or her pussy.

I pretend to fight back a bit, half-assed lifting my arms up, wiggling around the mattress, kicking my feet, kneeing Willa in the ass, and growling while trying to bite her tongue, because that's what she likes. Willa gets off on conquering me, the little minx.

"Stay still," she warns in a sultry voice, and I listen. I'm thoroughly enjoying this fucked up game we play, because I know I'm the only person on the planet she'd ever trust enough or be comfortable with doing this. I freeze my muscles, watching her body language for hints on what's coming next.

Letting go of my wrists, lifting to sit astride my hips, "Good boy," she praises me. The lips may be moving, but my eyes dart to her fingertips. Deftly unbuttoning her white blouse– the woman wears white all year long, every single day. Virginal white. After slowly popping button after button, driving me fucking insane, she parts her blouse down the middle, exposing her bra and the tiny tits hidden beneath.

Flicking the front closure on her bra, Willa bounces on my lap, tearing a, "No fair," from my parted lips. Panting, I suffer through the severe grind of her ass on my dick and the way her titties jounce when she bobs up and down. "You're doing that on purpose," I whisper breathlessly. "No fair."

"Don't pop in your pants, old man." Willa taunts me, smirking while grinding with evil intent. "I can feel your willy dancing, and your recovery time probably sucks."

"Hey, I'm not *that* old." My hands retaliate, flashing out to grip a palmful of tit. Groaning, cock jerking in happiness, I get a few squeezes in before she's swatting my hands away like a pesky fly. "No fair," I pout, resting my palms on the mattress.

"Good boy." Willa rewards me by not closing her blouse. She runs her palms underneath my t-shirt, grazing my bare skin. "You were always a fast learner." My nipples get tugged playfully between questing fingertips, and try as I might, the succubus can feel my reaction. "Mmm… somebody always pretends they don't like me torturing their nips, but the willy in your pants never lies."

"Free my willy," I mutter lamely, receiving an eye roll for my efforts. "From my pants."

Willa chuckles, "Dumbass," underneath her breath, but I feel it's a win since I got her to smile.

There's no two ways about it; it's been over a year since we touched like this, and many, many years since we touched in a healthy way. It's why we held off, spending time building intimacy through a brush of a touch, a whisper in an ear, holding hands. It was always rushed before, and painful in the aftermath.

So if Willa wants to taunt and tease me, turn this playful or violent, I'm going to let her. But we'll be ending the night making love and falling asleep in each other's arms, and waking up together for the first time in our lives. It's a lot of pressure, and I fear I'll disappoint.

"Do whatever you want to me," I offer. "My mind, body, heart, and soul belongs to you."

Smiling wryly down at me, "I think I better take good care of it, because I don't want to wear it out."

"Ah-ha-ha-ha…" I mock-laugh. "The old fogey jokes never get old."

Willa's laugh is a real one, tinged with naughtiness. "Let's free that willy, shall we?"

"We shall." I become super helpful, lifting up so Willa can pull my t-shirt off my back. With the flick of her wrist, it lands somewhere in the vicinity of the bathroom door. I get a bit overexcited when her palm grazes my hard-on as her fingers work the button and zipper on my jeans. It's a struggle, but as soon as fresh air caresses my dick, I don't give two shits that my jeans just hit the bedroom door— Willa's got an arm on her.

Panting, biting back a *please*, in slow perusal, Willa's gaze skims over my body. When her eyes light on my cock, the little guy jerks up, trying to get at her, begging like an eager puppy. Fists clenching in the quilt, toes curling, I lock my muscles down from reacting, because all I want to do is pounce on the woman and get inside her. Now.

A pitiful, "Please," slips out before I can stop it. "Touch me."

"Ask and you shall receive." A sweet kiss is placed against my lips, but it vanishes as quickly as it arrives. But I'm not disappointed, because Willa's lips pass over my nose, dampen my forehead with her breath, and then dip down along my jawline to my neck. Her teeth nipping every few inches on their journey, I wiggle around restlessly, unable to contain the pleasure.

"Jesus Christ," I cry out when her teeth latch onto my left nipple. "Harder!" I shout, needing more than the tip of her tongue teasing at the bud.

Sleight of hand, Willa's mouth occupies me so I don't notice her fingertips twisting in my chest hair until it's too late. With a sharp yank, I grunt in pain. A few hairs snap off from the force.

Pre-cum drips out the tip of my dick to dampen my belly, and if he likes it, I decide I must as well. "I liked that." Breathlessly gasping for air, I press my chest into her palm. "Do it again."

Leaning forward, Willa whispers against my lips. "It's about the element of surprise, Royce-baby."

Neck arching, I release, "Demon spawn from Hell!" when my nuts get twisted. Delicate skin fisted in her palm, it only lasted a split-second, but the pain was unbearable. "Yell *surprise* next time before you do that," I turn surly.

The burning pain slowly recedes, spreading to other parts of my body. In its wake is an intense, tingly sensation. I can even feel the movement of air caressing my balls, I'm that sensitive.

Turning boneless, eyelashes fluttering, the only part of my body at attention is my dick. Voice thick, I slur, "I've missed you and your depraved ways, Willamina." Completely relaxed, I melt into the mattress. "I think I needed that."

Willa hovers over me, but I don't have the energy to take over just yet. I tilt my chin, silently begging for a kiss. "Mmm…" I moan. Parting my lips, my tongue darts out to mingle with hers. We take our time, leisurely kissing. No harshness. All soft and welcoming. The texture of taste buds scouring my lips, the inside of my cheek, then the roof of my mouth is a surprising stimulant.

Feeling adventurous since I already had my balls squished, my fingertips venture up Willa's supple inner thigh as we kiss. Hiking up her skirt, I skate my fingers along the seat of her panties, dipping in when I find a bunch in the elastic.

Willa whimpers against my lips as I tug the seat of her panties to the side, exposing her damp heat. Opening her mouth wider on a moan, my tongue darts in at the same time my fingertip traces along her slit, slowly parting her nether lips.

Returning the favor, I tug sharply at the girly hair between her thighs, and Willa has a similar reaction. Pressing into my palm, she grinds her pussy against my fingertips. "More," she moans. "Harder."

The sound of her voice combined with her sneaky hand headed toward my dick, has me barking out, "Don't touch it!" I breathe through the need to come, praying that the wash on my belly is only pre-cum and not the real deal.

Impatient, I focus all of my energy in divesting Willa of her panties. Ripping the fabric off her ass, I toss it, not caring where it lands.

"Gimme those lips," I rasp, not sure which set I'm begging to touch. Willa takes away my indecision by kissing me roughly and pressing my palm between her legs. The woman never had any shame when it came to taking what she wanted. "You're so damn hot deep inside."

Flipping around with amazing speed, or maybe it's because my sluggish, lust-filled mind can't keep up, Willa rotates and lands on top of me. Stunned, all I can do is stare at the fuzzy pussy inches from my chin.

"Well, we've never done this before," I murmur in surprise, cock totally down for it. Gripping the firm globes of Willa's perfect ass, I spread her nether lips with my fingertips, revealing the delicious pink core. I'm eagerly diving in with a groan before Willa can even fasten her lips around my cock.

Stimulation overload, I never thought pleasure could hurt. It's too much, too soon. The intoxicating scent and taste of Willa combined with the sensation of my cock rubbing against the roof of her mouth and her wicked tongue flicking the tip, I'm unable to concentrate on what I'm doing because I'm a heartbeat away from emptying my sack down Willa's throat.

"Tell me I'm the best you've ever had." Willa demands in a husky voice that's dripping with the need for validation. Her mouth is no longer wrapped around my dick. She's pressing her face into the crook where my thigh meets my groin. Her words vibrate against my nutsack. Desperate, "Tell me. Lie to me if you have to."

Head popping up, I try to look at Willa, but her ass is in the way. "I'll never lie to you," I vow. "I'm not comparing you to Annie. *Ever.* Especially not today." Thumbs parting her pussy hair, my tongue darts in to lave her button. Circling her clit with the flat of my tongue, Willa wiggles around on my chest. "It wasn't the same, being married to Annie, because you're not Annie and Annie's not you. There is no comparison."

Distracting her, because I can practically scent Willa's hurt flavoring the air, my tongue glides from her clit to asshole in one long swipe. Then I stab her pussy nice and deep a few times, getting her wetter and wetter with my saliva.

"But if you're concerned about sex…" I lean up a bit, wrapping my lips around her clit, and then I suck as hard as I can. Willa's grunt of surprise is payment enough. "Ninety percent of anything we've ever done, was the first time I've ever done it. Including this position right now, Willa. So never feel insecure. Okay?"

"Okay," Willa whispers, and I can't stand how unsure of herself she sounds.

"Succubus?" I slap her ass firmly, getting off on how the flesh jiggles. "Where did my confident succubus go? Hmm?" Hands gliding down the sides of her spine, I rub her back, her hips, and decide I prefer her ass. "You're not Annie's replacement, Willamina. That thought has never crossed my mind. You're you, and I don't expect you to be anything else. I fell in love with you, bad diction, stubbornness, flaws and all."

"I speak proper English now," Willa grumbles, but I can hear the smile in her voice. I must have done or said something right, but hell if I know what, because she starts nuzzling at my dick with the tip of her nose.

Deciding it's funny and not tarnishing Annie's memory, I let Willa on to a little secret. "You were right about the drunken blowjobs. Remember?"

"Holy shit." Willa whips around to look at me with huge blue eyes. "I was right? I was just taking a stab in the dark with that one."

Chuckling underneath my breath, I say more than I should. "The only time oral was on the menu was if I could get two bottles of wine into Annie, and sometimes that was still a no-go. This is my first sixty-nine–" and *I wish it wasn't being interrupted*, I mentally add. "She liked slow and steady. The only position was missionary, with her legs flat on the mattress and her hands on my shoulders." I feel like I'm betraying Annie's memory, but I can't stop the words from tumbling out of my mouth. "I loved Annie. She was my best friend. My wife. Brennan's momma. But there was no spark in the bedroom, and we both knew it. It wasn't important to her, so I pretended it didn't matter to me."

Willa's sad eyes are bleeding *I'm so sorry*.

"Since the day I met you, no matter how depraved it was, being around you was like being lit up by a livewire. I knew I was going to be consumed, but I couldn't wait to catch on fire."

Back arching off the mattress, this time I know I said the right thing. Willa swallows my dick whole– to the root. Another first for me. "Jesus Christ, woman. You better git to riding my face before I blow my load."

Pussy hair tickling at my chin, my succubus is back. Completely shameless, Willa grinds against my lips as she works my shaft with the expertise of a well-seasoned whore. I feel the need to drop down to my knees and pray to God for gifting this creature to me.

Dick throbbing for release, it gives a few warning spurts of pre-cum. Understanding my body as well as I do, Willa slips off my dick with a loud slurp. Chuckling, I go back to my feast between her legs, tongue-fucking the hell out of her pussy.

Balls captured in the warmth of Willa's mouth, "Yeah, you do that," I encourage breathlessly. Bending at the knee, I can't stop my thighs from spreading as far as they will go while seesawing back and forth in pleasure. Thrusting my hips up and down to get Willa's tongue to drag over my sack, my dick bounces on my belly.

Lost to the pleasure, it's too late before I'm barking, "Willa, don't!"

Drunk on lust and power, Willa's voice is slurred. "You licked me there. Fair's fair."

"Don't," I warn firmly. "I'm scarred down there." Nails biting into Willa's thighs, of course she ignores me. "Please stop," I beg of her.

"Royce, *yes*." Willa uses her momma voice on me. "Every inch of your body belongs to me, and that bastard is not going to haunt you anymore. I'm going to take the hurt away and leave an impression of me on your skin."

Eyes slipping shut, I clench my lids, unable to stop Willa, even when I tell her no. Counting backward, I try not to conjure all those who came before Willa– an endless stream of doctors and nurses stitching me up, cleaning my wounds, and every humiliation imaginable. But before them came Sean, leaving scars after ruining me with his body and with my granddaddy's truncheon.

It's just Willa. It's just Willa. It's just Willa. I repeat as I try to ignore the insistent tongue flicking along my taint, not quite having the balls to venture to my scars. Fists clenched, I relax into it. I was so far gone I hadn't realized Willa was slowly stroking my cock in time with the flick of her tongue.

Tears dampening my sideburns, I give in, knowing to hold back is to prolong this agony. Tilting my hips, I spread my legs farther apart to give Willa more space to work with. Taking my acquiescence as permission, her tongue dips into me.

Teeth gritted, fists clenched, I try to concentrate on the small things: the warmth of the saliva trailing down my crack. The way Willa's breasts sway against my torso with her movements, pebbled nipples etching at my skin. The soothing rhythm of her tongue swirling in a pattern along my scar tissue.

"Willa!" I shriek when her fingertip goes where it shouldn't.

"Shh… relax," she coaxes. "I'll never hurt you. You know that. You're just afraid."

"I'm not afraid," I mutter petulantly, and Willa laughs against my skin.

Ignoring all sensation, my mind goes on repeat again. *It's just Willa. It's just Willa. Sean is dead because Corbin is your hero. Wait! What? I didn't mean that. It's just Willa. It's just Willa. Jesus Christ, I do owe that bastard a thank you, for at least giving me Wynn. Definitely for giving me Willa. Okay, for saving my life. It's just Willa.*

"Royce? You're thinking so loud I can hear you," Willa breaks into my insane ramblings. "How are we doing here? We good?"

"Huh?" I grunt, then I realize why she's asking as sensation slowly filters back in. My body freezes, thinking it should freak out, but it's too late. Willa already has two fingers shoved deep inside my ass, and she's slowly but surely stroking me like she's coaxing a kitten.

"How scarred am I?" spills out before I can stop it, curiosity getting the better of me.

"No clue." Willa's fingers wiggle around experimentally. It feels odd, but not bad. My flesh burns but it feels full in a good way. My skin gets all shivery the more she moves her fingertips. "I've never done this before, so I don't have another asshole to gauge it against." Snickering loudly. "C'mon, old man. Even you gotta see the humor in that."

"Ha-ha," I mock-laugh, but then it warps into a sound of true amusement. "Okay, pretty sure you've cured me of the fear of my own asshole."

I have no idea what possesses me, but I reach down to grip my balls. Groaning, I decide I rather like that, especially mixed with whatever the hell she's got going on down there and her tiny hand fisting my cock. Randomly squeezing my sack, I wait Willa out. Tipping my chin forward, I try to reach the sweet pussy in my line of sight, but it's just out of reach. A drip of arousal hanging off her girly hair has me whimpering in need.

"I think…" Willa's breathless. "You're really, really soft– and fucking hot," she mutters wryly. "Like a goddamned furnace. But a few ridges near the outside aren't soft, so I guess those are your scars. I can see some on the outside where you were stitched up, and I kinda like how they felt underneath my tongue."

Gripping my balls tighter, I might not have liked how they felt under her tongue, but I like that she liked it. "Dr. Feelgood? You about finished down there?"

"Yeah, okay." Shifting, her knee bumps me in the side. "We should do this again sometime."

Grunting deep from my chest, my, *"Definitely not,"* is cut off when Willa rotates her fingers as she pulls out. Gripping my balls even tighter, I close my eyes and pray, *"Whatever the hell that was, please make sure Willa didn't notice."*

But it's Willa, so of course she fucking noticed.

My stomach muscles lock up on the second pass. By the third pass, I'm biting my lip to contain a moan. Shivering, my entire body lights on fire. My dick feels so full I fear it will burst. By the tenth pass, I can't come on her hand. A man has got to have some pride.

"Oh, God," I breathe through the need as I yank her fingers from my body. With speed I didn't know I possessed, I'm picking Willa up and tossing her ass at the foot of the bed. "It's high-time you learned what doggie-style really is, little girl."

My dick is lined up and sheathed deep inside Willa's body in an instant. Willa's keen warping into a grunt is the most satisfying sound I've ever heard. Knees levered on the edge of the bed, hands gripping tightly at Willa's waist, I pound her into the mattress.

With every thrust in she grunts sharply, with every thrust out she moans deeply, and in between she has to relearn how to breathe. Willa's fingertips are twisting into the quilt as she tries to hang on during the onslaught.

Headboard pounding against the wall, my teeth are chattering with the force. "Oh. My. Fucking. God." Willa's words vibrate with our movements, sounding like she's humming into a fan. I reduce my woman to a begging, pleading wanton creature, and it makes me feel like a goddamned man. "Don't stop! Don't stop! I'm so close! Don't stop!"

I stop.

"You're Satan." Willa's awed voice reaches my ears as I roll her over onto her back and crawl between her thighs. "Pure evil. I was having a good time."

Chuckling, I slide into her slowly, luxuriating in the silky feel of her body surrounding mine. "Fucking is fun, but I'm not going to cum inside you like that– at least not tonight." Propped up on my elbows, I brush the hair off her forehead with my fingertips. "I'm warning you that I'm gonna last like three thrusts, but I wanted to do it face-to-face at least."

Lips curling sweetly at the corners, I expect something girly, something romantic to flow from Willa's mouth. "My clit is vibrating and my pussy feels different inside, like when I come I'm gonna die."

Unable to stop myself, I roll my eyes in response.

Flexing my thighs, we moan together. Flexing my thighs again, I add some hip action to the mix, and it feels even better. Not one to sit back and be ridden, Willa wraps her legs around my waist, anchoring her heels into my ass. Then the claws come out— fingernails forcing me to thrust deeper. Harder.

"That's three," I grunt through gritted teeth. "I lasted longer than I thought." Eyes glittering with silent laughter, Willa and I reach a height together like never before.

Willa chooses the oddest time to finally tell me. Voice thick with emotion, tears dotting her flushed cheeks, "I love you, Royce. I love you so much it scares me."

There's no doubt in my mind she truly means it. I never had to hear her say the words because I just felt it to my core. It's like, the sky is blue, the grass is green, I love Willa and she loves me.

Good God, I'm the romantic in the relationship.

Fully connected in all ways, we both let go with wild abandon, and I'm terrified the kids can hear us two stories down below, outside the house, and all the way into their tents.

"S'up, boss man?" Warren calls to me as I lurk around the old pharmacy, which is now his domain as the shop. "It's been a good first day, eh?"

"Yeah." My head nods up and down, mulling over how surprised I am. "Penny's been busy in the Welcome Center. A lot of people came pouring in to sign up for different classes. She's also taking suggestions."

Crouched next to a five-gallon bucket, Warren beams up at me with pride. "I think it's the mascot." I wait, having no idea what he's talking about, while he places a few tools in the bucket. "Copper, dummy. Everyone's coming in to see my beautiful boy."

"Yep. Right you are, War. Right you are." Chuckling, my eyes dart about, looking for someone. "It has nothing to do with getting a proper education to tackle life."

Light skin blushing bright pink, Warren's blue eyes practically glow with happiness. "Copper is manning the suggestion box. Nobody can resist a chubby baby, so we're getting loads of suggestions."

"Ah!" Feeling warm inside my heart. "Yeah, the little guy nabbed me too— suave feller ya got there. I almost filled out a card. You'll be beating the girls off with a stick. So… what's on your agenda for the afternoon?"

"Well." Warren blows out a deep breath, wiping a hand across his brow. "Since I showed Kade how to change his oil, and only Hayden took to the instruction, I figured a lot of townsfolk don't know squat about auto maintenance— something about higher education pushing basic skills from your brain."

A loud snort ricochets around the shop. "Asshole," Kade says as he strides in. "You're a piss-poor teacher."

Warren and I share a loaded look. Kade. God love him. He is dumber than a box of rocks until you beat the knowledge into his head. Repeatedly. With the instruction manual. But once he learns something, he never forgets.

"You didn't tell me to put the pan underneath the car before I pulled the plug." Kade gestures wildly, face bright red with embarrassment. "Oil. Every-fucking-where. It was like the motherfucking Exxon Valdez. I went into wildlife protection mode."

"Not my fault!" Warren shouts while I murmur, "Common sense is not your strong suit."

"Yeah… well, I'ma tackle that bitchin' task this time around." Kade puffs out his very large chest, looking intimidating as all hell. "I'll be the best dang grease monkey Mechanic Franklin has ever seen. He'll be ditching his asshole son-in-law and taking me on to apprentice. I'll prove I can do it all. Getting my Master's yet knowing a trade."

Baying like a wild animal, Warren loses his shit. "Bro, shut the fuck up. I'm gonna piss my pants laughing." The bucket overturns in the commotion. "Just stop. Go back to pushing your papers."

"Rat-bastard," Kade grumbles. Stomping back to his office, a pair of Chucks doesn't have the same effect as his usual Wolverines. He's pounding extra hard, and gets frustrated. "Ahhhhh!" he shouts. "Fuck you!"

"Ain't ya glad you got him at sixteen?" Warren smirks at me. "That's the best he can do for an adult temper tantrum. When he was five years old…"

"Good Lord." My eyes bug out imagining a kid with gangly uncontrollable arms and legs pitching a fit. "You get that it's people like Kade who need the Life Skills Center the most, right? We just tell the townies it's for the hillfolk."

"We best keep that a secret," Warren says with a wink.

Eyes darting around, I look into the Welcome Center, and then peer into the Study Lab. "Have you seen your sister around anywhere?"

"In The Kitchen with a smile on her face and a hitch in her step. You did good, boss man." Warren flashes a naughty grin at me and waggles his eyebrows. "I'd suggest the pantry. It's nice and dark, and has a lock. Be forewarned: if you don't see me or Penny around, enter at your own risk."

"The Life Skills Center has a fuck booth?" I mull that over, liking the sounds of that. "Good to know." I wander away with The Kitchen as my destination. "Good to know."

The Study Lab is dark and appears to be empty as I enter, but as I get farther into the room, a high-pitched voice filters to my ears. Looking around at all the desks, peeking behind the bookshelves, checking out the seating area, I see nothing.

"What the hell?" The Study Lab used to be the insurance office, so it's just as deep as every other building on the block. Checking out all the nooks and crannies, it's always the last place you look.

Huddled together at the desk in the far back corner, used for people who can't study without isolation, I find Brennan and Jack talking to a laptop.

"Dude, pan your webcam around and show us your room," Jack's demanding.

"Did you just call me dude, sugar?" A tiny voice reverberates from the laptop speakers. "A dude? I'm a queen."

"Just do it." Bren's voice contains an eye roll. "I'm living vicariously through your *Big Gay College Dorm Life*."

"I like the sounds of that. I'll have to do webcasts for a new reality show." Creeping up behind them silently, I peer over their shoulders. "For you–" Franny is sitting at a desk with a cinderblock wall at his back. He spots me and smiles but doesn't tell the boys. "For you, sugar, I'll do anything."

Panning his camera slowly, Francis shows us his dorm room. Two twin beds. Two dressers. Two desks. Two wardrobes. Nothing different than any other dorm room. Half the walls are covered in Pride propaganda and feather boas, and the other half is covered with poster-sized book covers featuring half-naked men and a huge dry-erase board with a detailed schedule.

"I'm guessing your roommate is a gay English major who is anal retentive," Jack observes for me, but his voice is flat, like he's jealous. "How'd ya manage that feat?"

"Spot on!" Franny is glowing from the screen when the camera pans back to him. "Sage is most definitely gay, an English major, has a stick up his ass about being on time and doing your best, but he sure is pretty as a picture."

"Got a picture?" Bren leans closer like he can spot one on the desk somewhere.

Lips twisting up deviously, Franny's eyes twitch between Bren and Jack. "I ended up with Sage Fischer because they dump the gay kids together, fearing we'll infect the straight kiddies, and it terrifies their mommas and daddies."

"Assholes," Jack mutters. "West Virginia U just pretends we don't exist. I wouldn't have roomed there if Wynn wasn't."

"I lucked out. Sage and I were named The Queen and The Twink. Everyone is very sweet to us. Helps because his family is real big in medicine and politics. His uncle is some low-level politician scumbag."

"Eww," Bren and Jack say in unison while I grimace.

"It gets worse," flows a soft voice, and then the sound of the door closing warbles the speaker. "The Sages of Massachusetts are right-wing conservative Christians. I'm real fun at cocktail parties for the Catholic hospital."

We get the view of a purple shirt as the kid comes into view. "Hi, I'm Sage Fischer. I'm gay. And I'm a liberal," he announces with obvious pleasure, no doubt his practiced, standard greeting to rub his family wrong.

We all lean forward, waiting for the roommate to come into focus. Tiny with delicate features, he's beautiful. Skinny as a rail, the kid sits down next to Franny, sharing the same seat.

Bren and Jack lean in closer, looking awed and murmuring odd noises from their chests that I wish I could remove from my ears. Clearly this Sage kid is a ten, judging by the boys' reactions.

Grin showcasing perfect white teeth, the kid musses up his white hair while a blush creeps up his cheeks. "You're giving me an ego," he purrs, and it's creepy how seductive he sounds.

"How much time do you spend on your hair every day, pretty boy?" Jack turns feral. "Your shirt costs more than my car."

Pointing at his roommate, "Sage rolls outta bed like that," Franny bursts Jack's bubble. "No joke. I've got a case of the green-eyed monster."

"Conservative family, remember?" Hurt mars the kid's expression. "It means we have money but we don't spend it. My mom only allows me to have seven shirts, three pairs of pants, and two pairs of shorts. Plus the five suits and the tux. Opal Fischer might be a Mensa member, but she underestimated me. She forgot to put a monetary cap on my wardrobe. But Mom fell for a shopaholic– Ginny. So my other mom sneaks me goodies."

"Nice," Bren drawls. There's a deep flush creeping up the back of his neck that freaks my ass out. "Very nice."

"Mmm… this one here will grow up to be a fine looking manly man." He points at Bren while eyeing me, obviously knowing I'm the daddy.

Jack winces, jerking backward like he was just slapped. Lurching forward again, he growls at the laptop screen.

"Put your claws away, tiger." Sage curls his fingers and scratches the air. "I'm taken. And none of you are my type." Stretching, shifting closer to the screen, Sage holds our undivided attention. "I can't go home for like… seven years. Statute of Limitations. Can't besmirch the impeccable Sage surname."

"What'd you do?" Jack and Bren say in unison, and I fight back the urge to speak myself.

"My sort-of-boyfriend is blond, blue-eyed, cute as a button, and glows like the sun. He's six-four, two-hundred pounds of boy-next-door. He's Fairport's rising star on the football field. But he's also the Chief of Police's baby boy."

"And?" Jack's getting impatient, and so am I.

"Massachusetts isn't Pennsyltucky," Sage says with an evil smirk.

"West Virginia, ya prissy douchebag," Jack snarls, but it only sparks the kid to keep riling us up.

"Pennsyltucky. West Virginia. Same difference." Insert menacing eyebrow raise. The kid is a consummate actor. "I just turned eighteen five days ago. Let's just say I want to be an English teacher, Chief Malcolm Mason has a major hard-on for the law, and Massachusetts has very strict age of consent laws. I have to stay out of the state until Chief Mason's anger subsides, or I won't be able to teach if I have to stay so many feet from a school zone."

"Dude, what did you do?" Bren gets impatient this time.

"Seriously, stop saying dude!" Franny bitches through the screen. "You're not a *bro*. You can't pull it off."

Sharing a laugh with his roommate, Sage decides to put us out of our misery. "Even though I've known the kid for five years, it's technically child molestation to accept the gift of a fifteen-year-old's virginity on your eighteenth birthday, even if he's the one holding you down on the mattress and a blink away from sixteen."

"Bullshit," I snarl, making myself known. "Total bullshit."

"I knew you were there." Bren leans back into me. "I've got Dad-dar."

"It's not bullshit." Sage nods his head up and down rapidly. "Trust me. I'm well-educated on the age of consent laws in my state."

"Nah, Sage." Bren leans forward again. "Dad believes ya. He's saying bullshit 'cuz he fell for a fifteen-year-old child bride and it turned him into an idiot. 'Round here, no one gives two shits unless you're gay."

"Ah, well…" Sage points at Franny's rainbow walls, and then at himself. "That's an issue for me, too."

"Hang in there, kid." Since I can't pat Sage on the shoulder, I rest my hands on Jack's and Brennan's instead. "Let the feller grow up some. His daddy will come around."

"*Damn*," Sage mouths. "That accent."

"Down boy," I chastise him, blush riding my cheeks because I'm flattered. "This old man has got to go find his woman."

"God, love a caveman," Sage's voice follows me as I walk away. "Franny says this one is bi," no doubt talking about Brennan. "Some guy ought to snag him before the breeders do. He's gonna age like fine wine."

Striding into the building we dubbed The Kitchen, still blushing like crazy, I find the rest of my family digging into some grub. Hayley and Hayden are fisting sandwiches while sitting on stools at the counter, their feet kicking at the lower cabinets. Kade and Wynn are shoveling chips by the handfuls, sharing a whispered conversation.

… And Willa. Back turned to the room, she's humming to herself while organizing ingredients for this evening's class on bread baking. She's wearing a virginal white dress, and my heart starts beating in my dick.

Announcing my arrival, "Bren and Jack have Franny on Skype." I hitch my thumb over my shoulder. "You better go check out his roommate."

"Sweet!" Wynn drawls, dropping the chip bag and charging out of the kitchen. Kade's on Wynn's heels, but he's being slowed down by two kids trying to overtake him.

Squealing, "Franny!" Hayley's super excited to see her friend again. Francis was always really patient with the kids, especially Hayley. She liked to be dressed up like a living doll. Hayden wanted nothing to do with it, except to document the humiliation on film.

"You sure do know how to clear a room, Mr. Kennedy." Turning to face me, Willa's smirking. "So, tell me about the roommate. Ah! You're blushing."

We both hitch our heads to the side when a "*Damn!*" flows in from the room next door.

"Pretty sure that was Kade. He always did have a thing for twinks. Never could understand his fixation with Wynn, seeing as how he's the total opposite of one." Blush deepening, I clear my throat. "Yeah, we should have followed them in there and watched the drama unfold. I'm positive Kade and Wynn are exactly that flirty kid's type."

Lips quirking up at the corners, "Coming onto ya, was he?" Willa sashays toward me, white dress swaying around her hips. I just back up, allowing her to think she's herding me to the pantry. "I've missed you."

"Have ya, now?" I reach behind me blindly to twist the knob. "I missed being inside ya, Mrs. Kennedy."

Eyes sharp, stalking me like a predator, Willa traps me in the pantry. "I think we could remedy that, Mr. Kennedy." My audible swallow is loud in the quiet pantry.

Allowing Willa to feel powerful, to feel in control like she's won, I stand in the dark room, watching as she shuts us in and locks the door. Then I pounce.

"Uh!" a grunt is torn from Willa's chest when I pin her face-first against the door. Stunned frozen, I use the opportunity to fetch both of her fragile wrists in one of my palms. Arms raised over head, her dress hikes up. Knee parting her thighs, I press into her.

Lips fluttering at her ear, "Welcome to the fuck booth, Mrs. Kennedy," flows, flicking her *on* switch. Free hand fishing between us, my fingertips hook into her panties. *Rip.* Willa jerks with the force but she remains completely silent.

"You're never allowed to wear pants," I rasp against her ear, then give it a little lick. Wiggling against my chest, Willa turns liquid. "And I'm seriously debating on never replacing your underwear."

"Hurry up!" Willa pants, turning impatient. Her ass grinds into me, always trying to usurp control. The push and pull struggle between us is what keeps it interesting. Using my free hand, I try to tear at my fly. "If I gotta wear a dress, you better invest in some workout pants."

"You're so smart," I mutter breathlessly, complimenting her. "We'll hit Amazon in a few minutes. But first–" Zipper down, I reach in, tugging my boxers out of the way to free my willy.

Surging forward, ass flexing, I thrust my hips, driving my cock home. "Ahhh!" Willa and I moan together, relieved after being apart for five excruciatingly long hours. Shivering, my body falls lax, all of my weight pressing Willa against the door.

Taking my time, my hand roves up the front of Willa's body. Her dress tickles at my forearm. Palm cupping first one tit, and then the other, I take my fill. I'm not rough, knowing her nipples are abraded from last night and this morning.

"Are you sore?" I swivel my hips, dick getting sucked by her lady parts, making sure she knows what I'm curious about.

"Yes," Willa breathes back, but then she counterthrusts. Hard. My dick bottoms out, cockhead smashing deep inside her. "But I love how alive it makes me feel. That little edge of pain makes the pleasure more intense."

With a smile in my voice, "That's my girl," I sing.

Using her raised arms as leverage, I release my passion for Willa that I usually have to contain and dampen. Legs spread wide, I force up into her over and over again. Her fingers curl around my thumb, nails branding my skin.

Hand leaving her tiny breast, I cup her mound with my palm. Hoisting her up by the pussy, I slip a finger deep inside right alongside my cock. I fuck the living daylights out of Willa, pressing her face to the door to quiet the animalistic sounds pouring from her throat.

Unable to last, I'm pouring when the first of Willa's spasms suck at my cock. Trying to ride out our orgasms in silence, the only sound escaping is our labored breath and the scratch of Willa's nails on the door.

"I'll build my stamina back up," I promise. I pull free of Willa's body, shuddering as her constricting muscles try to recapture me. "We went too long without." Tucking myself back in, I take a step back to give Willa some room.

She rolls from her front to rest her back on the door. Completely boneless, Willa sprawls, not caring about my semen running in rivulets down her inner thighs.

Dropping to my knees, the tile floor jarring me, I press my mouth to her girly bits and get to cleaning up my own mess. I lick her thighs clean first, then I spread her wide open with my fingertips. Mouth latched, I suck at her opening until all I taste is her essence. Tongue curling around her clit, Willa breaks apart again. Head rocking back and forth against the door, stifling her cries she bites her own fist.

Once the last shudder passes, I pull away, seeking her discarded panties. "What was that?" Willa's voice is rough, throaty. Blushing, I wipe my face clean with her panties, and then tuck them in my front pocket.

Rising to my feet, "You don't have any underwear, and you can't walk around with my cum trickling down your legs all day. It'll drive me nuts and freak the kids out."

Willa sounds embarrassed yet awed. "I planned on hitting the bathroom."

"My way was more fun." I flash a smile, then lean in to lay a wet smacker on her lips. "You got off a second time, and you don't have to chance a walk of shame if anyone is in the kitchen."

Pulling out her cellphone to use as a light, "Good point." Willa shakes her head, still looking shocked. "Do I look okay?" She pats her mussed up hair and tugs her dress into place.

"You look perfect," I reply honestly. Willa looks like I just fucked her six ways to Sunday and back again. Curls sticking out in every direction, lips ruddy and swollen, face and chest flushed– *I* did that.

"C'mon, Mrs. Kennedy." I unlock the door, squinting when I open it and get hit by the bright light. "We have a center to run."

A few minutes later, Willa's back to organizing tonight's baking lesson and I'm sitting on a stool eating the huge after-sex sandwich she made me. Could the woman be any more perfect?

All the kids pour into the room, mad chatter following them. Popping a piece of tomato into my mouth, I try to absorb this, because it's the last time. Tomorrow afternoon the boys head off to college, beginning a new era for all of us. Plus, I'm pretty sure Wynn is never going to forgive me when I drop the fact that I'm the twins' father into his lap.

Not looking forward to *that*.

Mmm... Teeth sinking into ham, salami, and Muenster, I watch my kids with great amusement. The twins hop up on stools on either side of me. Their Gillette lineage showing, they turn to thievery. Hayley steals my pickle, but Hayden steals half my freaking sandwich. I issue a warning glare, but the little brat takes a big bite.

"You're just like your brother licking Kade's sweets," is on the tip of my tongue, but that secret is still hovering over us. But not for long.

Shrugging, the three of us eat quietly, all smiles when Willa plunks another sandwich before us. As entertainment, we watch the interplay between the others like we're eating in front of the television in the den.

Jack and Bren are whispering furiously in the entryway, evidently arguing as usual. I have no idea what's been going down with Bren, but whatever it is has pissed his buddy off royally. If Bren isn't moping, he's fighting with Jackson.

Wynn and Kaden are leaning against the counter wearing blushes. Even the tips of their ears are bright red. Staring at the floor in front of them, their eyes keep darting to the side to look at the other.

"Sage Fischer liked ya, didn't he?" I nosh on a pickle. "The both of ya?"

Embarrassed, Wynn turns his back to us. Laughing heartily, Kade blushes more for the both of them. Then he's leaning over to peck a quick kiss to Wynn's neck. "That boy is trouble. Jesus. Unrelenting little shit. Apparently Wynn is the spirit and image of the guy's homeboy. Some kid named Weston."

"Sage said Weston is off limits, but I'm not." Wynn's shy voice is quiet, wavering with mortification but also a hint of something else entirely.

Baffled, Willa and I share a look, unsure how Kaden and Wynn are attracted to the same guy but he's the complete opposite of who they are. We shrug at the same time, letting it go.

"Two choices," Willa announces, calling out to Bren and Jackson. "Either eat, or take your teenage angst outta my kitchen." My son glares at her but doesn't speak. Jack flashes Willa an apologetic look.

"How about a third choice, sis?" Wynn pulls the recipe out of Willa's hand. "How about I help you set up for later?"

"Ever the golden boy," Kade mutters, voice amused. "*My* golden boy."

"Last I checked," the Kennedy erupts in me. We're jealous and possessive. "Wynn's my golden boy until tomorrow."

"We'll share," Kade surprises me. Then he turns to Wynn and says, "I'm willing to share," and it holds hidden meaning.

Pointing at the doorway. "Take your pissing contests outta my kitchen," Willa orders in her momma voice. "Eat or help."

The twins and I eat, and the boys get to helping.

Antsy, I've been patrolling the house all morning, unable to sit still. "Cupcakes?" I stare down at the spread Willa's putting on the coffee table. A mix of sweet and salty, and it's all fattening. "It's ten a.m. and we're not having a party."

"I'm being hospitable," Willa says innocently, batting her eyelashes at me. Annoyed, I swat her ass for good measure.

"It's our kids." I just gawk at her, trying to get her to see how ridiculous cupcakes and fried cheese bites are for a dirty secret reveal.

"Fat is better than passing out booze to get through this," Willa reminds me. Shifting the platter on the table until she thinks it's perfect, Willa stares down at the cupcakes in Old Gold & Blue for West Virginia University's Mountaineers. But we're not having a going away party.

Pointing down at the absurdity, "What are the tiny blue and pink ones for?"

Willa stares at me, not blinking, so I wait her out. Challenging each other, we listen to the kids running around upstairs. How such tiny creatures can sound like buffalo is beyond me. It's almost as odd as having cupcakes on a day like today.

"Open one," Willa orders me.

"You're such a weirdo." I snatch a pink cupcake off the platter, glaring at the woman. "Succubus thief." I mutter a few unsavory compliments underneath my breath as I split the cupcake in half. "The fuck…"

"Think of it as a gender reveal for a baby shower." Willa takes the piece of paper out of my hand. "This is insurance in case you don't have the balls to say it out loud."

"I'll show you balls, little girl." I just stop myself from cupping my nuts.

The pink cupcake had a note inside saying **Royce Kennedy is Hayley Kennedy's biological father.**

I tear into a light blue cupcake, knowing damn well what I'm going to find. **Royce Kennedy is Hayden Kennedy's biological father.**

Sputtering, flabbergasted, nearly speechless… "What is this, Maury Povich meets Martha fucking Stewart?"

Maintaining a straight face, "Royce, you *are* the father," Willa mimics Maury.

I ignore her, knowing she's laughing on the inside. I grab to find out what's in the huge gold and blue cupcakes. **IOU: Daddy buys your textbooks.**

"A truth reveal and a bribe?" I stare down at the slips of paper, mind reeling. I stalk to the kitchen, pitching the cake, wrappers, and incriminating evidence in the trash. "Wait a cotton picking minute!" I charge back into the den to confront Willa. "You don't think I'll do it?"

"Now I know you'll do it," Willa says with a smirk.

Finding her irrational, "Do all the big cupcakes have textbooks in 'em? I mean, there's at least three dozen West Virginia U cupcakes. How many textbooks do Kaden, Wynn, and Brennan possibly need?"

"Thirty cupcakes to be exact." Willa's still wearing that satisfied smirk. "Three sets of ten different prizes. If they get duplicates, they only get it once, and the other kids lose out. It's about teamwork. Now one of them is out some textbooks. Pity."

"What about those?" I point at the evil cupcakes. "Do they have prizes?"

"Nah…" Willa's grin gets larger. "Having you as a daddy is reward enough for the twins."

"You're enjoying this, aren't you?" I tug Willa into my arms. "You love yanking my chain and twisting my balls."

Nuzzling the side of my neck with the tip of her nose, she whispers to me like I always do her. "You have nothing to be scared of, Royce." She flips my off switch and I relax into her. "The kids instinctively know you're their father. Always have. Always will. This is not a surprise for them."

"Wynn," I whisper my biggest fear.

"He'll get over it. Eventually." Willa squeezes me tighter. "It's in his nature to forgive."

"Oh, but it's also in Wynn's nature to turn into the world's biggest asshole."

Willa's evil chuckle is answer enough.

"Royce?" Kade's hesitant voice flows in from the entryway. "Dr. Cassidy's here. Do you guys need a minute?"

"Do I need a minute?" I laugh without humor. Try another decade. I pull away from Willa, heart beating out of control. "Nope, guess not."

"It's nice to finally meet you, Dr. Cassidy. Warren is always singing your praises." Kaden escorts our therapist into the den. "You're a miracle worker. What classes do you suggest I should–"

"Son," I call out to stop him in his tracks. "Go get the kids." I catch Willa rolling her eyes in my peripheral vision. Whether it was meant for me or Kade remains to be seen.

Hiding something behind the sofa, Dr. Cassidy distracts me with her words. "I see you baked the cupcakes I suggested."

"Of course she did," I mutter, dropping down onto the sofa, and Willa joins me. My eyes roll heavenward when the stampede moves through the upstairs hallway to the staircase.

"Old floors?" Dr. Cassidy smirks– sarcastic old bat. "Don't go blaming me for your current predicament, Mr. Kennedy," she answers my unspoken thoughts. "Once this is over with," looking at her watch, "I'd say ten minutes from now. It will be my job to make sure you don't make any further lifelong mistakes. But we'll cross those bridges when we get to them."

"Sorry," I mutter, properly cowed. I dig my elbow into my knee, and then rest my cheek in my open palm. "I know I'm being an asshole, but I'm terrified. Either I'm closing in on a panic attack, or this old man is gonna have a heart attack."

"Royce," Dr. Cassidy says firmly. "You're gonna get through this and be stronger for it."

"Starting now." I snap to attention when the herd of children descends.

"And you're not old," Willa reminds me, and Dr. Cassidy adds, "I'm closing in on old, and even I'm not there yet."

"Cupcakes!" Wynn licks his lips while plopping down on the loveseat, with Kade landing next to him. "Can I have one, sis?"

"Me too!" the twins chirp together, deciding to sit inches from the coffee table where the treats are. They stare, refusing to blink, like the treats will disappear before their very eyes.

"Mountaineer cakes are for the big kids. Tiny cakes for the little ones." I turn to face Willa, horror etched across my expression, and all she does is smile sweetly at me.

"Oh! What's this?" Bren fishes out a piece of paper, then pops the cake in his mouth. "Mmm... Yummy! *IOU: One pass at saying it's none of our business. Daddy promises not to meddle.* Sweet! I'll be keeping this piece of paper handy." Bren digs out his wallet, and tucks the IOU behind his license.

"I got an Amazon code for a fifty dollar gift card," Kade mumbles, obviously disappointed. "The note attached said it's for school supplies. Can I switch? Please!"

"Thanks!" Wynn says brightly, snatching the code from Kade's outstretched fingertips. "I could use some Sharpies. This one is definitely for you."

Taking the paper, Kade reads it in a flat voice. "Kentwood County Obedience School. Really, Willa? *Really?*"

"I was really praying you'd get that one." Willa flashes an innocent smile. "I put extras in the cupcakes just to be sure."

"Uncle Kade?" Hayden tries to gain his attention. "Is that where they spank big kids?"

A miracle occurs. Dr. Cassidy barks a laugh, finally proving she's human. She covers her mouth with a palm, obviously embarrassed. A flush is creeping up her cheeks to hide behind her bifocals.

"Kid, it's for Perty. Willa's not looking forward to cleaning up his accidents while I'm away at school."

"Not to be rude or anything," Wynn begins hesitantly. "But who is she?" He points at Dr. Cassidy, and then his eyes light on the paper in Hayden's hand. "What was in your cupcake?"

Hayden's fingertips clench, hiding the evidence. Freezing like a scared rabbit, his eyes connect with mine, and he says absolutely nothing.

I can't look away from my youngest son, neither one of us knowing what to do. But one thing is certain, Hayden wasn't surprised. Panic setting in, I begin to sweat profusely. My skin feels tight. I can't get enough oxygen in my lungs. My heart is stuttering.

What do I do? What do I say?

"What's going on?" Wynn demands. Eyes flicking from face to face. "Sis?" When she doesn't speak, he tries Bren. When Bren doesn't react, he seeks the most reliable source. "Kaden, if you don't answer me, you'll regret it."

Kaden just stares at me, mouth hanging open, words frozen on his tongue.

When the twins were toddlers, I didn't stop them from calling me daddy. But after the assault, I was firm about them calling me Uncle Royce. The cupcakes weren't for the kids. They were for me. Willa and Dr. Cassidy wanted to assure me that Hayden and Hayley already knew. It took away some of my stress so I could deal with Wynn.

Dr. Cassidy isn't here to mediate. She's here to manage me. They're all here to manage me. My kids are leaving in a few hours– moving away from me. And Wynn may never speak to me again. The good doctor is here to make sure *I* don't lose my shit.

I can't get the words out. My brain won't move my tongue. My lips won't form words. I can't do it.

I can't.

"Just rip the Band-Aid off and get it over with, Dad." Brennan leans forward, grabbing a pink cupcake. "Catch!" In slow motion, we all watch it arc across the coffee table to land directly in Wynn's outstretched palm.

Wynn already looks betrayed because we all know something he doesn't, and I don't think I'm ready for him to grow up and realize I'm just as flawed as his actual father.

Desperate, "Don't!" flows from my mouth, hand held out in a stop motion. But it's too late. Wynn is splitting the cupcake, then his deft fingers pluck the piece of paper from the center.

I can't breathe.

No one speaks.

All eyes are on Wynn.

Molars grinding, jaw clenching, fist obliterating the cupcake to crumbs, Wynn stares directly in my eyes with utter betrayal written across his face. Lunging to his feet, I can't get a single word out before he's out the front door and tearing across the yard.

Stunned, I want to go after him, but I can't get my limbs to move.

"Warren's waiting in the yard. We knew this was exactly how it would play out." Kade tries to reassure me, but it doesn't work. "Don't worry about Wynn, Royce. He just needs to cool off. Warren's gonna drag his ass to see Corbin, anyway."

"Great! Just what he needs," Brennan mumbles, and he's not being sarcastic.

"Are you okay, Daddy?" Hayley sets her tiny hand on mine, and I choke on a sob. Suffocating, I can't seem to relearn to breathe. All my sins have been brought to light, and the person with the most goodness in their heart will never see me the same way again. I'll never be Wynn's mentor– his dad.

"Mr. Kennedy?" Dr. Cassidy's no longer calling me Royce, so I know that's a bad sign. "It was under your control when, how, and whether or not you ever told the truth. It is *not* under your control on how the other person will react to said truth. You are not responsible for how Wynn feels. But you will be held accountable for your actions and the consequences they create."

"You mean losing my son?"

"No, I mean finally acknowledging your children." Dr. Cassidy reminds me, causing my eyes to flick down to meet first Hayden's then Hayley's eyes. They're sad, only because they're worried about their daddy.

"I'm fine," I mutter numbly. "We all knew how this would go down."

"Royce?" I'm Royce again. "Wynn will either come around or he won't, and that is entirely up to him. Let him know you're open to answering any questions he may have, and that you want to rebuild the trust back, but don't push."

Hayley crawls into my lap, resting her head against my shoulder. I wrap my arms around her tightly and thank God for what I do have.

"This is for you." Dr. Cassidy retrieves whatever was hidden behind the sofa– the Sunshine Bear. I take Wynn's yellow teddy bear from her, and Hayley and I share it. "The teddy bears were to comfort only *you*. They represent the most important people in your life. Royce, you need to learn to let go. The bears are your focus objects."

"Like Suicidal Tendencies is mine." Kade reaches over to shake Sunshine Bear's hand. "Sometimes– sometimes how we feel is overwhelming and if we unleash it on the people we care most about, we'll push them away. Talk to the bear, Royce. Yell at it. Hug it. Punch it. Whatever it takes. But don't keep putting on your dad uniform and calling yourself an old man. Live."

"On Monday, we start individual counseling, Royce." Dr. Cassidy drops a bombshell. "I allowed you to use Willa as a crutch in our sessions all summer so that you'd actually come and get some help. It's time to move past that and really heal."

"What is this?" Those particular words together should sound defensive, but they come out confused and terrified. "Is this *my* intervention?"

"Yes," Willa answers for everyone without hesitation. "Yes."

"Fine," I mutter belligerently. "I'll go. But until then I need to process. No more managing Royce for the rest of the weekend."

"That's very fair, Royce. And I appreciate that you called yourself Royce just now, not Daddy." Dr. Cassidy gets up from her chair, and I assume she's leaving. But instead, she starts dragging teddy bears out from behind the sofa. It's so bizarre I start laughing hysterically.

Hayley crawls out of my lap, and she and Hayden jump into the pile of teddy bears. Hugging and squeezing, guessing whose bear is whose. I better not add any more important people to my life, or I will need to build a room just to house the dang things.

I turn to Willa. "What's your focus object?"

Smiling sadly, she leans into me to whisper. "You are, Royce. You're my focus object. I can always count on you, no matter what. You believe you need to take care of us, so you won't allow us in. That's why you have the bears. You need to trust that we will always be there for you, and someday you might allow us to do so in the flesh."

"Royce, you're not alone," Dr. Cassidy states the obvious. "You counted on Annie and your father, and when you lost them it terrified you. You clung to the notion you had to be everything for Bren, and you never again allowed anyone to take care of you. Maybe a little bit with Donny, but he let you down in the worst possible way, and you still refuse to be angry about it. It isn't selfish to put your needs above others."

"I don't want to talk about it anymore today," I mutter, emotionally exhausted.

"Then I'd suggest you stop asking questions that open avenues to things that we must acknowledge." Eyes narrowed, I stare at Dr. Cassidy like she's nuts. "You asked Willa what her focus object was. She told you. The answer opened up for more questions. You're in control."

"She means *shut up, Royce,*" Willa teases me.

I don't shut up.

Sunshine Bear is still clutched to my chest. "Kaden, why didn't you go after Wynn?" I'm surprised. I would have thought Wynn would have been priority number one for Kade.

"Because there's a part two." Kade flashes a sad smile while pointing at Bren. "Batter up!"

"I'ma use this right now." Bren pulls out his wallet and searches around inside for the IOU.

"Brennan," Dr. Cassidy turns her doctor voice on my eldest. "I suggest you rip your own Band-Aid off this time."

"I pity your children." Kaden chuckles, and Dr. Cassidy joins him. "I wanna grow up to be just like you."

"Then you have better study hard, Mr. Marx."

We all bust out chuckling at Kaden's expense. A much-needed laugh about something that isn't funny. A cathartic release.

"Young Mr. Kennedy, we're waiting."

"Rip the Band-Aid. Wish I'd thought of a cupcake. Maybe a hand grenade." After muttering to himself, shifting on the love seat, staring at Kade for moral support, Brennan takes in a big gulp of air and releases it in a gust. "Jesse's pregnant."

Several gasps light around the room, but no one asks who the father is. Hayley's, "Oh, another baby! YAY!" has me acting without thought.

"Kids, we need to have an adult conversation. Go upstairs and play."

"Ah, do we have to?" Hayden whines.

"You can take the bears with you."

Scooping them up into his arms, Hayden marches up the stairs like he weighs nine thousand pounds, with Hayley picking up the teddy bears he drops along the way.

Once the kids are out of earshot, it's a relief that this is something I can take charge of. We don't need Dr. Cassidy to intervene. This is a job only a father can perform for his son, especially when it's a mistake he's already learned from.

"NO!" I state so strongly the single word borders on violence. Bren starts to speak but I don't let him. "No. Absolutely not. No."

"But I love–"

"*But I love Jessica* is what you were going to say. We already know it. She's been one of your best friends since kindergarten." I put my hand up when Bren starts to balk. "You love Jessica like I loved your mother. I get it. But no."

"Why the hell not?" Bren lunges to his feet, furious. "I'm a grown fucking man! I'm going to take responsibility for my child, so I don't have to deal with a bullshit intervention in the future. I don't want to be an every other weekend dad who pays child support while Jessica flounders. I want *my* baby every day. Give me some credit, Dad."

"I want more for you, son." I shake my head sadly. "So much more. Don't you get that?"

"Apparently not!" Bren shouts, flabbergasted. "I'm going to marry Jessica, Dad. I'm going to marry her. I'm going to love her. I'm going to take care of her and our children."

"And you won't be happy," I remind him. "No, don't shake your head at me. You won't be. You have to hear me out."

Standing over my seated form, Bren speaks to me in a way he never has before. He bellows at me, losing his temper. "*No*, you have to *hear* me!"

Feeling gutted, I admit the truth. "Brennan, I loved your mother with all my heart. I miss her like crazy every single day. She was my best friend, and I wouldn't trade a second I had with her for anything. But there are different kinds of love… If your mother had been alive when I met Willa, I can't make any promises I would have remained faithful."

"What the fuck?" hisses out from between Kaden's lips. "Oh, shit. Royce. Don't go there."

"I loved your mom, but I was never *in* love with her, and there is a difference. I'm sorry that I have to tell you that, son." I clutch my chest– the ache unbearable.

"Dad?" My words hurt Brennan, but he's finally hearing me through the haze of anger.

"I'm not saying I love Willa more. I'm saying it's *different*. Different like how I feel about Donny and you kids. How I even love Jackson and Francis– Jessica. Because I watched them grow up beside you. But it's not the same thing."

Taking a deep breath, I wipe the tears from my eyes with the back of my wrist. "So much for shutting up so I don't open anymore *therapy avenues*," I mutter sarcastically. "I would have lived my entire life in ignorant bliss with your mother. We would have had a basketball team full of kids, and we would have died happy in our old age. But you are *not* ignorant."

Baffled, Bren takes a few steps back, and then falls onto the loveseat. "What the hell does love have to do with an education?"

"It doesn't," I twist my words. "I know you and Jessica love each other, and right now Jesse is on board because she's ignorant to how it could be. But you both deserve more. I know she likes girls and she doesn't think she'll ever find one. Maybe she wants to be a wife and mother, and she found this great guy who she can love– a guy who takes the loneliness away and loves her in a different way than she loves him."

With narrowed eyes, Brennan lunges to his feet like he wants to murder me because he doesn't want to hear the truth. I don't flinch. I pour it all out there, wishing someone would have done this for me when I was his age. No matter how hard Bren tries to evade my eyes, I don't allow it. He will look me in the eyes and see that I speak the truth.

"But the thing is, you're *not* ignorant. I can tell by the pained expression on your face that you get what I mean by comparing your momma and Willa. If you'd never met Jack, and if Jessica never meets a girl who will rock her world, you could die happy in ignorant bliss because you do love each other. You're just not *in* love. But it's too late because you've already met Jack, and I can tell you've already had a taste."

My son turns his back to me, refusing to look me in the eye, and I *ache* for him. "I bet you've had more than a taste. I bet it happened after you committed to Jessica. Probably last night. Jack is on his way to school right now with a broken heart, isn't he?"

"I had no other choice." Bren's voice warps from defiant to devastated. "My kid will come first. You taught me that."

Ignoring the dig that this is my fault, I soldier forth. "You can tell yourself that you'll be faithful, but it's impossible. You can tuck that boy in his dorm room far from your reach, but you'll still miss him and ache for him. You can have your brother make sure Jack doesn't shake his ass at every guy he meets to take the pain away. But then you'll get a whiff of it and get jealous, and you'll break your vows to your wife."

"I won't! I won't cheat," Bren vows, but I can tell even he doesn't believe it because he undoubtedly already has.

"Someday, could be next month or ten years from now, Jessica will make a new friend because she can't play pretend anymore. There'll be a spark with this woman and your marriage will fall apart. It will hurt your children more than if you would've just started a healthy routine and parental relationship from the start. Just be friends raising your child, that's all I'm saying. You both deserve what will make you happy."

"It's not gonna be like that for me and Jesse!" Bren's false outrage warps into a whine. "It's not!"

"Bullshit." I finally admit the truth. "My brother is my best friend– without your momma, you and Donny were my whole world –and look what I did to him, Bren. Look!" I bark out sharply while pointing at Willa. "I can make excuses about an extortionist, but it doesn't change the fact that even if Donny was in love with Willa, I would have actively tried to get into her pants. There was nothing on this planet that would have altered that fate, no matter how depraved it was."

"You wouldn't have done that to Uncle Donny." Bren has more confidence in me than he should.

"I would. I did. He was my brother, not just a girl I've known since the sandbox."

Bren is purposely being stubborn for some reason, completely conflicting with the son I've always known. "Dad, Jessica and I are not the same as you and Willa."

"No, shit! I'm talking about you and Jack, dumbass." I sigh in exasperation. "I'm stopping you from living an endless cycle of jealousy, hurt, and guilt and shame. Where Jack gets a boyfriend, and you snap. You both cheat with each other, say you love each other, and then leave because you feel responsible for Jessica's happiness. Because that's what's gonna happen until you get your head out of your ass and think selfishly for yourself but selflessly for Jessica, Jack, and your unborn child. Just because it's the moral thing to do, doesn't mean it's the right thing for you."

"Fuck," Bren gasps out, choking on the single word.

"I told you so," Kade taunts, but he sounds like he's going to be sick. "I told you to talk to Dad first. I tried to warn you but you wouldn't listen."

"Because he's doing what I knew he would do. He's making my decisions for me, not letting me be my own man."

"You're too young to be your own man," flows in unison from Dr. Cassidy, Kade, Willa, and me. I finish it off with, "You're too young, son. But you're old enough to make mistakes. It's my job as your father to share with you the wisdom I've learned from making mine."

"It's too late for that," Bren cries out, clutching at his chest. "Way too late."

"It's never too late," I whisper sadly. "*Never*."

"It is!" Bren shouts. "It is. I married Jessica this morning."

~Coming Soon~

STAINLESS

Rusty Knob #3: Brennan Kennedy

-ACKNOWLEDGEMENTS-

A lot of work goes into writing a novel, and it isn't just by the writer herself. **My parents:** for their unconditional support. **My readers**: thank you for reading my twisted words and spreading my books to the masses. For without you, no one would have ever heard of my stories. My readers are my lifeblood. A shout out to the members of the **M&M of Restraint Group on Facebook**: thanks for the endless entertainment and inspiration. Thank you to my street team: **Erica Chilson's Deviants!** You guys ROCK! **Wicked Reads**: (in all its incarnations) **Angela G.**, thank you for taking over and making Wicked Reads better than I could have done by myself. & thank you for helping promote my work and the work of other authors. Angela? Have I told you lately how much I appreciate you? A huge thank you to the **Wicked Writer's Betas** for keeping me grounded and encouraging me to keep trudging along when I get frustrated. Your thoughts and observations are invaluable. ((Hugs)) Beta readers who worked on Rusty Knob: **Kris D, Suz A, Darcy V, Di C, Angela G, Diane P, Jacki G, Linsey T, Alexis W, Alicia P, Billie Jo H, Shelby H, Tassie M, & Liz S.** Someday, I'd love to meet you all in real life- it would be the experience of a lifetime.

ABOUT THE AUTHOR

Erica Chilson does not write in the 3rd person, wanting her readers to *be* her characters. Therefore, writing a bio about herself is uncomfortable in the extreme.

Born, raised, and here to stay, the Wicked Writer is a stump-jumper, a ridge-runner. Hailing from North Central Pennsylvania, directly on the New York State border; she loves the changes in seasons, the humid air, all the mountainous forest, and the gloomy atmosphere.

Introverted, but not socially awkward, Erica prides herself on thinking first and filtering her speech. There are days she doesn't speak at all. If it wasn't for the fact that she lives with her parents, giving her a sense of reality, she would be a hermit, where the delivery man finds her months after expiration.

Reading was an escape, a way to leave a not-so pleasant reality behind. Reading lent Erica the courage she gathered from the characters between the pages to long for a different life. Writing was an instrument of change, evolving Erica into the woman she is today– a better, more mature, more at peace thinker.

Erica has a wicked mind, one she pours out into her creations. Her filter doesn't allow all of it to erupt, much to her relief. Sarcastic, with a very dark, perverse sense of humor, Erica puts a bit of herself into every character she writes.

Erica Chilson loves hearing from readers. If you would like more information on release dates, works in progress, teaser chapters, and random bits of madness...

FB Fan Page: https://www.facebook.com/thewickedwriter
Website: ericachilson.com
Via email: wickedwriter.ericachilson@gmail.com

DEVIANTS ONLY, if you'd like to join Erica Chilson's SECRET Facebook group, M&M of Restraint: SIGN-UP Form available on website. 18+ due to mature conversations and content.

www.ingramcontent.com/pod-product-compliance
Lightning Source LLC
Chambersburg PA
CBHW072219170626
46813CB00003B/1010